MISSING YOU IN ATLANTIC CITY

Jane Kelly

Plexus Publishing, Inc.
Medford, New Jersey

First printing, 2014

Published by:
Plexus Publishing, Inc.
143 Old Marlton Pike
Medford, NJ 08055

This is a work of fiction. Names, characters, places, and incidents either are the product of the author's imagination or are used fictitiously. Any resemblance to actual persons, living or dead, is entirely coincidental.

Printed in the United States of America.

Library of Congress Cataloging-in-Publication Data

Kelly, Jane, 1949-
Missing You in Atlantic City / Jane Kelly.
pages cm. -- (A Meg Daniels Mystery)
ISBN 978-1-940091-00-6
1. Women detectives--Fiction. 2. Atlantic City (N.J.)--Fiction. 3. Mystery fiction. I. Title.
PS3561.E39424M57 2014
813'.54--dc23

2014012517

President and CEO: Thomas H. Hogan, Sr.
Editor-in-Chief and Publisher: John B. Bryans
Managing Editor: Amy M. Reeve
Production Manager: Norma Neimeister
Book Designer: Kara Mia Jalkowski
Cover Designer: Denise Erickson
Marketing Coordinator: Rob Colding

To the memory of the Kelly Family Dancers
and their brief but illustrious career.

To Rosemary, Fred, Rick, Beth, Ricky, John, Susan,
John, Kelly, John, Frederick, and Heather.

And to the dancers of the future Chloe, Jack,
Jack, Elizabeth, Olivia, and Nicholas.

Acknowledgments

In researching this book, I had a lot of fun revisiting 1964. I appreciate the assistance of my friends who did the time travel with me.

I owe thanks ...

To Carolyn Marconi Andersen and Denise Marconi Leitch for sharing their memories of the real Bella Napoli and helping me create the fictional version where Betty Boyle worked. Thanks for the stories, the hospitality, and the memories of the summer of '64.

To the Dudek family—Gary, Nicholas, Caroline, and especially Lisa Marconi Dudek who drove through pounding rain to trace Meg and Andy's steps.

To Bill Andersen for sharing his expertise on sailing and the music of summers past.

To Dottie and Bill Maher who paid their first, but not their last, visit to the Knife and Fork and other Atlantic City hot spots so that Meg and Andy's dinner date would be accurate.

To Marilynn Benz and Carole Turk for visiting the spots that Meg and Andy frequent with me and tasting all the treats the Atlantic City Boardwalk has to offer.

To Linda Geiger for relating her stories of modern day Atlantic City and her recollections of marching in Lyndon Johnson's birthday parade.

To Barbara and Victor Aprea for sharing their knowledge of Bernardsville and Middlesex County so that Meg knows her way around the state.

To Pat and Wayne of Wayne Jewelers on Wayne Avenue in Wayne, Pennsylvania for making sure I didn't let Andy pick out an inferior product.

To Rick and Beth Kelly for the time spent reading my drafts and talking about times gone by.

To the Atlantic City Public Library—everyone should be aware of the help and information available at the Atlantic City Public Library and specifically in the Heston Collection of Atlantic City history.

To Plexus president Tom Hogan, Sr. who brought me into the Plexus family, and to the Plexus staff who supported this effort. To managing editor Amy M. Reeve for being a pleasure to work with and for coordinating the efforts of those behind the scenes, including Kara Mia Jalkowski, Norma Neimeister, and Denise Erickson whose cover design captures the sadness of a missing mother's "Johnny Angel" so well. To marketing coordinator Rob Colding who approaches marketing with great focus, energy, and humor.

Finally, to my editor, John B. Bryans, who suggested I take Meg Daniels to Atlantic City and who went along on the ride. Many thanks for a relationship that extends back more than fifteen years and has produced three novels. I hope there will be more to follow.

Chapter 1

Johnny Boyle was not Italian but he wanted to be. Not just Italian, a specific Italian, another Jersey boy: Francis Albert Sinatra. Frank. Ol' Blue Eyes. The Chairman of the Board.

So Johnny used an Italian stage name: Johnny Angelini. The first time I saw him, he was crooning "In the Wee Small Hours of the Morning" in an Atlantic City casino bar. Johnny sounded less like a Sinatra impersonator and more like an acolyte, performing in the image of his musical God. With his insouciant attitude, a classic repertoire, and a classic tuxedo, Johnny Angelini screamed Rat Pack.

When he finished singing "Come Rain or Come Shine," in chatter reminiscent of his idol, Johnny thanked the composers. Looking around the room, I was willing to bet the names Harold Arlen and Johnny Mercer were lost on the patrons. For the next number, Johnny picked up the tempo, moving back and forth across the stage, assuring everyone in the audience that, despite their overwhelming indifference, he got a kick out of them.

"He's pointing at you," I said, nudging Andy.

Andy didn't even open his eyes to reply. "He points at everyone when he sings this one. I've seen him do it before."

"The microphone cord makes me nervous. I'm afraid he'll trip over it."

Andy was unconcerned. "He's a pro."

Up on stage, Johnny ended the song without a misstep. "Thanks to Mr. Cole Porter," Johnny said. "Stick around for another of his best when I come back."

The audience members, probably hoping to return to the gambling tables before Johnny returned to the stage, did not appear to care. The entertainer did not appear to mind. Maybe he'd grown used to a lukewarm response. I, however, could not listen to the scattered and weak applause without contrasting the fantasies of the young Johnny Boyle with the reality of the middle-aged performer. Surely he hadn't spent hours perfecting his moves in the mirror in the hope that his reflection would be replaced by twenty people talking over his act.

"Watching people perform in places like this makes me sad," I said. "I don't think any singer dreams of this gig."

Andy opened his eyes. "Not true. For one thing, it's steady work." Andy didn't think that Johnny saw anything tragic in warbling American standards under the gaze of the saints, prophets, and cherubs of the fake Sistine Chapel ceiling and over the bells, whistles, and general clamor of the casino. "He has an education that could land him a high six-figure salary at a prestigious New York law firm—or at least he would have when he graduated from Yale Law twenty years ago."

Andy's point was that Johnny "Angelini" Boyle preferred crooning at the Artistical Hotel and Casino in Atlantic City, New Jersey, to the career of a high-powered attorney. "And it's a credit to Johnny that the hotel has kept him on for ten years," he said with conviction. "Management wants its customers happy."

It seemed to me the audience wasn't so much happy as rude. Apparently, Johnny didn't agree. Tepid applause was still applause. The singer had a big smile on his face as he left the stage and headed our way.

"Andrea Beckino—I heard you were around, mi buddio!"

Why bother learning Italian when you could take perfectly good English words and Italianize them? I wondered.

"Johnny!" Andy stood and wrapped an arm around the singer. It did not encircle the man's entire body. Johnny wasn't fat, just wide. Very wide.

"This is my friend, Meg Daniels."

"Friend, eh?" Johnny raised his voice to be heard over the noisy lounge chatter. "I had my eye on you two romantics during my set."

What the singer viewed as romance was actually Andy dozing on my shoulder after a twelve-hour day at his desk deep in the bowels of the Artistical. Andy wasn't cut out for office work.

With great theatricality, the singer winked at me. "I would say that you are far more than friends."

"Good friends," I clarified. "For over six years now."

Johnny had more to say on the subject but Andy interrupted. "Johnny, please sit down and chat—about something else. Buy you a drink?"

Andy pulled out a chair—just one example of the Artistical's interpretation of 16th-century Italian seating—and Johnny dropped onto the velour seat. A waitress materialized beside him with a tumbler. I guessed two things: that the glass contained Johnny's usual and that Johnny's usual was whiskey with ice. Johnny drank the liquid down and began to talk, not only about something else, but about everything else.

Apparently, voice training was required to make oneself heard over the casino clatter. It also allowed Johnny to talk for long periods of time without taking a breath that would permit anyone else to get a word in edgewise. I didn't mind. Johnny's stories weren't what I would call interesting, but his delivery was entertaining. Years of handling audiences, I guess.

Eventually Johnny circled back to his original topic. "So, Andy, tell me about you two." Johnny leaned forward and winked again with theatrical exaggeration. "I recognize *amore* when I see it."

"We both work for the Artistical's resort in the Bahamas. I handle security, and Meg's the VIP concierge. I was asked to come to the Atlantic City location to do a security audit, and since we don't get a lot of celebs in the Bahamas in July and August, Meg decided to use some vacation time and join me. I'm in the middle of—"

"Yeah, security," Johnny interrupted. "That's something I'd like to talk to you about."

The singer removed a Gucci wallet from his back pocket and laid it open on the faux marble tabletop. In the space where most people would store a driver's license, Johnny kept a picture. "That's my mama. Beautiful, wasn't she?"

Andy picked up the billfold and studied the photo before passing it to me. The woman, wrapped in the arms of a young man, wrapped a baby in her own.

"Is this ... ?" I pointed to the baby.

"Yep. That's me as a *bambino*, on my christening day with Mama and Papa."

The woman in the black-and-white photo was young, or had been when wildly bouffant hairdos were in style. Her hair, as dark as Johnny's, contrasted with her pale complexion. I suspected that her eyes, pale in the picture, were the same bright blue as her son's. Her smile, small and tentative, made me wonder if the big hair and heavy makeup disguised a shy woman.

"She disappeared fifty years ago." Half a century later, Johnny's sadness at the loss of a mother he never knew percolated just under the surface. "Vanished without a trace."

"Johnny, I am sorry." Andy grasped his friend's knee in that way that guys do during life's emotional peaks—like during a missed fourth down in the closing minutes of a playoff game. "I never knew."

"I never told."

Neither Andy nor I asked any questions. If Johnny wanted to talk about his mother, he would. And, it turned out, he did.

"Mama was nineteen, and I was only six months old when she disappeared into thin air. She left the restaurant where she was waitressing one night in '64 during the Democratic National Convention and hasn't been seen since. Cops never found a trace of her. No purse. No wedding ring. No nothing."

"It must be really hard, not knowing ..." Andy's voice was as soft as it could be and still be heard above the noise.

"Standing on that stage, I always scan the audience hoping that one night she'll be sitting out there. When I was a kid, I convinced myself that she'd hit her head and got amnesia and that all she'd have to do was see me and she'd remember everything."

I passed the photo back to Johnny and he stared at it as he spoke. "My Papa—Andy, you met my father once or twice—he's always been convinced she was murdered. He's dying now. He had cancer before, and we thought he had it beaten, but it looks like it's back." Johnny shook his head. "He won't consider treatment this time. He won't even go to the doctor to find out for sure. He lies on the couch all day, ready to die. And now that he knows he's going, after years of not talking about Mama at all, I hear him crying over her. I know he feels responsible. Time and time again, I hear him say, 'I shouldn't have let him get away with it.'"

Andy asked the obvious question. "Do you know who he's talking about?"

"He says he means whoever it was who killed my mother—that he should have tracked him down at the time. Before the trail went cold."

Andy knew where this conversation was headed. "Johnny, I wish I could look into this for you, but I'm not a PI anymore. I'm up here on assignment, working twelve-hour days. I've only got two weeks left. I wish I could help, but I can't."

Johnny took a long look at the picture, then put his wallet back in his pocket. This big man looked small. "I've tried not to dwell on this, Andy, but with Papa dying, I can't get it out of my mind. What happened to her? Why would anyone want to hurt her? Sometimes—and this is the worst—sometimes I wonder if maybe she didn't love us, didn't love me, and ran off with someone. Papa says no. He says he knows she's dead. He says a husband knows. He can't tell me why or how. He just knows." In an attempt to keep the tears welling in his eyes from flowing down his cheeks, Johnny looked to the ersatz Sistine Chapel ceiling. His effort failed. Tears left his eyes and headed for his jaw line.

I followed Johnny's gaze and looked at God's fingers reaching across the ceiling to Adam. The digits were not as delicately etched as the ones in Rome but the image still reinforced my need to reach out to Johnny. My eyes met Andy's. It seemed we were helpless to ease his friend's pain. Or were we?

"Johnny, I'm not a professional investigator but I've helped Andy on a few cases. Maybe I could gather a little background information for him to review." I looked to Andy. His shrug said 'Okay with me.'

"Oh, no. You're busy working." Johnny wiped a tear from his cheek.

"*Andy* is working," I said. "I'm on vacation. I'll be happy to take a break from sunbathing to ask around about this. Do a little research at the library."

"No, no."

I thought 'no, no' meant he was going to refuse my offer, but it didn't. It meant that going to the library would not be necessary.

"Papa kept a file," Johnny said. "I have all the clippings. Are you staying here? I'll drop them off tomorrow."

Chapter 2

At 8:55 the next morning, I was still in bed with my head under my pillow, avoiding the glare of the bright summer sun off the Atlantic.

"Later," I responded to the knocking at my door. It must have been Marjorie's day off. As the regular housekeeper, she knew I wasn't interested in service before 10 AM.

It took a moment for me to realize that the banging was not going to stop. I went to the door.

"Johnny says I should make sure you get this." A bellman handed me a large brown envelope and departed.

I squinted to read the writing on the front:

Meg Daniels, as promised
Johnny Boyle (Angelini)

I grabbed my morning Coke from the mini-bar, sat on the edge of the bed, and stared into space for several minutes. The Mid-Atlantic region had been locked in a heat wave for close to a week. No matter how enticing the beach looked, I knew the truth and wouldn't be able to handle it, not on a 100-plus-degree day. I couldn't handle much of *anything* on a 100-plus-degree day.

Even in my air-conditioned hotel room, it took me a few minutes to muster the energy to open the envelope. Inside I found two items: a binder containing newspaper clippings and handwritten notes neatly tucked into plastic sleeves, and a smaller envelope full of photographs.

I settled onto the bed with the files and got lost in the world of Betty and Buddy Boyle and their young son Johnny. At least until my phone buzzed.

Help me!

The first text message of the day from Andy. Working in an office seemed to bring out his inner middle-school child:

Wish I were on the beach

Sitting at a desk = BORING

Can't wait to meet u ;)

Did I mention that this man had passed his fortieth birthday?

I typed back *44 minutes*, the time left until our daily 11 AM meeting at Café Monet for breakfast—well, my breakfast, his lunch—and the only time I saw Andy wide awake. His status at our evening beach rendezvous ranged from dozing to out cold.

Thanks to abundant man-made flora and fauna, Café Monet looked like an oddly static garden, but the clatter of the casino's bells, whistles, and sirens was a constant reminder that a fortune might be waiting only a few steps away.

"How many times have you used the word *cacophony*?" I slipped into the booth across from Andy.

"To my knowledge, I've never used the word *cacophony*. Although I would be happy to right now, as in, How about that cacophony coming from the casino floor?"

"After three weeks living in this hotel, the cacophony is really getting to me." I rubbed my temples.

"Well, try to remember that the cacophony is part of the casino experience, created for the enjoyment of the Artistical's paying customers. Employees staying here in comped premium rooms need not complain. That racket pays our bills."

"I know, I know, but you can't get anywhere from our room without passing through the casino. Look at the ocean, right out there." I pointed to the window visible only to patrons seated in the restaurant. "Without that window, who would even know there was an ocean around here?"

"Hey," Andy protested. "Let's pay a little respect to the hotel architects. An ocean is not an easy thing to hide. A pond, a lake, even a river—maybe. But an entire ocean? That wasn't easy."

"I know the casino has rules about no clocks or windows, but wouldn't it be more relaxing if the restaurant, at least, was open to the crash of waves on the beach?"

"If it was, gamblers might venture outside and squander valuable betting dollars on frivolous things like bathing suits, beach towels, and sun screen—which those of us who have spent the last month locked in windowless rooms lit only by monitor glow could definitely use." He looked at his once-tanned arms. "Lucky you can get to the beach before the sun goes down."

He exaggerated, since the sun wasn't *completely* down at 7 PM when he got off work. However, I had to admit that his tan was fading and that the sun-streaks in his hair were beginning to suggest gray more than blond. But I felt certain that his physical condition was as temporary as his current work assignment.

He pointed to the envelope in front of me. "What's that?"

"Johnny didn't waste any time. It's everything the family saved about his mom's disappearance. A bellman dropped it off before nine, which, considering Johnny's last show ended at 2 AM, is rather impressive."

"Are you sure you want to take this on?" Andy appeared concerned. "This is supposed to be a vacation for you."

"We live at the beach. I can miss a day or two of my seashore vacation." I unfolded a sheet of white lined paper with a rough edge that had been torn out of a copy book, the old bound kind, without spirals.

"This is the saddest thing." I held the page up so Andy could see the childish printing. "It's signed 'Johnny Boyle, Age 10, August 27, 1974'—the tenth anniversary of his mother's disappearance."

Ignoring grammar and spelling errors, I read the words aloud just as young Johnny had written them.

My Mother:
Was beautiful
Was married to my father
Liked going to the movies with her parents
Learned to dance with her father
Sang to me "Johnny Angel"
Culd sew
Made my christning dress
Made a lot of her clothes
Loved the color purple
Liked violets as her favorite flower
Wanted to go to school
Wanted to be a travel agent
Wanted to go to Paris
Will be nineteen years old forever
Loved me very much

"How old did you say he was he when he wrote that?" Andy asked.

"Ten."

"Hmmmm. 'Will be nineteen years old forever.'"

I nodded. "That struck me as a rather sophisticated concept for a ten-year-old to grasp." I pulled out a group of black-and-white snapshots and handed them to Andy. "A note on the envelope these came out of describes them as the only surviving photos of Betty Brophy Boyle's childhood. When she got married, she must have become the house photographer because there are loads of pictures of her two boys. Not many of her."

While Andy studied a photo of Betty as a child, standing at the ocean's edge in overalls, I ordered French toast for me and the usual for Andy. He turned the photo over and read aloud. "Betty, age 5." I took the photo from his hand. Even at five, the child's smile seemed tentative. If the writing on the envelope was to be believed, only one other picture of Betty's childhood survived. Standing in the midst of a large group of girls in long white dresses, she wore the same shy grin. Someone had printed *Eighth grade graduation, 1958* on the back.

Only in the next picture, which was a copy of the photo Johnny had showed us the night before, did Betty's eyes match the smile on her lips. Wrapped in the arms of a young man with slicked-down hair—her husband, Buddy—Betty rested her cheek on the head of a chubby, happy baby in a long white christening gown. A notation said the photo was of John James Boyle, the man I'd seen perform as Johnny Angelini.

"They look like a happy family," Andy observed.

"Did Johnny ever suggest otherwise?"

He shook his head. "I don't know Johnny all that well. By the time I met him, he must have been forty or close to it. If I even realized that his mother wasn't around, I would have assumed she'd died of natural causes. No one ever said a word to me about her disappearance." He laid the photos on top of the folder.

I moved on to a collection of color photos. "Pictures of Johnny as a baby." I pulled out one fading snapshot. "Look at this one. Notice anything?"

"It's what we'd call a 'selfie.' Betty snapped the picture by holding her arm out. Can't see much of her but she did an excellent job getting Johnny in the frame."

"Notice anything else?"

He shrugged.

"Anyone else?"

He studied the photo.

"Everyone is looking in one direction because ..." I led him to the answer.

"Because they're looking at Martin Luther King, Jr." He whistled. "Look how close she got!"

"You could also say, 'Look how close she got Johnny to Martin Luther King, Jr.' She made sure Johnny was part of the action when the convention came to town."

"Who's the cowgirl?" He held up a photo of a pretty young girl in a straw hat holding baby Johnny.

"A Jersey Johnson Girl. They served as hostesses at the convention. Story's in one of the clippings." I passed him another photo. "Betty found someone to handle the camera so she and Johnny could get into a picture with some of the civil rights protestors on the Boardwalk."

"That's pretty sweet how she took the kid everywhere with her." Andy spoke softly.

"We can't know what she would have become, but she certainly appeared to be a doting mother during his first six months."

"What are the facts of her disappearance?" Andy was still a private investigator at heart.

"Thursday, August 27, 1964, she worked a party at the Bella Napoli restaurant on the 2300 block of Pacific Avenue. She left sometime around midnight. No one provided a precise time."

"No timecards?"

"Not even a sign-out sheet as far as these records show. According to the notes, she worked later than usual and was in a hurry to get home. She was wearing a white uniform, a black apron, white rubber-soled shoes, and carrying a straw handbag." I flipped through the yellow sheaves of paper. "A note from Johnny says his grandparents and father compiled these files. It looks as if they got as much information as they could from the police, then interviewed several people themselves to verify what the cops had told them."

I handed the pages to Andy. He glanced through them. "I'll read them later, assuming I can stay awake tonight."

I wasn't overly optimistic about that possibility. I continued, "According to the notes, the police interviewed Betty's coworkers at Bella Napoli, but the only names mentioned here are the two owners and a cook. All three of them passed away in the late '80s." I paused. "Why no additional names—kitchen staff, other waitresses? Even if the police did a superficial investigation, Buddy went looking for Betty the next day. Wouldn't he have spoken to her coworkers?"

"I doubt he started writing everything down the first day. These notes were probably started after the police stopped actively working the case—most seasonal workers would have been long gone by then."

"Everyone at the restaurant assumed Betty left via the back door that night, but no one remembered seeing her leave."

Andy flipped through an original copy of the 1964 Democratic National Convention program. "Thursday was a big night. Last day of the convention, and it ended with a birthday party for LBJ—went to midnight according to the schedule, although I thought I saw a clipping that the events ran late."

"Streets should have been busy, unless everybody was up on the Boardwalk for the parade and fireworks. She could have disappeared into the crowd," I said.

Andy gazed out the window and sighed. "This might be the only time I see the ocean today."

"It's a mere seven-and-a-half hours until our rendezvous on the beach. In the meantime, I thought I'd try to track down some of the people in these clippings."

"Fifty-year-old clippings?" He appeared amused. "Good luck."

"I want to at least be able to tell Johnny we tried. I'm going to work on the assumption that she was murdered. If she'd had an accident, her body would probably have turned up. As hopeful as Johnny's amnesia theory is, I don't think it's feasible. And I can't believe she is still living with an abductor after fifty years."

"Suicide?"

"It doesn't seem her family even considered the possibility. If I uncover something to suggest it, I'll investigate, but I'm not headed down that road."

Andy leafed through the newspaper clippings. "Not much to go on here. It doesn't look as if the story got much play."

"Most of these articles are about the convention. There are only two about Betty's disappearance, and reading between the lines, the cops thought she ran away." I picked up the photo of Betty holding baby Johnny in his christening gown. "I know looks can be deceiving, but from this photo, I'd say there's no way she would have left her little boy behind. I'm going to start by testing that assumption."

"Uh huh." Andy had become engrossed in fifty-year-old political news.

"One of the few names I have to work with is a next-door neighbor, Lorraine Wasserman." I pointed to a handwritten notation on a sheet from a yellow legal pad. "Looks like the Boyles lived on Arctic Avenue at the time."

Andy glanced at the note. "That was decades ago."

"Yes, but Lorraine Wasserman is still listed as living there according to an online search. I think I'll walk over and check it out. Do you have a better idea?"

"Not about a fifty-year-old case." He held up the yellowing front page of a copy of the *Atlantic City Press.* "Poor LBJ. It looks as if Kennedy's ghost was haunting Convention Hall. Johnson had to deliver his acceptance speech after a huge ovation for Bobby Kennedy's intro to a movie about JFK. This article also talks about the unveiling of the Kennedy bust on the Boardwalk just before the convention started."

"Betty and Johnny attended the dedication—there's a picture with that written on the back." I found the snapshot and passed it across the table. "Andy, I'd like to help Johnny. But I have to know why such a highly educated guy talks the way he does. Using double negatives and words like *broad* and *dame*? And didn't people stop 'digging' everything sometime in the last century?"

"Johnny's father was a huge Sinatra fan, and I guess he got Johnny into the Rat Pack thing. He tries to affect that same hip kind of speech—you know, a playful, kind of wise-guy banter. You may recall that he actually uttered the phrase, 'Ring-a-ding-ding.'"

"He must not have been exactly the epitome of cool in the '80s."

"True, idolizing the Rat Pack wasn't so cool then for kids Johnny's age, but he learned at his father's knee."

"His birthday is so ironic."

"In what way?"

"He was born on February 9, 1964."

"So?"

"That was the day the British invasion began."

"The British invaded America in 1964?"

"Don't be coy. The night Johnny was born the Beatles appeared on *The Ed Sullivan Show.*"

"You weren't even born yet, so where did you pick up that bit of trivia?"

"I was a history major."

"But you never studied."

He was right about that. Most of my knowledge was not the result of book learning. "My parents and grandparents were big on reminiscing, but my newfound encyclopedic knowledge of the social history of previous eras is the result of my slideshow project."

I'd recently scanned photographs of my ancestors, added captions, and set the results to period music. Andy's ears had found the barbershop quartet renditions of "On the Boardwalk in Atlantic City" playing over photos of my great-grandparents in 1920s swim garb particularly painful.

As he groaned at the memory, I continued. "I know my parents' and grandparents' world as well as I know my own, if not better—which brings me to the irony of Johnny's birthday. From what you told me, he always aspired to be a crooner. Those singers held on during the Elvis years and, then, on the very day Johnny arrived, the American pop music scene changed forever and the crooners got left behind. I wonder what time he was born ... Ed Sullivan might even have been on the air!"

"Come on, that world didn't *disappear*. Even *I* know who Frank Sinatra is."

"Yes, and in 1986, when Johnny got out of college, how popular was that crooner scene?"

"Okay, you win." Andy held up his hands in surrender. "You've been winning a lot lately. You might want to think about losing a few, so as not to damage my fragile ego."

"Sure." I focused on organizing the Boyle files. "I'll think about it."

Chapter 3

Lorraine Wasserman looked tired, as if worn out from drinking too many beers and smoking too many cigarettes. She leaned hard on the screen door to push it open eight inches, just enough to get a better look at me. I don't think she wanted to talk about Betty Boyle but resisting would have required more energy than the senior citizen appeared to possess.

"You might as well come in. Hotter than Hades out there. You look wiped out."

I could believe that. I left the Artistical from its entrance on Pacific. My zigzagging walk from there to the Wasserman home on Arctic Avenue, near Florida Avenue, had left my forehead dripping with sweat and my clothes clinging wetly to my torso. I *really* wanted to come in.

I yanked the door open and followed Mrs. Wasserman into a kitchen that contained one attractive item: the window air-conditioner. What did I care about the stacks of unwashed dishes and the piles of newspapers in the corner? The room felt *cool*.

My hostess gestured to a chrome-and-plastic kitchen set that transported me back to 1964 before I'd asked a single question about Betty Boyle. I dropped onto a chair as if I'd just completed a fifty-mile hike.

"You're here about Betty Boyle who lived next door? Johnny's mother?" Mrs. Wasserman pulled a BIC lighter from her apron pocket and relit a half-smoked Marlboro from a plastic ashtray well on its way to overflowing. "That was a long time ago. Don't hear that name very often. I was a young mother with three children who still loved me when Betty lived in that apartment over there." She waved her cigarette at the window. "Second floor."

I turned to look but saw nothing of note, just a brick duplex with one apartment upstairs and one down, each with a wide porch covering the front of the building. On the porch of the apartment where the Boyles had lived, a gray cat stretched out along the wooden railing watching the traffic on Arctic Avenue.

"She lived there with a roommate at first. I don't know why she moved out of her parents' house. Most girls back then stayed at home until they were married. I got no idea how she afforded the place, even with a roommate."

She took a moment to stare at the duplex next door, and I followed her lead. When it was new, the building would have been what my father liked to call a "humble abode."

"When she moved in, she was no more than a kid." Mrs. Wasserman added that she did not want to speak ill of the dead, but she appeared to be quite good at it. "Betty was different from me. Not to be unkind but, in my eyes, she was a bit of a tramp. You probably don't know this, but Johnny arrived seven months after she married Buddy." She waited for me to express shock and horror.

Instead, I empathized with Betty, pregnant in 1963, when rules for female behavior still prevailed and the social upheaval of the late '60s was yet to come. With limited options, marrying Buddy must have seemed like the easiest choice.

"Before she got married, she ran with kind of a fast crowd." Mrs. Wasserman exhaled into my face.

I tried not to recoil from the smoke. "Crowd?"

"Her roommate was this girl named Myra, and the two of them had lots of boyfriends, if you get my drift."

I did.

"Myra lived there until Betty and Buddy got married. As a matter of fact, she brought Buddy home one night and that's how he met Betty. Next thing you know, Myra moved out and Buddy moved in."

Mrs. Wasserman used the dwindling butt of her Marlboro to light another. I waited in silence.

"That Myra wasn't much better than Betty, but she didn't get caught fooling around and end up with a baby in her belly. Though I guess in the long run Betty did fine. Johnny was a sweet boy, and his father really loved him. That Buddy Boyle was a nice young man. He had a hard time for a couple years after Betty left, died ... whatever." She leaned forward as if conveying confidential information. "Depression. At the time, I didn't understand, but life—rotten husband, ungrateful kids—all that taught me about depression."

"Well, it certainly seems as if Buddy had reason to be depressed." I tried to remind Mrs. Wasserman that I had not come to talk about her problems.

"If it weren't for that baby boy, Buddy would have ended up a homeless drunk. For Johnny's sake he had to drag himself out of bed every day. Then, all of sudden, when the kid is about four, maybe five, Buddy pulls himself together, starts a business, and moves to a big house in Margate. Or Ventnor. Never know which town Marven Gardens is in. Marven Gardens. You know, like on the Monopoly board. You know Monopoly?"

It was hard not to. If you missed playing the game in childhood, you couldn't miss the giant Monopoly board on the Boardwalk in front of Bally's—with Marven Gardens misspelled as *Marvin* Gardens, just like on the real game board. I nodded.

"You play Monopoly?"

I shook my head.

"Me neither. I'm only asking because I heard that they added Arctic Avenue to the new version. I wonder how much the properties cost ..." She stopped to think. "Anyway, Monopoly was the reason I didn't even have to leave the house to know that Buddy must have done okay for himself. Marven Gardens was a high-priced square on that game board." She paused to take a long drag on her cigarette. "Johnny's kind of a sad man. No wife. No kids. Still lives with his father. Calls him *papa* now. Wants to be Italian. Calls himself *Angelini.*" She shook her head sadly. "Poor kid. He never got over not having a mother, and he and Buddy were more like brothers than father and son. Buddy got the boy into that ridiculous Rat Pack stuff. If not, maybe the kid could have made something of himself."

I changed the subject. "Do you remember the night Johnny's mother disappeared?"

"Nothing special to remember about that night. I do remember the next morning. Like I didn't have enough to do taking care of my own kids, Buddy Boyle showed up at my front door." Lorraine shook her head. After so many years, when she spoke, she still sounded annoyed.

* * *

There he was, Buddy Boyle, standing on Lorraine Wasserman's porch toting that baby of his. She knew where this was going when she spotted the bottles in his hand and the diapers under his arm. She hadn't even had time to make breakfast for her own kids. She didn't need another mouth to feed, but she had to open the door. He could see her through the screen.

"Lorraine, I hate to ask, but I'm worried about Betty. She didn't come home last night. I just know something horrible has happened."

Lorraine wasn't surprised to see that Buddy had been crying. She knew it was only a matter of time until that girl broke his heart. Buddy looked tough with the slick hair and the shiny suits, but underneath he was a nice boy. Not that Betty. Once a party girl, always a party girl was what Lorraine thought.

"I fell asleep on the couch last night. Johnny woke up at midnight. Betty wasn't there to nurse him. I was so tired, I just gave him a bottle and went back to sleep." Tears filled his eyes, but he blinked them back. "When I woke up this morning, Betty still wasn't there. You haven't seen her have you?" His eyes begged for an answer, any answer.

Did he think Lorraine sat up all night watching what the neighbors did? In truth, she *had* spent some evenings trying to figure out what was going on in the Boyle house but not since the baby arrived. She knew what went on in a house with a six-month-old. She had one herself.

"The baby hasn't eaten. If you give him some formula, I'll replace it," Buddy pleaded.

She knew he would. Buddy was that kind of guy. Honest. Hard-working. And jovial, usually. But not that morning. That day he was frantic. And the baby sensed that something was amiss. He acted fussy and seemed about to burst into full-blown wailing.

"Here, give him to me." She forced cheerfulness into her voice. "Hi, Johnny," she cooed. "You can stay with Aunt Lorraine while Daddy goes to find Mommy." She took the baby into her arms even though a second whining six-month-old was the last thing she needed.

"I have a really bad feeling about this, Lorraine. She knows Johnny needs to nurse. Where could she be?"

Lorraine had a lot of ideas. Maybe not as to *where* Betty was but certainly *why* she might be gone. From the moment she found out Betty had a bun in the oven, she doubted that she was capable of the hard work of being a wife and mother, at least for the long haul. But while she didn't expect Betty to take to motherhood, she never expected her to run off this soon.

Lorraine needed to go the Acme, but she could barely manage the market with her own three, let alone an extra baby in tow. Minding Johnny kept her stuck at home, which is why she was sitting on the porch when Myra stopped by the Boyles' place. Barely noon, and the tramp had her hair piled on top of her head and makeup all over her face. Her cover-up barely concealed her bathing suit, and her bathing suit barely concealed anything at all.

Say what you will about the girl, Myra was persistent. She knocked, she called, she knocked again. Lorraine didn't bother telling the Boyles' visitor that her efforts were futile. She wasn't in the mood to get involved.

"Excuse me, Mrs. Wasserman. It's me, Myra." Leaning across the railing of the Boyles' porch, Myra displayed more cleavage than any decent girl would. "Do you know if Betty is around?"

"They aren't home," Lorraine called across the small space between the houses.

"I thought Betty would be here. I came to meet the baby."

Lorraine didn't bother to point out Johnny in the playpen behind her. She didn't feel like entertaining someone who wasn't her friend and watching that someone coo over a baby that wasn't hers. It wasn't part of her deal with Buddy.

"I don't know where they are." That was true. She wasn't going to start any rumors—at least with Myra.

"Oh." Myra sounded disappointed. "I'll try again later."

Like Lorraine cared what that little tramp did.

* * *

"Later on, when Buddy convinced the police that Betty really was gone, the cops asked me a lot of questions about Buddy and what he did that night. I told them I didn't hear any odd noises at the house and that I didn't hear him go out. Of course, he could have sneaked out, and I wouldn't have heard a thing. But I knew Buddy Boyle would never have left that child alone. *Ever.* His family was the center of his world."

"Including Betty?"

"Yeah, Betty too. Fatherhood changed Buddy from a party boy to a family man in a snap." She tried to snap her fingers but her thumb made no sound as it slipped off her middle finger.

"Did Betty ever seem jealous of the attention Buddy gave Johnny?"

Mrs. Wasserman eyed me as if I were looking for trouble. I noticed a touch of approval in her gaze. "The girl didn't confide in me, but if you want to ask me if she ran off, ask me. I'll tell you that I don't *think* she would ever have left that baby while she was still nursing him. We didn't do that so much in those days. I used the bottle. But Betty read that Princess Grace had breastfed her kids. You know—Grace Kelly, the movie actress, from right up there in Philadelphia." She ignored my nod. "Not from your era, I guess."

"Do you have a theory about what happened that night?"

Mrs. Wasserman shrugged. "The Democratic Convention was in town. I got nothing against Democrats. I am one—on occasion. But during conventions, people get crazy. Betty worked at the Bella Napoli the night she disappeared. Nice, family-owned restaurant, right across the street from Convention Hall. There would be a lot of conventioneers there. I think she got in some sort of trouble."

"What kind of trouble?"

"She'd been home with the baby for six months. Glamorous strangers came to town. Maybe she felt the need to kick up her heels. Like I said, she had been a party girl. Maybe that lifestyle got the best of her. They never found hide nor hair of Betty. I always wondered if she went out on a boat with someone and fell overboard. I can't think of any other reason they never found a single trace."

Neither could I.

Chapter 4

It was 2 PM when I returned to the Artistical. I had just gotten a text from Andy that read *5 hrs til beach.*

I texted back. *Can't wait. Looking for Johnny now.*

Neighbor guilty? Andy asked.

Only of being a bitch. Got to find Johnny.

The information I was looking for came from the doorman, who told me I could find Johnny at the same place every day at 2 PM, sitting at the counter in the Botticelli Buffet.

I spotted the singer easily. He was the only customer wearing a tuxedo. Wide white napkin tucked into his open shirt collar, Johnny hunched over a king-size meatball hoagie. I slipped onto the stool beside him and, after adding his cell number to my phone so I could track him down, told him about my efforts so far.

"I talked to your childhood neighbor, Mrs. Wasserman, this morning."

His smile was genuine and, given the contrast of his whitened teeth against his tanned skin, a bit overwhelming. In the light of day, or at least daytime in the Botticelli Buffet, what I'd initially thought to be theatrical makeup was revealed as his natural skin tone. Not natural to humans, perhaps, but common to well-worn leather goods.

"Crusty old dame, isn't she?" His tone was affectionate. "I still drop by to see her on occasion. Her kids don't, and I probably wouldn't either if I had her for a mother." He took a big bite of his sandwich.

"She told me she cared for you the morning your mother disappeared. She doesn't remember anything else, apparently. I'm guessing she would have mentioned it to you if she had."

"Maybe. I've discovered that people tend to protect the children of murder victims. Even when the children are rounding fifty." He held his plate up. "You want a fry?"

I shook my head.

"Sure?"

I nodded. I was sure. Johnny's plate resembled a bloody crime scene.

"Mrs. Wasserman did mention a friend of your mother's by the name of Myra. She says Myra dropped by that morning—to get her first look at you, actually. Did that name ever come up?"

"My papa used to talk about a broad called Myra that really made good."

"How so?" I pulled out the notebook and pen I'd purchased on my way back from my visit with Mrs. Wasserman. New case, new notebook. Andy liked to say that I was more willing to help with his investigations if I could have a new notebook. New writing supplies always reminded me of the first day of school and the excitement and optimism that came with it.

"My papa said she married some rich doctor. She has a big house in Brigantine. Right on the beach."

"Did you ever meet her?" I smoothed the paper in my spiral notebook and made a note about Myra's place in Brigantine.

"Nah. Papa didn't keep in touch with Mama's friends."

"Do you know her last name?"

Johnny shook his head, wiped his mouth, and pulled his cell phone out of the inside pocket of his tux. "Hey, Papa." His voice, accustomed to drowning out the casino noises, was loud enough that he might have reached his father without telephonic assistance. "How ya doing today?" He listened intently and accepted whatever his father said. "You remember Myra? That chick that Mama knew, they went to school and then worked together? You told me she married some doctor. You recollect his name?" Again, he listened intently. "Nah, no problem. Just curious."

Johnny dropped his phone on the counter and picked up his sandwich. "He says he feels better. I don't know what to think. First, he says he's in horrible pain. Then he says he's okay. How do I know what to do? I'm no doctor, and he won't see one." He took a bite and chewed as he spoke. "And he doesn't know Myra's last name."

At that point, his phone played "Strangers in the Night." He picked it up. "You okay?" He paused. "Oh." He paused. "What kind?" He paused. "Thanks." Placing the phone back on the table, he looked at me. "Morris. Myra married a Dr. Morris. A surgeon."

"Assuming she's still in Brigantine, I'll go see her this afternoon."

Johnny wiped the sauce from his lips, brushed the crumbs off his hands, and pushed his plate away.

"I appreciate your doing this. If you understood what kind of lady my mama was, you'd be happy that you are helping find out what happened to her." He spun his stool so it faced mine but didn't make eye contact. His eyes lost their focus. "My papa told me a story about my mama during the convention. There were protestors out on the Boardwalk. Black people from Mississippi whose seats at the convention got stolen by white guys. My mama asked them why they were protesting, and they told her. She walked over to James'—the store right there on the Boardwalk—and bought salt water taffy for those people. To welcome them to Atlantic City." His eyes filled with tears at the tale. "Anyway, thanks. If there's anything I can do for you," Johnny's tone brightened, "like maybe sing at your wedding, you let me know."

"No need to warm up for that performance."

"What's the deal with you and Andy?"

"We're dating, that's all."

"And you share a house?"

"It's corporate housing. Andy is head of security, and I am the VIP concierge at the hotel."

"Nice gig. How'd you get that?"

"The owner liked Andy and lured him away from the PI business to handle security for him." Actually, he lured Andy away from sailing around the Caribbean between gigs. "A position for me was one of the lures."

"Lucky. He could have made you a housekeeper," he joked.

Not if he'd ever seen my apartment. I didn't mention that I couldn't even make a bed to save my life. "I have a marketing background. I guess VIP concierge was as close as he could get."

"Still don't see why you two shouldn't get married. Beck is a good looking guy. Big. Strong. Looks like an aging surfer, but with a better haircut and grown-up clothes. I bet he could still give a girl a run for her money. You should get him to marry you before some bathing beauty down in the Bahamas snatches him right out from under your nose."

I shrugged. "We're having a good time."

"Is that what you think life is about? Having a good time?"

I considered the question carefully. "Pretty much."

"What about *bambinos*?"

I shook my head. "Not for me."

"Has it occurred to you that you're getting to the point where it will be too late for you?" Johnny sure knew how to make a woman feel good about herself.

"Thanks for the reminder." I didn't fight my sarcastic tone.

"A woman should have a husband. Family life is good," Johnny said with conviction.

Maybe when you're one of the family members being taken care of—not the wife and mother who's responsible for meeting the needs of everyone in the house. "If family is so good, why don't you have one?"

"That is another story. We're talking about you." With Sinatra-esque flair, Johnny shot a finger in my direction just in case I felt confused as to who *you* was.

"You are beginning to sound like my girlfriends. I should point out that I have spent the last few weeks avoiding them."

"You avoid your friends?" Johnny scowled. "What kind of girl are you? What kind of friends are they?"

"The kind who advise me to dump Andy and find some guy with a nine-to-five job and a lovely home in north Jersey, southern Connecticut, or suburban Philadelphia, because that's what they did and they love their lives. And the thing is, I respect that they are happy doing something that I don't want to do. But they can't accept that I'm happy doing something they don't want to do."

Judging by his expression neither could Johnny. "I don't see any sparkle in your eyes. Maybe they don't either."

"I have dull army-green eyes. They *never* sparkle. Did you ever hear anyone say, Isn't it beautiful how the sun glimmers on that Sherman tank?"

Johnny dropped the subject of my eyes. "You and Andy have a good life together?"

"We have a great life, aside from these past few weeks when he's been so burnt out and depressed by office work that he can barely stay awake."

"Hmmmm." Johnny didn't meet my gaze.

"No, that's really the reason. It's his work, not me."

He returned to his main point. "So why not cement the deal? Are you afraid of getting married, afraid you two will end up in Splitsville?"

"No." I thought Johnny had just revealed a lot about his own reluctance to marry, not mine. "I gotta go." Before I begin to dislike you, I thought. "I want to see Myra Morris today if I can."

"I appreciate that. I do. Tell you what, to say thank you I'll set you up with Sylvia in the beauty salon. She'll make you look like a sexy dame."

"I've really got to get going. Really."

Chapter 5

I found an address online in Brigantine for a Maxwell Morris, with a household that included "Myra, aged 65–70," a likely candidate to be Betty's friend. I didn't call to check or to say I was coming. Andy had taught me the value of making unexpected appearances and observing facial reactions.

I sent Andy an email telling him that I was taking the rental car. Sequestered somewhere in the deepest, darkest recesses of the hotel, he must have ranked my trip in a rental car to the next town right up there with a getaway in a private plane to Cannes. I tried to think of something to add to make him feel better, but he was bored, not stupid. I just added *See u at 7.*

The Morris house left little space for a driveway, so I parked on the street. As I walked past the large, late model Mercedes in the driveway, I caught a glimpse of Atlantic City through soaring panes of glass. If this was Myra's place, I could see what Johnny meant. She had done all right for herself. And she got to live into the 21st century, something Betty Boyle never had a chance to do.

To me, Betty Boyle, gone before I was born, was a historical figure. Dead in the first months of the transition to the Beatles years, she remained frozen forever in the Elvis era. In the first instant I looked at Myra Morris, still vibrant and attractive fifty years later, I felt sadness about all the years and all the changes Betty Boyle had missed.

Aside from a shock of fashionably cropped white hair, nothing about Myra Morris suggested senior citizen. No, that was wrong. She did look like a senior, but the type for whom retirement is a lark—the type who smiles out from ads for expensive resorts and luxury cruises. She appeared energetic and beautiful despite wrinkles on her over-tanned skin. Her clothes, maybe a size two petite, were expensive in a casual, I-just-stopped-by-after-golf-before-I-head-to-the-club-for-dinner fashion. Her smile was quizzical. *I'm sure once I know who you are, I'll be happy to see you.*

"Mrs. Morris, I wonder if I could ask you a few questions about Betty Boyle."

"Betty Boyle?" Her reaction was sharp, but her controlled expression made sure I couldn't figure out why. Fear? Sadness? Distaste? Or simply surprise? I didn't know. "I haven't heard that name in years. Why are you asking?" Her polite smile grew tight, unnatural.

"Her husband is dying, and her son would like him to know the truth about his mother's disappearance before he goes."

"Buddy's dying?" The mask evaporated. Myra seemed shaken.

I nodded. "Cancer. They thought they got it the first time, but apparently it came back. This time he's choosing not to fight."

She gazed over my shoulder. "Life can be a challenge at this age." She pulled herself back from wherever she'd gone. "Are you a cop?"

"Just a friend who's making some inquiries."

She nodded as she considered her options. After a few seconds, she opened the door wide and stepped aside. "Please come in. It's hot out there." Then, in what I viewed as an effort to be a good hostess, she prattled on about heat and humidity while she led me through an overly chilled hallway. I followed her into an elegant room with unobstructed views of Atlantic City through windows with frost forming in the corners. Who thought to carry a sweater on a 98-degree day?

Actually, Myra Morris did. She had tied a bright pink cardigan around the shoulders of the crisp white blouse that matched her equally crisp white slacks. Her living room appeared as neat as she did but far less crisp, combining the warmth of a socialite's library with the coolness of modern style.

Following the wave of Myra's hand, I headed for a dark sofa designed for comfort. Before I sat, I admired a very formal portrait marred only by the excesses of 1970s fashion. "Beautiful family." A young man in glasses that were as oversized as his lapels and his tie had one arm wrapped around a young, ruffle-adorned Myra and the other around two little girls, one the spitting image of her father, the luckier one the spitting image of her mother.

"Thank you. Although I would suggest if you're going to have your family immortalized in oil, everyone should take off their glasses." The line gave the impression of being well rehearsed. She waited for me to chuckle, so I did as I lowered myself onto the couch.

Myra sat on the edge of a wing chair across a heavy mahogany coffee table with her back to what, even on a day made hazy by heavy air, was a fantastic view. I guessed she'd come to take it for granted over the years.

"I understand you worked and lived with Betty." I smiled, rather sweetly I thought.

"I wasn't working with her at the time she died, but I had worked with her before. I knew her from high school. We did share an apartment, but then Betty met Buddy. I moved out, and he moved in. I didn't see her much after that. I took some time off to travel. Why wouldn't I? We were young." She looked embarrassed. I detected a defensive tone that disappeared when she changed the subject. "I did see Betty briefly before she died."

She stared past me. Later, I realized that she could share the view in a large gilded mirror behind me, but I don't think that was what she was seeing as she gazed at the reflection of Atlantic City.

"I had only been back home for a month or so when the Democratic Convention came to town. Not exactly sure why they brought it here. The city was past its prime, and it was years before gambling came in." She leaned forward and opened an ornate silver box on the coffee table. She pulled out a cigarette and lit it with a matching silver lighter. Only after she exhaled did she ask if I minded.

How could I? I was in her house.

"I only allow myself three a day." She took another deep drag that said she really needed one of those three right now. "Anyway, as you might know, the Democrats nominated Lyndon Johnson here. A friend told me about a party for some of the Mid-Atlantic delegations at a restaurant behind Convention Hall. I sneaked in. Actually, I didn't have to sneak. I just walked in. No matter. There was Betty, working, serving drinks. That was one or two nights before she disappeared. I didn't go near the convention on Monday, the first day. So, I believe it must have been Tuesday. It's amazing to think such a significant detail—the last time I saw my friend—could slip away, but it has." She shook her head in amazement.

"Did anything unusual happen that night?"

She hesitated. "I have to say yes. I witnessed an odd, and by odd, I mean *bad* situation, but I don't think it had anything to do with Betty's disappearance."

"What happened?"

"I can't imagine that it matters."

"Everything Betty did that week matters."

"It was a long time ago."

"Not to her son. He lives with it every day."

Myra's expression grew sad, even wistful I thought. A full minute passed before she spoke.

* * *

Myra Morris would never forget that night. She knew that even before she saw Betty. Myra felt so foolish, thinking that simply by taking off her waitress uniform, she could rise from serving to mingling. She'd been so naïve to think that she could stroll into an event with the conventioneers and meet someone nice, someone who would care about her. She couldn't even remember who told her about the party for the Mid-Atlantic delegates. She didn't mind going alone. Being on her own made it easier to meet people, but the moment she stepped through the door, she knew it wouldn't matter at this party. She didn't fit in.

Chapter 5

In 1964, it was easy to pick out the kids who went to college. As she looked around the restaurant, Myra knew that she had walked into a room full of them. Sure, they had graduated anywhere from five to forty years earlier, but they were still frat boys and sorority girls. There were very few women in the room, but enough that she could compare her stylish haircut to their pageboys and her colored beads to their pearls. When she came back to Atlantic City, ten pounds heavier than when she left, she worked with her meager budget to purchase a versatile wardrobe. For church and special occasions, she'd tried hard to find something Jacqueline Kennedy would have worn, but as she looked around that room, she realized she had spent her dollars in the wrong stores. A fancy design made of cheap material was still a cheap dress. She was wearing the only cheap dress in the room. Cheap and loud.

It wasn't that everyone in the room was dressed in identical clothes; it was just that the people were all the same. She suspected that if they stripped naked, they would still be able to pick each other out in a crowd. Short, tall, skinny, plump—never fat—these women would recognize each other. She didn't understand what made them the same. Maybe it was the knowledge that they came from the right suburb, went to the right schools, and made all the right choices that bound them.

She was about to slip away and walk down the Boardwalk to the Chalfonte-Haddon Hall, where the Texas delegates, like their President, Lyndon Johnson, might be more down-to-earth. Then she spotted Betty. Tempted to pretend she hadn't seen her old friend, she averted her eyes but didn't turn her back. None of the women in pearls knew the servers, but Betty didn't deserve to be snubbed. She had never done anything *intentional* to hurt Myra. They had been the best of friends until Betty got involved with Buddy.

Within a day of Betty and Buddy's rendezvous with true love, Myra moved back home with her family. Within a month of Betty's marriage, Myra left Atlantic City. She'd stayed away for a year, returning only in early August. She hadn't called Betty to say she was back in town. She wasn't sure she would get in touch. She wasn't sure she would even say hello that night. She was still deciding when Betty called her name. "Myra!" Myra looked up to see the waitress smiling broadly.

The decision had been made for her. "Betty?" Myra feigned surprise. She moved forward through the tables crowded together to accommodate the crowd. "I was trying to figure out if that was really you," she lied.

"Myra! You're back!" Betty held an empty tray under her left arm and hugged Myra with her right. "I'm so happy to see you!"

Myra fought the urge to recoil. People must have been staring.

"You look beautiful." Betty eyed her friend's white and blue dress with the red trim. "Very patriotic. I love it!"

The comment sealed that dress's fate. The tags were still on her dresser. Maybe she could return it. "I've been meaning to call. I got back a few weeks ago."

"And you didn't let me know?"

Myra detected no tinge of disapproval in Betty's voice, just surprise. "I had a lot to do. I found a job. Waitressing. Over at the Claridge."

"That's wonderful, Myra. I hear it's a nice place to work."

"So you're still working here, I see." Myra tried to convey approval when what she felt was disgust. Betty had no ambition at all.

"I came back when the season started. Myra, you have to come see my baby. His name is Johnny. He's six months old now. He looks so much like Buddy."

"That's great." Myra tried to sound happy for her old friend.

"He sits up and smiles and laughs." Betty's face beamed. "He's a lot of fun."

Myra wasn't into that kind of fun. She didn't want to talk about Betty and Buddy's baby.

"I generally work lunch. Buddy tends bar at night. Between the two of us we do okay. This week we switched so I can work the convention events. It's so exciting. These are all important people."

People who think that they are important and you are not, Myra thought. She forced a smile and kept silent.

Betty sighed. "Of course, it would have been a lot more exciting if President Kennedy were here. I named my baby after him."

Myra could understand the sentimentality about the death of the handsome president with the beautiful wife and the adorable children, but naming your kid after him? Boulevards and junior high schools—

that she could understand. But your baby? Myra found that pathetic. "I thought you'd name him after Buddy."

"Well, I was going to, but after the assassination ..." The recollection appeared to affect Betty so much that she couldn't go on. "Wait here."

Myra didn't get people who reacted so strongly to the death of a man they didn't even know. There were a lot of them. If the memorials didn't stop, it would be hard to find a street in the country that didn't bear some variation of John F. Kennedy's name.

Watching Betty across the room, she wondered why the waitress who named her child after the president didn't join the ranks of women across the country who wanted to look like Jacqueline Kennedy. Betty's hairdo was badly in need of updating. How had they ever been such close friends?

Myra lit a cigarette and pretended she was waiting for her very important date rather than her waitress friend. She used the time to study the people she wanted to fit in with, the crowd she wanted to become part of. She needed a better life for herself. Better than she had. Better than her parents had. Better than her parents expected her to have. She'd been thinking about taking classes after work. Standing in the middle of the Bella Napoli that night, she realized night school might give her a degree but it would not make her look the way these people did. So confident, not only of their party's victory, but of their personal success. College kids.

While she was away, Myra had spent a lot of time with a different kind of college girl. That girl would have called the people in this room "Establishment," and she railed against the Establishment. She had shown her disdain by wearing black clothes, dark makeup, and long straight hair. She lived in New York City and called herself a beatnik. Myra had considered giving the girl's lifestyle a try, even though she found the poetry incomprehensible and the music boring. Then her cousin told her the Beat movement was dead. Myra never asked how a high school girl from Pittsburgh knew that, but she accepted her cousin's word. Besides, New York City wasn't what Myra wanted from life. She wanted a house in the suburbs, a Ford Country Squire station wagon, and a husband in a gray flannel suit who drove to his office every morning while she stayed home taking care of the kids—two boys and two girls—and a sheepdog. Once she got a little money together she would get away from Atlantic City, move to a big city, and meet a man who worked in an office. No bartenders in her future. She'd promised herself.

Maybe it was better that Betty had married Buddy. He had no aspirations. Neither did Betty. She smiled as she served drinks. Not a fake smile like the one Myra pasted on her face in the hopes of getting bigger tips, but a genuine smile. Myra wondered if Betty was a little slow. She seemed so easily pleased.

"Here." Betty handed her a glass. "It's only ginger ale. That's all the bartender will give me for free."

Myra said thanks—although a non-alcoholic drink was the last thing she wanted or needed right then.

"Have you seen a lot of the convention?"

"Not much to see, yet." Myra's delivery was as flat as Betty's was animated.

"But you work at the Claridge. *The Today Show* is broadcasting from there. Did you see Hugh Downs?"

Myra could not have cared less about some morning show host. "I don't have much time to roam around when I'm working."

"Have you seen the protestors out front of the convention center?" Betty's tone suggested excitement.

Myra's suggested disgust. "What is all that about?"

Betty explained, in a somewhat confusing fashion, how the Democratic Party in Mississippi had denied convention seats to the Negroes who were protesting.

"How do you know all this?"

"I talked to them."

"Betty, are you crazy? People will think you are like those boys who got killed down there. You read about them, didn't you? White people murdered them along with the Negro boy they were with. Killed them for trying to help the Mississippi Negroes."

"Don't be silly, Myra. This isn't Mississippi. This is New Jersey."

"Betty, don't be naïve. There are a lot of people right here in Atlantic City who don't want colored people mixing with white people."

"Well, that has to change."

"Betty, be careful. What about that biker in the apartment downstairs? The one with the Confederate flags on his motorcycle and in his window? God, Betty, he even had a Confederate flag beach towel. What if he saw you?"

A voice called, "Hey, honey, we need some beer here. You can have your own party, with your own kind, on your own time."

The words stung Myra but Betty didn't take offense. She still had a smile on her face.

"Look, I've got to go. Promise me you'll come see the baby. I can give you your bracelet back. You left it when you moved."

After what happened, Betty thinks she would care about a bracelet?

Myra made a promise she was fairly sure she would not keep. Then she noticed the spreading stain on Betty's dress, but she didn't say anything. If she had, the incident with the scion of the Braddock family might not have happened. But she said nothing. Myra let Betty walk away with a wet spot growing on her uniform where it covered her left breast. Betty should have been more careful. She'd been nursing for six months. She must have known that could happen.

Myra headed for the door but she'd only gone a few steps when she heard a tray crash and then a voice say, "Hey, thanks for being my drink."

Myra turned and saw Betty fighting off one of the frat boy types—a man, young but too old to act like a kid. He pulled Betty's breast out of her uniform and nursing bra. He tried to work Betty's swollen nipple into his mouth, while his frat boy friends looked on chanting: "Drink, Drink, Drink!"

Betty defended herself well. A young man wearing a seersucker suit and a worried expression pushed through the crowd but Betty had taken care of her attacker long before the guy reached the culprit. Betty planted two hands on the drunkard's chest and pushed him away. She probably couldn't have moved him if he hadn't been drunk. She probably wouldn't have *needed* to move him if he hadn't been drunk. Betty wasn't exactly this guy's type.

Less than a minute passed before Betty had regained her balance, straightened her clothing, and placed her hands on her hips. Her assailant registered only amusement as she spoke. "I have a husband and son who love me." She picked up a drink from the table and threw it in his face. "Who could ever love you?"

His friends hooted, but the man's smile disappeared. Myra saw his eyes narrow and his expression turn to hate. She had seen such an odious look at the movies, but never in real life. Betty returned the man's stare without flinching.

The incident was brief. The fellow in the seersucker suit signaled to one of the youngest of the frat boy types to stop laughing and help him control the inebriated lout. The younger man straightened up and moved fast. While he held the protesting drunk in his chair, the man in the seersucker suit whispered in the hard-drinker's ear. Finally, the over-aged frat boy shrugged, laughed, and acted blasé as he mopped the liquid off his summer suit.

He was still laughing when Betty retrieved her tray from the floor and headed back to the bar.

* * *

"Most of the crowd never even knew what happened, or they didn't care if they happened to see." Myra did not appear perplexed by the crowd's lack of concern. "It was the times."

"Did you know the man's name?" My question called Myra back from 1964.

"When I heard someone say he was Ward Braddock, I recognized him. At that point, his picture was always in the paper, especially in the society pages. He was marrying some girl from a family even richer than the Braddocks. Ward was the rising star of that family. Senator Braddock, Governor Braddock—*those* Braddocks. He was in the New Jersey State Senate at that point, waiting for a bigger job to open up, I guess. Everyone thought he'd be the Braddock to make president."

"What went wrong?"

"Apparently his behavior that night was typical."

Myra shrugged and lit another cigarette. "Anyway, based on the things Betty said that night, I think she really might have changed in the future, developed a real interest in politics, in causes—not just fancy events and celebrities. She acted so excited about seeing Martin Luther King, Jr. the day before. I didn't even know who he was back then." Despite her effort to speak well of Betty, Myra's tone indicated disapproval. "And Bobby Kennedy. She sneaked away from her job and into the convention hall to hear him speak."

Interesting, but I wanted to hear more about Ward Braddock.

Myra never saw him again, at least not in person. "He got in some sort of jam not long after. Never made a run for high office. And then he showed up on the news."

"What did he do to get back into the news?"

"Nothing. He became an anchor on a local channel. Some UHF station, not a major network. Kind of a low-level job for a Braddock. He tried to create the impression that he worked on television for New Jersey's sake, not his own."

"How was he as a newsman?"

Myra leaned forward and flicked the ashes from the tip of her cigarette into a heavy crystal ashtray. "He read the teleprompter, won some awards, and wrote a memoir. I should say *bought* some awards and *published* a memoir. Rumor has it he didn't actually write the book. He's retired now, but he's been mentioned in the papers recently because his son is running for governor."

"Is the son a jerk, too?"

"That I don't know, but the apple never falls far from the tree."

"After Betty disappeared, did you ever think Braddock might have had something to do with it?"

She thought long and hard before she answered. "No." She leaned forward and flicked her ashes again. "People like the Braddocks didn't even register that they'd insulted someone, hurt someone. I told the story to the police. I assume they interviewed the guy. Not that they would have given him any grief. In those days, cops didn't mess with the bigwigs."

"Did Buddy call you when Betty disappeared?"

She shook her head. "He didn't know I was back in town."

"How did you hear Betty was missing?"

"Newspaper. There was a small story maybe a week after she disappeared. My father saw it. Of course, eventually the cops tracked me down. Someone at Bella Napoli had told them about the incident with Ward Braddock and that I'd been there."

"What did you think happened to Betty?"

She worked hard at flicking her ashes and kept her eyes on her efforts. "I thought she just had some bad luck and ran into some crazy person who killed her." She paused. She had something else to say. I gave her time to figure out how she would say it. "Sometimes I wonder if supporting those protestors had something to do with it."

"You think a racist might have targeted her?"

Myra's eyes were still on the heavy crystal ashtray. "It wouldn't have been that shocking back then considering the attitudes. But that is pure speculation."

"What about that biker in the apartment downstairs?"

She shook her head. "He was a big talker." She abandoned her efforts with the ashes and leaned back in her chair. "A poser. Tried to look like a tough guy. I think the Confederate flag stuff was just part of the biker image he wanted to project."

"Do you know what happened to him?"

She shook her head. "Nothing good, I imagine. Why? Do you want to check him out?" She considered the idea and shrugged. "I guess it wouldn't hurt. Assuming he didn't fall off that bike and crack his head open, he must be close to eighty now. Name is Larry Donovan."

"Did he get along with Betty?"

"We all coexisted. Betty and I had to pass his porch to climb the stairs to our apartment. His friends would leer and make jokes because that was the only way they knew to deal with women. Even then I found them offensive. The jokes, I mean. I guess his friends, too. Bunch of losers. They had good motorcycles and bad jobs, when they bothered to work. Back then, being a bad-ass on a Harley with a black leather jacket and tattoos on your arms was something you did full time or not at all. Certainly not the kind of man I was interested in."

"Did you ever believe Betty might have just run away?"

Shaking her head created a bizarre display of smoke as Myra exhaled with the theatricality of a Broadway diva. "She and Buddy were totally in love. I know some folks said they had a shotgun wedding, but it wasn't. I mean, yes, she was pregnant, but no one had to hold a gun to Buddy's head." Again, Myra grew wistful. "Once Buddy met Betty, it was kismet." She paused as if debating whether to share. "I dated Buddy a few times. I liked him. I would have gone out with him again, but then he met Betty. After that, I became invisible. The rest is history. Then I met Max, and this is my history." She waved her arm at her house ending with a pointing gesture to direct my eyes to the view.

"Nice history."

"I was lucky. When I was younger, I did some dumb things, wanted some stupid things—like mingling with the Braddocks and their social set. Betty was smarter than I was, at least in that way. She had no delusions of grandeur. She didn't live to see Buddy become a success, but I don't think she would have cared if he tended bar forever. Buddy made the right choice, marrying Betty."

"Did you ever see her baby?"

She inhaled and leaned forward to grind out the cigarette as she spoke. "I stopped by her apartment a couple days after I ran into her, but she wasn't there. That cranky neighbor didn't know where she was. Turns out no one did." She shook her head as if amazed. "How could I know that she was really gone?"

Myra stared over my shoulder again. "After that day in 1963 when I moved out, Betty called one or two times. I did talk to her, but she was so caught up in her new life with Buddy that we never got together. Nowadays, I hear about Buddy once in a while. I did see Johnny sing once. He uses an Italian name, but I knew he was Johnny Boyle. He put on a pretty good show." She shook her head as if returning from a faraway place before letting her eyes meet mine. "No Frank Sinatra, but not bad. His father must be proud." She smiled but only politely.

"Did you introduce yourself to Johnny?"

"No." Myra reacted with surprise. "I didn't think he'd want to meet me." She shrugged. "If you see Buddy, please give him my best. I'll keep him in my prayers." Although she had already extinguished her cigarette, she ground it out again.

I took it as my signal to leave.

Chapter 6

Evenings on the beach are the most alluring time to me. In Atlantic City, by 6 PM when the lifeguards take off, parents have removed their children from the sun, heat, and sheer excitement of the seashore, and sunbathers without families in tow have already drifted off to the bars, the restaurants, and, most of all, the casinos. They were all gone by 7 PM when I followed the Artistical's wooden walkway to the beach.

I bypassed the action at the beach-side bar where singles scavenged for dates and seagulls scavenged for food. I found Andy hidden by high dunes from the happy hour crowd at the bar and the strollers on the Boardwalk. As I gazed at my aging surfer, as Johnny had dubbed him, sprawled face-down on a blanket, I saw a lot more aging than surfer.

I unfurled my beach towel and spread it on the sand beside his lifeless form. "Nice breeze." I plopped down and breathed in the ocean air. "It's such a relief from today's heat."

"How would I know?" His tone registered only one step above a whine. "I was stuck inside all day."

"Consider yourself lucky. Today was a classic triple H. Hot, hazy, and humid." Why was I impersonating a plucky TV weather personality? Nothing about Andy's mood suggested he wanted to hear plucky. I toned down my approach. "It's much better now. If you sit up, you can catch a little bit of breeze."

"Uh huh."

"And you're missing the view."

"We live at the beach." He didn't look up.

"This is different."

"I can hear the surf. I'll open my eyes in a few minutes. The ocean will still be there."

I couldn't argue with Andy's logic.

After a couple moments of silence, he asked, "Did you have a good day?"

"I am beginning to get a feel for the world Betty Boyle lived in. I talked to that neighbor and also one of her girlfriends. Listening to people talk about her transports me to the 1960s."

"If I open my eyes, am I going to find a hippie chick sitting next to me?"

"Not *that* part of the '60s—the early years when the '50s were still fading away. The world was starting to change, but Betty seemed to be content with her life. She adored her husband and their baby. I'm sure some people disapproved that she got pregnant before marriage, but she was thrilled to be a mom. And then, almost before her family life began, it ended."

"Any idea why?" Without opening his eyes, Andy lifted himself onto one elbow, found the effort too much, and fell onto his back.

"Not yet. Though her girlfriend Myra may have been carrying a torch for Buddy. She admits to having dated him before he met Betty, but I think she was downplaying how much she really cared about him."

"What makes you say that?" Andy opened his eyes to ask the question but they slid shut as soon as the words were out of his mouth.

"Woman's intuition."

"If I remember correctly, your intuition once told you I was trying to murder you."

"That was a long time ago. And your behavior *was* a little odd."

"I thought you were a heartless, cold-blooded killer." He yawned.

"I like to think of that as meeting cute." I closed my eyes and let the ocean breeze wash away any thoughts of the investigation in Ocean City that had brought us together—an investigation in which I was the prime suspect at one point. When I opened my eyes, Andy was still lying limp beside me.

"Let's go in the water," I suggested. "The surf will perk you up. It's refreshing."

By the time we got beyond the breakers, Andy had stopped complaining. He even found the energy to let me hold onto him and bounce with him in the gentle waves. "Tell me more." He was suddenly wide awake and interested. "Do you think this Myra was so infatuated with Buddy Boyle that she might have eliminated Betty to get him back?"

"I don't think so." As we drifted south with the current, I recapped Myra's story, including the part about Betty Boyle's public encounter with Ward Braddock.

"I always heard he was a low-life, but I don't know that much about him. By the time I got old enough to pay attention, he was no longer a player."

I concluded by telling him about Myra's visit to the Boyle apartment the day after Betty went missing. "Betty was already gone, forever as it turned out, but Myra didn't know that at the time."

"Or, did she?" Andy mused. "Maybe she came by as part of her cover story. Or to comfort Buddy when he found out his wife was dead—because she'd killed her." I saw Andy's expression turn to surprise. "Breaker!"

The wave tore us apart. I waited for the force to pass before I popped to the surface. Andy had washed toward shore. He fought his way back to me. "Surf is certainly picking up out here."

I didn't miss a beat. "Myra did okay."

"But back then she couldn't know that she would."

"I don't think she ever would have settled for Buddy. She told me she aspired to a lifestyle like the Braddocks had, and from what I've heard, Buddy would never fit into that world. Even if he had money."

"Given what I've seen in the news over the years, the Braddocks' world might not be a very nice place to live." Andy jumped over another big breaker.

I dog-paddled back over to him. "So, given your connections with the AC police, I thought you might be able to find out who handled Betty's case?"

I didn't hear his answer. A big wave sank me. Next thing I knew I was sitting in shallow water with enough sand in my bathing suit to fill a hazard guarding the 18th green at one of the Braddocks' country clubs. For at least a few minutes, I stopped worrying about Betty Boyle.

Chapter 7

When Andy left for his elevator commute the next morning, he wasn't optimistic about unearthing information on a fifty-year-old case but said he would try.

"It will get me out of this building, at least," he said. "And, by the way, I can't do lunch today—I have a meeting." He heard himself sigh and reacted with a guilty expression. "It isn't that I don't work when I'm in the Bahamas. I do. I work hard. Really."

I nodded. I knew he did. He was on call 24/7/365, but from the beach, the bar, and a hammock on our porch. He was rarely at a desk.

He headed for the door, remembered that he'd forgotten to kiss me goodbye, and returned to plant his lips lightly on my forehead. "I'll text you after the meeting."

Outside my hotel room, Atlantic City came to life. Joggers ran along the water's edge. Swimmers bounced in the waves. Shoppers strolled along the Boardwalk. I stayed in bed. I spent my morning munching on items from the mini-bar and searching the internet. Apparently Myra Morris lived the kind of life where your name shows up in the newspaper only when you're born, married, or dead. I found almost nothing about her online, in the *Atlantic City Press,* or any of the other expected places.

Ward Braddock, on the other hand, had gotten into a few scrapes over his lifetime that made it into one of the papers that did have an online history—the *New York Times.* I found stories about bar brawls as well as political battles. Given the era's more protective treatment of politicians, I could only imagine the incidents that hadn't made it into the press.

Among those that did, I uncovered an episode that transcended characterization as an "incident." Senator Ward Braddock had gotten into trouble with a capital "T"—and his father wasn't able to bail him out. In 1974, one of Braddock's aides tried to take the blame for a hit-and-run in New York City after a drunken Braddock ran down a homeless man in the street. Unfortunately for Braddock, not only were there witnesses, but witnesses who could not be bought off; though according to them, it wasn't because the Braddocks didn't try. The rising political star accepted a plea bargain and got probation on both hit-and-run and obstruction charges.

Make that *former* rising political star. Braddock's life-long dream of a run for the White House was over. By 1975, he had disappeared completely from public view, resurfacing a decade later as the news anchor for a local television station.

I could find nothing further about the aide who'd tried to cover for the senator in the hit-and-run, but an earlier reference to another Braddock aide in an obituary caught my attention. Apparently his aide Charles Speakes had taken his own life shortly after he was last seen on the day LBJ was inaugurated. The young man could have been tormented by any number of demons; I just wondered if Ward Braddock could have been one of them.

Not all of Braddock's aides came to such an unfortunate end. I found an article from the 1990s about the director of an Atlantic City community center who had once worked for Braddock. Anton Wisk left the senator's employ in April 1965, three months after Charles Speakes's death. I found the turnover on Braddock's staff interesting, but it really wasn't what I was looking for.

I called the public library to verify that 1964 issues of the *Atlantic City Press* were available and learned they were on microfilm. The librarian also suggested a special resource—the Heston Collection—that contained "a wealth of Atlantic City historic documentation." I made an appointment to see it.

Even though it was a short walk, given the heat, I took a cab. I got to see the part of Atlantic City that was not all about gambling and good times, the part of town that couldn't hide its economic woes. A lot of people work nights in gambling meccas, but I didn't think all of the people on the streets of Atlantic City were lucky enough to have jobs—night or day. The city suffered not only from the vagaries of the world economy, but from the dwindling fortunes of the gaming industry in New Jersey.

At the library, there were a lot of patrons using the computers, and I wondered how many of them were looking for jobs. I knew they weren't looking for old newspaper articles since I had no competition for the microfilm reader.

Because I had no desire to tease my hair, struggle into stockings, or apply copious amounts of makeup to enhance my research experience, I used my imagination to channel Betty. I envisioned the young mother, newspaper resting on her kitchen table, oversized pink plastic rollers on her head, cotton housecoat wrapped around her, snatching a coffee break while her infant son took his morning nap. She would have wanted to hear the slightest hiccup out of Johnny's mouth, so the radio would be off. Summer sounds drifting from the distance would make their way through the open windows. The crashing of the surf. The shouts of beachgoers. The drone of planes towing advertising banners up and down the beach. Sounds I heard in my hotel room, or would have if the hotel hadn't hermetically sealed the windows to keep extreme temperatures out and overextended gamblers in.

In the library, all I heard was the whirring noise of microfilm moving through the reader as I searched for the dates of the Democratic Convention. Betty could not have missed the stories about the Mississippi credentials fight that dominated the headlines from the first day. And given that she'd named her son after the president slain only nine months earlier, she would have carefully read the articles about the Kennedys, including reports that JFK's widow, Jacqueline, and his brother, Bobby, were coming to town. I imagined she was dismayed by the stories that embarrassed the city, of which there were several.

I found Betty's name once, in a short news item from September reporting that a young waitress and mother had gone missing two weeks before; it was one of two articles Johnny had already given me. In it, the police offered a public plea for the missing woman, asking her to call home right away to let her worried family know she was okay. They apparently hadn't anticipated that, five decades later, her family would still be waiting for that call.

I returned the microfilm and kept my appointment to see the Heston Collection. I scanned the files the extremely helpful librarian offered and was not surprised to find no mention of a missing waitress. The librarian was so accommodating that I didn't think she would mind if I made another request.

"Do you have any information on Ward Braddock? He was a local politician and state senator who later went into broadcasting."

"He wrote a book several years ago." She checked her computer and expressed surprise that it had been checked out. "We have quite a bit of information on the Braddock family," she said. "Even on Ward."

Given my instinctive dislike of the man, I loved her comment and the tone in which it was delivered. *Even on Ward.*

She produced an issue of a local magazine less than a year old. In it, I found a profile of the retired politician/newscaster. Now, however, they were referring to him as a philanthropist. The article did not convince me of anything except that Ward Braddock was a world-class egotist.

Chapter 8

When I left the library, I found four text messages from Andy.

Pen leaking. Fear lethal fumes.

Checked OSHA regs. Leaking pens do not cause immediate death. So they CLAIM.

Researching boredom regs.

Phone found on man dead at desk. Ignored OSHA reg re boredom. Advise where to send body.

I typed a reply: *Beach 7pm. Will revive.*

Seconds later his response came: *No beach. Working case for you when done here. Where have you been?*

1964, I replied.

Do not get hair done.

With no need to rush to meet Andy at the beach, I took a cab the ten blocks to Lorraine Wasserman's to see if she knew what had become of Larry Donovan.

"What do you mean, what happened to him?" Mrs. Wasserman's tone convinced me that she'd successfully defended the title of neighborhood grouch since the '60s. "He's right down there." She pointed to the Boyles' old building next door.

Atlantic City has had more lives than the average cat. Grand hotels rising and falling. Gangsters rising and falling. Casinos rising and falling. And all that time, Mrs. Wasserman kept the same next-door neighbor?

"He's lived there since 1964?" I was incredulous.

Mrs. Wasserman shrugged. "Why not? He has a sweetheart deal. He's probably there now. If not, you'll find him at St. Michael's, the Catholic church on Mississippi."

"Does he work there?"

"Larry don't work no more. Mass every morning ain't enough for him. Sometimes he goes back in the afternoon to pray."

For what? I asked myself the question, but Mrs. Wasserman answered. "He got himself into some sort of trouble. Big trouble. I don't know what happened, but all of a sudden he straightened up and got religion."

"Do you remember when he changed?" I was thinking, hoping, it might be the night he killed Betty Boyle.

"I don't know. Long time ago."

"In the last twenty years?"

"No, longer. He's been into clean living ever since. Looks like Arnold Schwarzenegger. Well, Schwarzenegger at eighty with a lots of tattoos and no hair. If you find him, ask him about his big change."

I would do just that. I didn't know how, but I would.

Larry's apartment was on street level, below the one Betty and Buddy Boyle had occupied some fifty years ago. I made my way to the door. The heavy railing and pillars, painted a deep red, made the first floor porch feel like a dark and dingy basement. The main decorative accent was a large Harley sitting in the corner. I figured if the bike was home, Larry was home.

I figured wrong—unless Larry refused to open his door to a stranger, a real possibility. No one answered my repeated knocks. I cupped my hands and stared into a living room furnished mostly with exercise equipment and weights. I glanced at the Harley. It looked ready to roll. I guessed Larry was also ready to roll. A biker approaching eighty must put in a fair amount of workout time. The bike was big and heavy.

Chapter 8

Even I couldn't produce a rationalization for taking a cab around the corner to St. Michael's. When the temperature hits 100, I restrict myself to meandering. So, I meandered the few blocks to the church on Mississippi Avenue.

As soon as my eyes adjusted to the dark inside the church, they focused on the guy in the back row rushing rosary beads through his fingers. This had to be Larry Donovan. He had a Schwarzenegger-style buff body, a Kojak-style bald head, and, most importantly, the name Donovan tattooed across his back in letters so large I could read them through the black mesh of his undershirt.

I stood near the holy water font and waited for Larry to finish his prayers. I thought he was done when I saw his fingers pass the crucifix and head around the beads for another rosary. Really though, I was in no hurry to get back into the hot sun. Plus, while he prayed, I rehearsed my approach. I still didn't have my script completed when Donovan shuffled to the end of the pew, stepped into the aisle, and genuflected.

The way Donovan crossed himself suggested that his actions were slow because of reverence, not age. He leaned on the pew but only lightly as he raised himself. The man really was in shape. Which is why I almost gasped when he turned around. Larry may have had the body of a man forty years his junior but he was definitely wearing his own face—a face that had not only lived eighty years, but eighty hard years.

Worried that a man of such devotion wouldn't respond to an approach within the church, I waited until he crossed the vestibule and had his hand on the heavy wooden door before I spoke.

"Mr. Donovan?"

He turned but said nothing.

"Mrs. Wassermann told me I might find you here."

"Yeah?" His expression was blank.

"I wondered if I could ask you a few questions about Betty Boyle."

His face remained devoid of emotion. He stared at me for a moment before he pushed the door open wide. "We'd better step outside."

He walked through the door and let it fall for me to catch. He moved down the steps to the sidewalk slowly but without obvious effort. I stopped on the second step so that my eyes met his. Mrs. Wassermann hadn't mentioned that Larry Donovan was a giant.

"You don't mean Betty Boyle, Buddy Boyle's wife, do you?"

"Yes, I do."

"But she died before you were born."

Aha. "So you think she is dead."

"Did she come back?" His sneer and his tone indicated he knew she had not.

I shook my head. "No, but we are looking into her case."

"Who's we? I know all the cops around here and you ain't one of 'em."

"I work with a private investigation firm. Betty's son has asked us to look into what happened to his mother."

"That kid turn out okay?"

I nodded.

"I never saw him after he was about five. That old Wasserman biddy claims he comes by to see her, but I've never laid eyes on the guy. Not that it matters. I didn't really know the Boyles, or want to. Especially the wife. Do-gooder. Not bad looking but a little clean-cut for my taste. In those days, I was only into biker chicks. Still am."

I guess he wanted to make it clear that he was not interested in my type either. He needed not have worried about advances from me, although I was fascinated by his veins. The man's arms looked strong but the blue veins that showed through his thin, creped skin appeared tired, old, and ragged. No wonder he masked them with a wide array of tattoos. "Surely, you must have felt bad when Betty disappeared."

"Not particularly. I regret that now, but at the time? I didn't care. I won't sugarcoat it. She was a silly young girl with silly liberal dreams. If she'd lived, she'd probably have had that kid of hers singing "We Shall Overcome" while I tried to sleep. I knew the world wasn't as rosy as she thought. I was ten years older. I'd been around. Been in the service. Seen a lot. Betty had never been out of New Jersey, as far as I know. But she thought she knew everything, thought everyone should be equal. She didn't even know any ..." he paused, "African-Americans." He let sarcasm drip from his words. "She got that crap from her mother, one of those jazz age floozies who hung out with musicians. Some of 'em black."

I don't know what Donovan thought he was saying, but I heard motive.

"Look, I used to be a self-centered prick who didn't take much notice of what happened to other people, let alone care. People don't believe that a man can change, that I could change, but I did. I guess you're talking to me because someone told you about the fight I had with her."

"Would you care to tell your side of the story?" I asked without clarifying that I had never heard any other side. Larry obliged.

* * *

Nazis on the Boardwalk? Larry Donovan never thought he'd see that happen. He wasn't sure what he thought about the American Nazi party. After all, he'd grown up hating Nazis, playing war—all with the Germans as the enemy. Some of his friends' fathers and brothers went off to fight the Jerries and never came back. Yet, there was something about these new Nazis' message to America that Larry found appealing. All these Negroes—he was supposed to call them Negroes—getting uppity, demanding more. This wasn't their country. The United States belonged to the white man who discovered it in the first place. The American Nazis understood that. And they understood the trouble all those do-gooders were making trying to help the colored folk. He wanted to know more about the party. That was why he took a stroll to the Boardwalk that day. To see if he could find any of these new Nazis to talk to, to learn about what they were doing.

Larry had spotted Betty on Florida Avenue and cut a block up Atlantic and sped down Mississippi to reach the Boardwalk ahead of her. He didn't want to walk with her and that bawling brat. Anytime he ran into her, it was the same thing. She asked a few polite questions and then went on and on about that noisy little kid of hers. Every night the damn baby got up in the middle of the night and cried. Woke him up. Sure, she shushed the kid right away, probably shoved one of those tits of hers into his mouth, but that didn't do Larry any good. He was awake. And stayed awake. Worrying. That's what he did since he lost his job at the garage. Worry. The old man made sure that no one would hire him. All because the boss's bitch daughter claimed he attacked her.

Attacked her? She attacked *him*. Said he looked like Ringo Starr with muscles. He didn't know what Ringo Starr looked like, so he felt flattered. Not that it would have mattered if he *had* seen the Beatle. The boss's daughter was stacked. How could he know she was only fourteen? She sure didn't look that young, or act it. She provided some really good tail but not so good that he should spend the rest of his life paying for one above-average lay. But her father thought differently, and the old man kept getting in his way, making him pay. The guy knew everyone up and down Absecon Island. And over the mainland too.

It wasn't bad enough that the boss ruined his chances of getting a job. No, to add insult to injury, he hired a colored kid to replace him. Larry couldn't believe it when he spotted the guy, sweat dripping down his dark brown skin, working in the bay, changing tires, moving fast to create a good impression, to make up for not being white. Larry lobbed some choice names at the guy that day. At least until the boss came out and told him to shut up, that he was lucky he wasn't in jail. Larry couldn't believe it. The boss sided with the colored guy. That just wasn't right. The Negro looked embarrassed and even sympathetic, but Larry knew that underneath he was laughing, enjoying besting a white man.

Larry roamed the area around Convention Hall looking for Nazis but didn't see any. How could he? The plaza outside Convention Hall was crowded with colored faces. Probably from Mississippi. He shook his head in disgust. And that was when he saw Betty Boyle, right in the middle of the protestors. Talking to them all—not only the white sympathizers who had joined the demonstration, but the Negroes themselves. Smiling and greeting them as if she knew them. Letting them coo over her baby. Hugging them. Touching their black skin. He couldn't believe it. She actually wrapped her arms around one of those uppity bitches. What gave people from Mississippi the right to make a scene at what should have been a nice event for Atlantic City? They were making his city look bad. Someone should put them their place. Someone should put Betty in her place.

He couldn't stop watching her. She treated the damn protestors better than she treated him, her neighbor.

He was pleased to see her coming in his direction. He wanted to let little Miss Freedom Rider know what he saw. He needed to tell her what he thought. "It will rub off on you, Betty. You and your kid."

She turned. She hadn't noticed him.

"I was watching you. I saw you. You and your Negro friends." He added a sardonic tone to the word *Negro*. Then, he grabbed her arm and studied it from wrist to shoulder. He rubbed his thumb on her forearm. "I thought I could rub this white off. I thought you'd be turning brown around now."

"Larry, are you drunk? It's not even noontime yet."

"I'm not drunk. I'm smart. Smart enough to see what those people want."

"They want the same rights we have." Betty jerked her arm away. "And, don't ever touch me again, Larry."

She kept her voice calm. No way she'd upset the baby. She did everything for that damn kid. She pushed the carriage away. Larry followed. "Believe me, Betty, I have no interest in touching you. I have no interest in touching skin that's been all over blackie skin."

She didn't stop the carriage. She just called over her shoulder. "Larry, it's 1964, not 1864."

His mother had taught him never to use profanity in front of a woman, so he kept his cursing mild. "Who the hell are you to go acting so superior? I understand dates, and I can count, Betty. Years. Days. Months. That little bastard of yours arrived a little early, didn't he? You got no reason to look down on me."

Betty turned and met his gaze. "I never looked down on you, Larry. At least before today."

Her calm, dismissive demeanor drove him over the edge. He forgot his mother's advice and released a torrent of curse words, ethnic slurs, and racial epithets at the top of his voice. His neighbor maintained her cool demeanor. All she did was push that damn stroller. Faster and faster. Ignoring him. Ignoring his problems. He stepped up his speed so he could walk beside her.

"Hey, buddy. Leave the little lady alone." A young man stepped in front of him.

Who was this? Some visitor. Some college kid. Probably a delegate. Neat little preppie. Khaki pants. Plaid shirt. Short haircut. Phony smile.

"Listen, buddy, I don't think the lady wants anything to do with you." The stranger laid his hand on Larry's arm. Lightly, as if he were a friend offering advice.

Larry didn't have any friends who looked like this guy. Larry didn't need any friends who looked like this guy. "Get your hand off me." He shrugged off the man's touch, but the grip got stronger.

"Let her go."

Betty kept moving, but Larry saw her eyes when she glanced over her shoulder. In that instant, he glimpsed anger, disgust, and, worst of all, pity. That was when Larry let it all out. He stood there with a stranger's grip restraining him and, at the top of his voice, spewed every hateful term he'd ever heard at her departing form. He didn't even remember most of what he said, but, later, after she disappeared, the police told him he said he'd kill her. He felt sure he didn't say that. Not exactly. He just said that he and his Nazi friends were going to stop people like her. Looking back on it, perhaps he shouldn't have used the phrase *Nazi friends*.

* * *

"So, did you join the Nazi party?"

"Not really."

To me, the answer should have been an easy yes or no. "Did you meet any Nazis at that convention?"

"Look, I've changed since then. That's clear. I might have had some contacts back then who were serious about the party. I wasn't. Besides, what I did back then doesn't matter. I'm a different person now."

I hoped so. "Was that the last time you saw Betty?"

"Must have been. She was gone by the end of the convention."

"How did you feel about that?"

"Anything that made that little brat cry more, I was against. If I had been a praying man in those days, I would have made a novena for her to come back."

"Did you see or hear anything odd the night she disappeared?"

"I told all this to the cops. I didn't see nothing. I heard a little extra crying. That kid would not shut up. I guess Buddy couldn't quiet him as fast as his mother could what with having to make formula and all. He must have dropped one of the bottles. I heard it smash on the floor."

I couldn't help thinking that maybe Buddy didn't simply drop a bottle. "Any yelling or screaming?"

"You mean aside from the kid? Nah, the only racket in that apartment that the baby didn't make was the creaking of bedsprings, if you get my drift. Those two were kids themselves. Even after the baby came, you could see that they were still hot for each other. I thought they were happy. All I told the police about the Boyles' relationship were positive things, which turned out to be a dumb move, because when they couldn't nail Buddy, they took another look at me. I don't know how, but they knew about my little fight with Betty. Who told you about it?"

"You did." I smiled, thanked him, and said goodbye. I didn't look back to see if the confusion on his face morphed into another emotion.

Chapter 9

Donovan went east toward the Boardwalk, so I headed west toward the White House, which in Atlantic City means the sub shop. The line for seating was long so I got an Italian sub to go. I just didn't know *where* to go with it. I'd planned on walking the reverse route that Betty would have taken home from work, but it was hot. I took a cab to the Boardwalk. I wanted time to think.

I found a seat in the plaza in front of what is now Boardwalk Hall but was Convention Hall back in 1964, the place where Betty spent so many of her final days. There was no shade, but at least the sun was at my back. All the benches faced the stage. Since there were no performers anywhere in sight, my imagination paraded my suspects across the empty platform to the accompaniment of pop music blaring from the mini-golf course beside me.

Ward Braddock. Of course, I put the politician on stage first. Why? I just didn't like the guy.

Myra Morris. Hell hath no fury, but a young Myra hadn't let her breakup with Buddy ruin her life. Actually, losing Buddy improved her future.

Larry Donovan. If neighbor killed neighbor based on political differences, the streets of America would be covered with dead bodies.

Buddy Boyle. I couldn't rule out the concerned husband. What was the big bang Donovan heard coming from upstairs in the Boyle apartment the night Betty disappeared? Simply the sound of a glass baby bottle crashing to the floor? I made a note to find out when plastic bottles became the norm.

By time I finished my lunch, my list of suspects had changed slightly. Buddy didn't make the cut, but Myra Morris and Larry Donovan held their positions along with my favorite, Ward Braddock.

Enjoying the minimal breeze drifting from the ocean onto the plaza, I envisioned Betty snapping photos all around the plaza as it had been in 1964. What was this growing emotional tie to Betty? Was I forcing the issue? Of course I was. But why? Because I'd gotten bored sitting on the beach? Because I was becoming more and more interested in her era? What did it matter? Understanding Betty would help me with the investigation.

I walked down the Mississippi Avenue ramp past the place where Trump Plaza customers entered and the spot where their trash exited. Once I reached Pacific Avenue, a few steps to my left put me opposite the spot where the Bella Napoli had done business until the mid-'70s. I stared across Pacific Avenue at the three-story building and willed myself to feel something profound, but I didn't. The old building was just a building, albeit a very different place than it had been in Betty's day. Observers would no more mistake the gentlemen's club for the Bella Napoli than they would mistake its members for gentlemen. It required a lot of imagination to see a wholesome family restaurant with wide, welcoming windows replacing the cold, cement walls.

I tried to envision the last known activities of Betty Boyle. I pictured her rushing down the narrow alley to start the brief walk home to her boys. Half a block south on Pacific Avenue and two blocks west on Georgia to Arctic. At that point she had less than a block to go. Such a short distance. With Buddy at home with Johnny, Betty had to walk that route every night, no matter what the weather. Why was the night of August 27, 1964 unusual? The answer was obvious. The convention was in town. Delegates. Press.

Protestors. Atlantic City was very different that night, and that night was very different for Betty Boyle.

In my effort to identify the killer, I was rooting for Braddock, who came to town with the Democrats. I still clung to that possibility at 8 PM when Andy found me sitting in our room, reviewing my notes and listening to music.

"Braddock?" Andy wasn't convinced. "I don't suppose you have any proof."

"No more evidence than I have against Myra Morris or my latest suspect, Larry Donovan." I patted the bed. "Sit down and I'll fill you in about Donovan."

Andy grabbed a few crumpled salt water taffy wrappers from the bed. He used his eyebrows to ask why they were there.

"I just happened to be passing James' on the Boardwalk on the way back from my investigation."

His eyebrows said he understood. And he did. In one way. He knew of my love for all things sugary. He didn't know that Betty Boyle had bought this same salt water taffy for the protestors on the Boardwalk. Salt water taffy made with the same recipe as the candy I'd chomped on that night.

I didn't go into the history of Betty's connection with James'. "You know how I love fudge."

Again, his eyebrows agreed.

"Well, I figured if I brought a pound of fudge home, I'd eat it all in one sitting."

"They do sell smaller portions." He spoke. The concept was too complex for his eyebrows.

"Yes, but I don't buy smaller portions. Anyway, I decided switching to salt water taffy was a good idea. Given all the chewing effort involved, it takes longer to eat." I pointed to a box on the dresser. "Help yourself."

He didn't. Instead, he cleared the candy wrappers off the bed and flopped beside me. He reclined with his eyes closed as I described Donovan's interactions with Betty Boyle. "He had a motive, and I'm sure a guy like that had the means to hurt Betty. Plus he had the opportunity, since the stairs to Betty's apartment ran alongside his porch. He could have easily pulled her into his place."

Andy wasn't sure he had sufficient motive. "Then again," he mused, "*no* murderer really has sufficient motive." He rubbed both eyes but didn't open them. "If he did do the crime, he had the problem of getting the body out of his apartment. I suppose he might have held her there for awhile, though from what you say Mrs. Wasserman wasn't one to miss any unusual goings-on next door."

"I got the impression she delights in finding dirt on people." I unwrapped a taffy with bright blue trim on the paper and popped it into my mouth. I didn't know what the flavor was, but it was my favorite. "I doubt the cops even searched Donovan's place."

Andy opened one eye but let his eyebrow ask me to repeat.

I waited until I finished my salt water taffy to continue. I was afraid I'd lost him while I chewed but he nodded when I explained my thinking that Donovan would have complained to me about a police search. "He said the police *questioned* him."

"So you now have three suspects—Myra Morris, Larry Donovan, and Ward Braddock—and the same amount of evidence against each of them. To sum it up, none."

I considered his statement for a few seconds before I answered. "Yep, that sounds right."

He sat up and raised a hand to silence me. "What are we listening to?"

"*The Best of Shelley Fabares.*"

He pointed his index finger to request clarification. "This is the best?"

"She wasn't really a singer. She was on *The Donna Reed Show* and someone got the idea she should make a record. And, before you ask, I know because I looked it up." I paused before I realized that Andy might not know who Donna Reed is.

"Just because I am currently living in the 21st century, unlike some others who shall remain nameless, I am not ignorant," Andy claimed. "I never knew she was on a television series, but it was hard not to know who she was since we watched *It's a Wonderful Life* dozens of times every Christmas when I was growing up."

"Anyway, Johnny said his mother sang 'Johnny Angel' to him. I downloaded it."

"I'm sorry to hear that. I am also sorry I have nothing new to add to your investigation." With a loud groan, Andy fell back on the pillow.

"Your eyes aren't closed, are they?" Dumb question. I could see that they were.

"Just resting them. I'm tired from doing your bidding. I had a drink with a buddy from the Atlantic City police. My friend wasn't even alive when Betty Boyle disappeared—never even heard of the case until I asked about it."

"And?"

"Checked it out and came up with nothing. So, given your suspicions about your favorite politician, I asked about any incidents with Braddock. Conventional wisdom is that even now no one goes on the record about any of the Braddocks, but the general feeling among old-timers is that Ward was kind of a jerk. It's come up lately because of his son Paulsen's run for governor. Apparently, they are a little skeptical about the current generation's grab for glory."

"I found articles about the son's campaign, but there's not much being written about his father these days," I said. "He wrote a book awhile back, but it wasn't on the library shelf. I bet he hires people to check it out periodically so the library doesn't discard it."

"According to my buddy, Braddock supports some local charities, but …" Andy's tone made it clear there *was* a but, "they figure everything he does is for appearances. Apparently, he gives his money but not his time—aside from the shows he puts on for the occasional photo op."

"Well, he must be eighty."

"Which is how old I feel." Andy yawned and snuggled with his pillow.

"So Braddock finally grew out of his more flagrant misbehavior. Makes sense."

Andy's eyes were closed, but he was still talking. "He may still be a major jackass, but he was never a murder suspect as far as my friend knows."

"Do you think he would have heard about something like that?"

He paused before answering. "Probably, but not necessarily. We're talking a time gap of fifty years, and Ward Braddock isn't the hot topic around the PD that he is around here. No one is still around from the 1964 investigation." He rolled onto his side and burrowed into the pillow.

"I didn't think any of the original detectives would still be on active duty."

"None of them are even on the *planet*, and my buddy says the case files are useless—nothing in them we don't already know from the notes Johnny gave you. This was one lightweight investigation, and I'm sure the cops didn't push very hard when it came to the Braddock angle."

I had a plan. I'd been thinking about it all day. "Maybe I should try to talk to Ward Braddock."

"Don't get him mad at you. The Braddocks are a powerful family." At least that's what I thought he said. His words were delivered through a huge yawn.

"I'm not even a New Jersey resident. I don't see what he could do to me."

"People like that have their ways. The Braddock family tentacles reach into every aspect of life in this state." He yawned again and his head rolled to the side. I heard him mumble "allegedly" over his shoulder.

"I found a recent profile on him in a magazine at the library," I said. "Apparently he walks the beach in Spring Lake early every morning. I'm going to take the car tomorrow and see if I can manage to bump into him."

Later, Andy said he knew he was asleep at that moment because if he hadn't been he would have told me to forget that idea. I didn't. Headphones in place so I wouldn't disturb his beauty rest, I popped a salt water taffy in my mouth and watched the only YouTube clip I could find of Ward Braddock as a young politician with a narrow tie, lapels, and point of view. It wasn't that he opposed civil rights, he said, he just wasn't sure the country was ready. I could only assume *he* wasn't ready. It was May 1964, less than two months before LBJ signed the landmark Civil Rights Act of 1964.

If the more recent video I found next was any indication, Braddock's broadcasting career was devoid of editorial content, at least on serious political issues. Probably tall—who can ever tell on TV?—but definitely dark and handsome, not to mention distinguished looking, he peered into the camera and commented on the "cruelty" of an increased number of speed traps on the local beach road.

Something about him made me root for the radar gun.

Chapter 10

Spring Lake would be a beautiful town even without the ocean on its edge. A walk from the beach along tree-shaded streets, past elegant Victorian homes with spacious and meticulously groomed lawns, to the large fresh water lake that gave the town its name reveals that Spring Lake is the embodiment of an American ideal. Anytown USA—for people with money and taste. People like Ward Braddock.

I'd gotten up hours earlier than I would have liked to make sure I found the best spot to catch the current patriarch of the Braddock family on his morning walk. In the unlikely event that *I* ever took a morning walk, if a stranger approached me, I would probably turn it into a morning *run*. I calculated that this would not be the case with Braddock for two reasons. First, in his glory days he'd grown accustomed to being approached by strangers; now that his fame was at best a faded public memory he would probably relish any attention. Second, and more pragmatically, even if he happened to be one of the few eighty-year-olds who still ran, he probably didn't move that fast.

I spotted him from the Boardwalk. By the time I found the stairs and crossed the soft sand to the water's edge, he had a one-block lead on me and was extending it. I kicked off my flip-flops and ran along the water's edge to catch up.

"Senator Braddock?" The pride on his face confirmed that I'd been right to dredge up his old title. The man stopped, turned, and reached for the pocket of his meticulously pressed shirt as if expecting to sign an autograph.

I should have caught my breath before starting this conversation but it was too late to reconsider. "My name is Meg Daniels," I gasped.

His bright eyes registered confusion. He didn't understand why I was telling him my name or why I thought he would be interested in knowing it. "Did you want a photo?" he blurted.

"No. Thank you. I mean, I'd love a picture of you but that's not why I'm here." I struggled to relax my breathing. "I wondered if I could ask you a few questions."

He glanced at the notebook in my hands. "Are you a reporter?" His eyes, a dark blue that was a perfect match for the sea behind him, opened wide. Hoping for good press, he pulled his shoulders back and his stomach in, as if his natural good looks, deep tan, and Ralph Lauren wardrobe didn't already make him resemble a model ready for his close-up. Or long shot. Or medium shot. Even at eighty, Braddock would take a striking photo from any angle. "I'm always happy to speak to members of the press."

"I'm not a reporter."

His eyes asked, *What are you?*

"I'm a historian." The way I saw it, I'd spent the previous day doing the work of a historian. It wasn't as if he could ask for my license.

"I see." He seemed disappointed that his name would not be going into the daily news, but I watched him come to the conclusion that having his name appear in *any* publication was a good thing.

"I'm researching the 1964 Democratic National Convention."

He stopped and gazed down at me with a stare that I read as curiosity mixed with a touch of hostility. I reacted with fear until I remembered that although he was a lot bigger than I was, he was also eighty. I could take him if I had to.

I read his smile as stiff, forced. "Why would you want to ask me about that convention? Which one was that? Kennedy?"

"Kennedy was 1960. 1964 was LBJ, in Atlantic City."

No New Jersey Democrat of Braddock's era could forget where the 1964 Democratic National Convention was held. Well, no New Jersey Democrat who still had all of his faculties, and Ward Braddock appeared to.

"How silly of me. Of course!" He let out a huge sigh. "Old age takes a toll on one's memory, Ms. Daniels."

Not so large a toll that he couldn't remember my name, apparently.

"Yes, poor Lyndon," he continued. "Such a tragic figure, don't you think? To get everything you hope for and then lose it because of that damn war in Southeast Asia. That kind of loss must be exceedingly painful."

Despite his forced grin, or possibly *because* of his forced grin, I didn't think he was talking about LBJ anymore.

"I didn't come to ask you about Lyndon Johnson. I wondered if you recalled an incident at a party during that convention. It involved a young waitress named Betty Boyle."

His wide eyes turned to slits but only for an instant. Even after years of retirement, the former politician and television anchor remained the master of his facial expressions. He wiped the shock off his face, but that one second told me he knew exactly whom I meant.

"You're asking me to think back quite a few years. Betty Boyle, you say? A waitress ..." He shook his head, slipped one bare foot out of a boat shoe, and watched his toe mold the sand into a small mound. "I must have been served by dozens of waitresses during that convention, and the interactions were understandably brief." He issued a deep guttural noise that, I suspect, was meant to express amusement. "Is there any reason I should remember this one?"

"She disappeared while the conventioneers were in town."

"Are you talking to all fifty-two hundred of them?"

He couldn't remember the convention, yet had an instant recall of the delegate count? Interesting.

"I believe she threw a drink in your face."

He shook his head and laughed, a low rueful chuckle that distanced him from the activities of his past. "Ah, to be young again. I did some rather foolish things way back when. For excitement these days I take long walks on this wonderful beach. Isn't it lovely here?"

I would have agreed, but he barely paused for breath.

"I stay here from May through mid-September. The only reason I leave in September is that I relish the autumn on my estate in Somerset County."

The magazine profile had told me all about his 200-acre estate, his mansion, and his orchards. I didn't need a full description but that didn't stop him. "I love to be up there in the autumn to pick apples and make cider. That's something I've been doing since I was a boy."

Braddock appeared willing to give me a full account of each of his eighty years omitting only the night he met Betty Boyle. I had to interrupt him in the middle of a sentence. "That sounds lovely, Senator, but I'm wondering if you remember anything about the woman who poured the drink on you. Betty Boyle."

"Was that the waitress's name? The police did come to tell me about a young woman who had apparently disappeared not long after we had a minor altercation. Is she the one who told you about me?"

"No, as I said, she's the one who disappeared. You don't remember anything about that?"

He didn't need much time to prepare a response. "I'm sorry. I do recall the police having some questions about a waitress, but I don't remember the nature of the questions. Had she run off with one of the conventioneers?"

"No, she vanished. She's never been seen since the night of August 27, 1964. Two nights after your encounter with her. I believe you met her on Tuesday, August 25, 1964."

"Not that I would remember the date. If you recall, I got the year wrong."

Yes, I thought, I've taken note of your alleged memory problems.

"That's very sad," he continued. "I never knew the resolution of that … of the young lady's disappearance."

"But you do agree there was an incident involving the two of you?"

He thought long and hard before he answered. "Yes, there was." He spoke as if he had just searched his memory and was surprised to find the information was stored there. "Although I have to say I cannot recall many details. I do remember the police visit."

* * *

Ward Braddock slipped the Ian Fleming novel he was reading into the drawer as soon as he heard the knock. He preferred living in the fantasy of James Bond's world to the reality of his own office, but duty called. His family always answered the call. He'd been told that since birth. "Yes?" He shuffled a few papers to create some noise and the impression he'd been working.

Anton Wisk stuck his head through the door to his office. "There are two policemen from Atlantic City here to see you, Senator. They'd like to talk to you about the waitress you had a problem with Tuesday night at the convention."

Wisk was a good worker, but he lacked common sense. The cops could hear him, and the idiot just spat out that there had been a "problem," and, even worse, he'd sounded nervous about it. After the election, the kid would have to go. He was too damn earnest and naïve. Braddock kept those thoughts to himself. The expression he let show was one of puzzlement.

"The waitress who threw the drink in your face."

"The police are here about that?"

Wisk nodded.

"I wasn't going to press charges." He spoke loudly in case the cops could hear. He couldn't understand why the police were wasting time investigating an audacious server throwing a drink in a customer's face, even if the customer was part of an important event and an influential family.

"Please show the officers in, Anton."

Braddock rose, walked around his desk, and extended his hand to each of the two officers, detectives in plain clothes. McGinty. Mangione. Straight out of central casting. A mick and a wop. Not that he would ever say those words out loud. Not if there was any chance his mother would hear him. She wouldn't be upset by the actual prejudice, but by his forgetting that micks and wops were voters, too.

"Gentlemen, I am surprised to see you. I had no intention of registering a complaint. The convention days were a busy and, I am sure, very tense time for the service staff."

McGinty shook his head, which was topped with stereotypical red hair. Yep, definitely central casting. It was all Braddock could do to keep from smiling. "Actually, the woman's husband came to see us," the cop said.

"Oh." Braddock nodded with great solemnity. "I am sorry if the young woman filed a complaint, although it was she who threw a drink on me. Or so I am told. I did attend the gathering at Bella Napoli, and, apparently, my behavior was inappropriate, but I do not recall the specifics very clearly. I'd had some champagne—a bit too much, it seems. What is the woman claiming?"

The younger Italian detective with the carefully slicked back hair spoke. "She isn't claiming anything."

"So, I am perplexed." Braddock's expression confirmed that. "And rude. Please, officers. Have a seat." He moved back to his desk chair and waved the cops into two mahogany Chippendale guest chairs that he hoped impressed them. You didn't have to be a connoisseur of fine things to know that his office was beautifully and expensively furnished. It couldn't hurt to use his surroundings to remind the cops who he was. "I'm afraid your visit confuses me."

"We have to look into everything Betty Boyle did that week." McGinty sounded apologetic.

"Betty Boyle?"

"The waitress. She's disappeared."

"Has she committed a crime?"

"No, not that we know. She didn't come home Thursday night."

"That's over a week ago now." Braddock admired his own ability to keep his expression wide-eyed, uncomprehending, and, above all, innocent.

"Right," Mangione said. "We figure she ran off, but the husband thinks she's come to some harm."

"Husbands are always the last to know." The senator smiled knowingly, thinking of the clueless husbands of his conquests. Sometimes his lovers even introduced him to their mates. The fools never had a clue. They were all social climbers, pure and simple, thrilled to meet the likes of Ward Braddock.

"We're sorry to bother you, sir, but one of the owners of the restaurant said there was an altercation between you and Mrs. Boyle at some point during the party," McGinty said. "We have to look into the situation. Now that the Democrats have left town, we have time. Did you enjoy that party?"

"As I said, so I've been told." Braddock feigned an embarrassed grin, trying to prove that despite his breeding and position, he was just one of the boys. Hard work, but worth the effort. He could tell that meeting a Braddock impressed McGinty; the Irish cop wasn't going to create any problems for him. So he focused on Mangione. He smiled as he continued the charm offensive. "I attended quite a few social events that week. A few too many. I can assure you that I will not behave in similar fashion again." He smirked. "At least not after my wedding next month."

Success. Mangione laughed. An empathetic laugh. They'd bonded.

"It's looking good for your boy," McGinty said, his tone suggesting he wasn't particularly pleased. "I guess LBJ will get his four-year term."

"If we allowed gambling in New Jersey, I'd bet on it." Braddock smiled with the full confidence that he was charming the two cops.

"Sorry, Senator, but I've got to ask you a few questions." McGinty shook his head as if cursing the bureaucracy that employed him.

Braddock didn't deny the detectives' version of the incident, even though he didn't clearly remember the specifics.

"I simply wanted a drink, and she was chatting with some friend of hers who, I should point out, did not belong there. I called her over. She was, after all, a waitress. Apparently, I made an inappropriate comment and was rewarded with a cold shower of alcohol. I am sorry to say I don't even remember what the young lady looked like."

"Were you angry when she poured that drink over your head?"

"Angry hardly describes it—but only for a few seconds. My father, you know the senator ..." Another reminder about the family they were dealing with couldn't hurt. "My father raised me to be a gentleman but also to realize that, under the right circumstances, anyone is capable of behaving like a cad. When that happened, I heard my father's voice advising me to admit my mistake and move on. Unfortunately, I've had to take his advice more than once."

"Did you attempt to apologize to Mrs. Boyle?"

"Even had I wanted to beg forgiveness, I didn't know her name."

"You knew where she worked."

"Yes, but that incident did not remain in the front of my mind. The week was so busy. I had no time to go back, but you make a good point. Once the convention concluded its business, I should have tried to find her and apologize." He painted his face with concern and looked from one cop to the other and back. "I do hope no harm has come to her."

"So you never saw her after that night?"

"No, as I said, there were so many events. I visited that particular establishment for just the one party." He heard the annoyance creeping into his voice. Who were these cops to harass him? He'd already told them he hadn't seen her again.

"Did you have any other contact with her that night?"

He fought to quash his irritation. "No, I did not."

The Irish detective handed him a picture.

He saw what appeared to be a happy family. "She's attractive, though not my type, certainly." He handed the picture back. "I hope you find her unharmed."

The detectives apologized for having bothered him. He didn't expect to hear from them again, and he didn't.

* * *

I worked hard to keep a look of amazement off my face. Did this man hear what he'd said, what he'd revealed about himself? I could have dismissed his openness as a result of senility, but I suspected lifelong arrogance was responsible. Ward Braddock said whatever he felt like saying.

"I am so sorry," he added. "And so embarrassed."

Maybe I was wrong. Maybe he *had* heard himself. Maybe he was going to explain to me that it was a different time back then. That attitudes were different. That he was different now. But that wasn't the case. It turned out he was only sorry that his memory sometimes failed him.

"One would think I could readily recall something so terrible." He raised a shaking hand to his cheek. I hadn't noticed any tremor before. "And perhaps I should have followed up to see how her story ended."

Was it terribly cynical of me to suspect that the tremors were an act? I didn't think so. After all, this doddering man was the same figure whose confident stride I'd admired from far away.

As if he could read my mind, he added, "I get so upset with myself when I can't remember things. Now what was it you wanted to know about LBJ?"

I thanked Braddock for his time and headed across the beach. His handshake might have been feeble, but there was nothing weak about his stare. I felt it even after I crossed the Boardwalk and reason told me he could no longer see me.

I backed out of my parking space a little too quickly. Remembering that I was in Braddock's town, I let off the gas a bit. The last thing I needed right now was a traffic citation—in case I wasn't just paranoid and Ward Braddock was still pulling strings.

Chapter 11

Andy was waiting at our regular table in the Café Monet when I returned from my trip to Spring Lake. He'd ordered the usual for himself and, because I was working my way through the breakfast menu, banana crepes for me. I knew this because he'd sent a text at 11:04 telling me and asking how far away I was. I was reading the message as I plopped onto the seat across from him seconds before the waitress slid my breakfast in front of me.

"Traffic was unbelievable."

"Yeah, what's going on? It's a mob scene around here."

I looked at him to see if he was kidding, but he wasn't. "Andy, it's the weekend. You didn't notice?"

"Why would I notice?" I heard true frustration in his voice. "I never get out of my hole." Andy worked to suppress his whining.

Okay, I *liked* to think Andy worked to suppress his whining. In truth, he wasn't putting in much effort.

"So you had a tough elevator commute?" he asked.

"Elevator? No. Car. I drove to Spring Lake this morning."

Clearly he did not remember the previous night's conversation. "And?"

"I'm never going to make it big in New Jersey politics."

"What did you do?"

"I ran into Ward Braddock on the beach in Spring Lake this morning."

"I know I dozed off," Andy replied between bites, "but I do recall warning you not to antagonize the Braddocks."

"I was polite. The old guy is still handsome and spry, even at eighty-something. His hair is white but his eyes still sparkle."

"So he charmed you."

"No, I think he killed Betty."

"Would you like to present some evidence?" Andy made no attempt to hide his skepticism.

"Braddock knew exactly what happened the night he and Betty Boyle tangled but when the cops asked him he pretended he didn't."

"He told you that?"

"No, but as he told his story, he chose his words *so* carefully. Painfully honest about some things. Revealing such unpleasant truths about himself that I couldn't doubt he was being honest. Glossing over other topics. And you should have seen him. One minute he's sharp as a tack, remembering the precise delegate count at the convention. Next minute he can't remember the year the convention was held."

"He's an old man, Meg."

"It was an act. I'm convinced."

Andy wasn't. He interpreted Braddock's reticence differently. "He might remember what happened and be embarrassed by it. I bet he did a lot of things as a young man that the senior citizen now finds humiliating. He really didn't give you anything."

"There must have been other witnesses to the incident between Braddock and Betty."

"It doesn't matter. He didn't deny the incident took place. Besides, I don't think it's going to be easy to obtain the guest list for a party held in the summer of 1964."

"I'll give Myra Morris a call and see if she's remembered anything else."

Chapter 12

I returned to my room and dialed Johnny's cell number, hoping for information about his father's condition. When he didn't answer, I left a message with my room extension and my cell number. While I waited for his call back, I spent my time watching the crowd on the beach and downloading music from the summer of 1964.

Andy would probably be happy that the Beatles had usurped Shelley Fabares's position at the top of my playlist. I wondered if the Fab Four had even made Betty's top 20. She was a busy young mother when the moptops were taking the U.S. by storm. I bet she would have liked the Peter and Gordon song "A World Without Love" that I sang along with as I watched a sailboat traverse the horizon and disappear to the south.

I grew frustrated waiting and started organizing our stuff. Andy and I had made enough of a mess that I continued through "Little Old Lady From Pasadena," "Where Did Our Love Go?" and "Everybody Loves Somebody Sometime." By the time all the papers in the room were in neat piles and our clothes and shoes were in the closet, I'd finished listening to the *Hard Day's Night* album and Johnny still hadn't called back. I needed something to do. I dialed Myra Morris.

When she heard my name, the woman sounded almost frightened.

"I am just calling to say that I did not forget your request for information about Buddy Boyle's condition. I haven't heard from his son."

"I'd love to know." She gave me the impression she felt both puzzled and relieved. "But please don't go out of your way."

"No problem. My mind is on this case anyway. You didn't happen to think of anything else, did you? For instance, if there were any other witnesses to the incident between Ward Braddock and Betty Boyle?"

"Of course, there were dozens of witnesses."

"Were there any you knew personally?"

"I already told you I didn't know anyone there. People like the Braddocks did not hang out with the likes of me. Ward Braddock's entourage could tell you who the other witnesses were. Not that any of them would say anything bad about him." I heard her light a cigarette. "I don't know why you're dwelling on that incident. That was a night or two before Betty disappeared."

She had a good point but I had a quick response. "It's the only incident I have to look at."

"You don't think you're going to make a case against a Braddock, do you?"

"I only want to find the truth."

"There were a couple of other waitresses working at the Bella Napoli that night. I don't remember their names, if I ever knew them. I hadn't worked with them before. One was a college kid the restaurant hired for the summer."

"Do you know anyone who would know their names?"

"No. No one that's still alive."

"Did you know of any men who gave Betty trouble?"

"Betty appealed to a lot of guys." I could hear impatience in her voice, yet Myra continued to answer politely. "Maybe Marco Angelini, but he turned out to be a good guy."

"Did you say Angelini?"

"He sang at the Pub Club. It's holding on by a thread now, but it was a pretty nice place back then. The two of them, Buddy and Marco, couldn't hang out at the real 500 Club with the real Rat Pack, so they used to act the Rat Pack part at the Pub Club, which they thought of as their own little 500 Club. To them, it was a game. Drinking, smoking, picking up women. Then Buddy met Betty and all that changed."

"Angelini resented Betty?" I asked, wondering how Johnny came to use this man's name as his stage name.

"Partly. I ran into Marco a couple of times when Buddy and Betty first started dating. Marco complained about how she took up Buddy's time, but I could tell by the way he talked that he had a crush on her. Too bad for him. Betty only had eyes for Buddy."

"You said Angelini turned out to be a good guy. What do you mean by that?"

"I don't have any firsthand information. I lost touch with Buddy and Marco, but I heard a little about them when I worked as a receptionist in Atlantic City before I got married." She took a deep breath. "After Betty died, Marco helped Buddy with Johnny. I guess that wasn't all good. The kid grew up watching Buddy and Marco play Frank and Dino, although Buddy's voice was no great shakes. He would have made a better Joey Bishop, although he wasn't that funny, either. Anyway, the two of them loved the Rat Pack, with the exception of Sammy."

"Sammy Davis Jr.?" I asked. "Were Buddy and Marco racists?"

"I wouldn't call them racists. It was the times. In our world, white people seldom met black people. *Negro* was the correct term back then."

"Is Angelini still alive?"

"Still singing at the Pub Club. I've seen his name on the marquee out front. I'm not sure how often he's there."

"Thanks. For the information and for your time."

"And thank you for getting back to me about Buddy." I waited while she exhaled. "Tell him I was asking for him. You'll let me know, won't you?"

The intensity in her tone surprised me.

Chapter 13

I found a few mentions of Marco Angelini online, all related to his singing career. I didn't find anything incriminating but neither did I find anything that said I shouldn't add him to my parade of suspects. After that, I paged through my notebook and found the name of the aide who had stopped working for Braddock in 1965 and was now executive director of the Absecon Center for Hope and Charity: Anton Wisk.

According to his bio on the organization's website, after a brief career in politics Wisk served in the Peace Corps in Malawi for two years, then returned to found the privately funded community center in the Inlet neighborhood. He'd been running it since its opening in 1968. I wanted to ask him about Braddock at the '64 convention.

I found Absecon Hope's phone number, made the call, and was put right through to Anton Wisk. To his voicemail, I should say. I left my cell number and my reason—*alleged* reason—for wanting to speak with him. He returned my call fifteen minutes later. Though his voice was that of a man well past the normal retirement age, he was still working and was anxious to talk about his pet project—especially when I reminded him that I was gathering information for a social history of Atlantic City. As with

Braddock, not quite a lie. The information I collected could be used in a book. I just wasn't going to write it.

Wisk claimed to have a busy day ahead, but after hemming and hawing to guarantee I understood what a huge favor he was doing for me, especially on a weekend, he conceded that if I dropped by in the late afternoon he would squeeze me in.

I went back to my online research, and, between breaks to watch the sun glittering on the water and to respond to Andy's forlorn texts, I found a few articles that discussed Absecon Hope, mostly its successes. Apparently, Anton Wisk was in the opportunity business. Scholarships. Sports contracts. Meetings with influential people, including one 1998 meeting with Ward Braddock who was, not surprisingly, a generous contributor to his former staff member's nonprofit. A quote from Braddock said he was proud to support the efforts of his former aide, a true humanitarian who did so much for the people of Atlantic City.

When Johnny finally called, I had a new question for him and wanted to ask it over lunch. I checked the time. 2 PM on the dot. "Start without me. I'll be right there."

In the Botticelli Buffet, Johnny was sitting in a booth with a big, sloppy cheesesteak in front of him. Instead of red sauce, this sandwich leaked mayo. "I thought this would be more comfortable than the counter. You have questions. Fire away."

"Did your grandparents ever tell you why your mother moved out of the house before she was married and got her own apartment? I don't think doing that was common back then."

Johnny didn't ask why I wanted to know. I could hear the pride in his voice as he responded. "My mama and my grandmother—she lived here through the Roaring Twenties—both felt a girl should be independent. Besides, my grandparents ran a small boarding house. They didn't protest because when she moved out, they got the best room in the house to rent out."

"I'd like to see your mother's childhood home. Where is it?"

"Somewhere under the Resorts parking lot. That's how my grandparents profited from gambling in Atlantic City. People say it didn't work, but what would the town be without gambling?"

Johnny stared at me as if I might have an answer. I had nothing to say, but Johnny always did. "The old grand hotels had deteriorated and the ones that weren't falling down were being torn down. Atlantic City's time had passed. Of course, I approve of gambling because the casinos gave me a place to sing." A grin covered his face. "I'm no Frank. I know that. Some people think I'm an 18-carat loser, but I'm happy. The Artistical is a first-rate hotel. So what if I don't play the big rooms? So what if a lot of the time I'm crooning to a half-empty room? I'm making a living doing something I love. I believe my mama would have approved. She liked music, but," he slapped the side of his head, "she had the worst taste—except, of course, for Frank. Papa got her to listen to Frank and the crooners."

Speaking of crooners ...

"Johnny, why did you take the name Angelini as a stage name?"

"Did you ever hear the song "Johnny Angel"?"

"Many times." I didn't elaborate that many of those times were last night. "The song is mentioned in the notes you gave me."

"My mama used to call me Johnny Angel. So I thought of that when I wanted a stage name, something Italian, like Frank's name. Marco Angelini, a friend of Papa's, sings at the Pub Club. He has, off and on, for over forty years. Even though it's kind of a dive now, he still has his fans. He was kind of a role model for me. So, I took his name."

"He helped you get started as a singer?"

"Yep, and more than that. When my mama first went away, my papa had some problems. People tell me that Marco stepped in and helped Papa out. I don't remember a time when Marco wasn't there for me. He's been like a second father."

"Did Marco ever talk to you about the night your mother disappeared?"

Johnny thought it was a dumb question. He didn't tell me so, but his scowl and tone did. "Marco wasn't there, so why would I ask? He didn't know anything. We talk about Mama all the time, but he says to remember only the good things."

"Do you mind if I talk to him?"

"Go ahead. Tell him I said hello. If I didn't have to work myself, I'd be over to catch his act. He only performs weekends, so you're in luck. You can go tonight. You'll have a good time even though I doubt he can help you." Johnny cleared his throat. "So you going to take Beck with you?"

"I'll ask him to go along."

"He still falling asleep on you?"

I shrugged. "Andy doesn't handle sitting in an office all day very well. At home in the Bahamas, running around all day keeps him peppy, but sitting at a desk here knocks him out."

Johnny shrugged and nodded.

"What?" I knew he had more to say.

"I just wondered if that's really his problem. I mean, I don't know the guy all that well, but I know how guys are."

"And?" I asked knowing he had even more to say.

"And, I'm just saying that if I were you I'd be a little worried that maybe your boyfriend's job isn't the only reason he's falling asleep on you."

"Thanks for your concern, Johnny." It seemed like the right time to change the subject. "I know your father is sick, but I would like to talk to him, too."

A strange noise, something between a grunt and a sigh, was his first response. "I don't know about that," he said, shaking his head. "He doesn't talk about my mother's death."

"This could be his last chance, Johnny. It might be easier for him to talk with a stranger like me about it than with his own son."

"I'll think about it." He stuffed his mouth so he wouldn't have to say anything more on the subject.

I just hoped he could think and chew at the same time.

Chapter 14

I took the rental car and headed to the Inlet neighborhood at the northern tip of Absecon Island in search of the Absecon Center for Hope and Charity, commonly known as Absecon Hope. After rows of businesses on Atlantic Avenue, I passed some neatly maintained houses that could have been either public or private housing; I couldn't tell for sure. As I continued north, I saw fewer houses and more vacant lots. Sad rows of five or six houses sat alone on full city blocks. I speculated that high hopes had accounted for the demolition and reality accounted for the lack of development.

But my mind kept wandering from the problems of Atlantic City to my own, as identified by Johnny Boyle. Was I so trusting, so naïve, so gullible that I'd missed a major issue going on with Andy? Maybe he wasn't bored with his job, maybe he was bored with me. After all, he didn't fall asleep on his job, he fell asleep on *me*. I shook my head in a futile attempt to drive these thoughts from my head before I created problems that didn't exist. Luckily, before I conjured up a major conflagration in my relationship, I spotted Absecon Hope sprawled across one side of a city block that was otherwise empty except for a lone house on the far corner. A chain link fence topped by razor wire surrounded the center's parking lot, a reminder that I was visiting an area that had to deal with more than its fair share of crime.

Although every window was protected by iron bars, the front entrance was unlocked. I figured that someone, somewhere, must be watching to see who came and went. At least I *hoped* someone, somewhere, was watching. Just in case they were, I painted a smile on my face as I pulled open a door with metal mesh woven through the glass and stepped inside. Here the scene was happier. The bright green walls were decorated with children's art. Stick figures painted on a yellow line on the linoleum floor indicated that I should follow them to the director's office. There, more wire mesh in another window, this one with the words "Executive Director" painted on it, marred the cheerful décor. Looking through the glass into a gray-walled room, I saw a gray-haired man in a faded gray plaid shirt bent over a gray metal desk that looked as if it might have been bought for Absecon Hope's opening in 1968. I rapped on the glass. When the man glanced up, I realized that his complexion was as gray as his surroundings. Had he grown to match them? What good was living at the beach if you never got out of your office?

I calculated that Anton Wisk was in his early seventies but he bounded out of his desk to greet me with more energy that I could have mustered in my thirties. He opened the door with a big smile on his face. "Ms. Daniels? So nice to meet you. I'm happy to help anyone interested in writing about Atlantic City."

Wisk's enthusiasm made me feel guilty. Andy would call my lie a cover story, but I recognized a lie when I heard one. And I hated to lie. Maybe I really *would* write a book. At some point. In the future. The distant future.

"I certainly enjoy contributing to the historical record of this town," he added as he waved me into a molded plastic visitor's chair. "Is this your first book?" He settled behind his desk and leaned forward, eyes bright with interest.

"Yes." I spoke the truth. "Yes, it would be. Will be. It will be."

"That's the spirit. We teach the kids to stay positive. Writing a book is a big task, but if you stay focused and take one step at a time, you'll be done before you know it."

He'd probably delivered some variation of that encouraging speech a thousand times. Probably every day. Probably many times every day.

"Good advice," I murmured.

"Sorry. I'm sure you don't need motivating, but the kids who pass through here do."

"You never know what a little encouragement might do." Even make me actually do what I said I would. "I found so many articles about the good work you do here." Exaggerating was not lying, I assured myself.

"We try. We've had some successes and, sadly, some misses. Like Atlantic City itself, we've had our ups and downs. I guess you know that. So many big dreams that turned out to be less than we hoped."

"I'm writing about just that, the fortunes of the city. I'm particularly interested in 1964 when the Democratic Convention came to town."

His mouth said the event had been a high point but his eyes said something else. "I attended the convention that year."

I didn't ask a follow-up question and let the seemingly garrulous man search for words. I wondered what he would tell me about Ward Braddock but, when he spoke, he talked about the vagaries of Atlantic City's luck. "The city had such high hopes. Everyone was so excited, thinking the convention would bring lots of business and positive press."

I knew from my time searching the Heston Collection that it had not turned out that way.

"Instead, such utter disappointment. The city was on a downward slide and continued on that path until Governor Byrne signed the gambling bill. Then we experienced something of a renaissance. Well-intentioned people thought gambling would be the salvation of Atlantic City, but I'm sure that you know that. If you drive around you will see that, again, things didn't work out exactly as planned. And now," he shook his head, "you no longer have to come to Atlantic City to gamble." He launched into a long explanation of the spread of gambling to nearby states.

"Did you live in Atlantic City in 1964?"

Wisk appeared surprised and maybe a bit insulted that I had taken the conversation back to the convention year. "No, I only attended the party conference. I worked for a state senator back then."

"Ward Braddock. I saw that in an article online."

His eyes met mine briefly. "Ironic, really. There I was at the Democratic convention hoping that I was working my way to Washington, D.C. Who would have thought that a few years later I'd be back in Atlantic City doing this? I grew up in North Jersey, in a New York suburb. What a surprise to find myself living and working here."

He continued as if he knew what my follow-up question would be. Good thing. I didn't have a clue about what to ask next.

"Kennedy's inauguration speech in 1961 inspired me to enter politics. Sadly, it did not take me long to learn I wasn't cut out for the realities of political life. But I did discover an interest in public service, so here I am fifty years later at Absecon Hope." He hopped to his feet. Okay, it was a septuagenarian variety of hop, but a hop nonetheless. "Let me show you around. It's a little late in the day but there's always something going on around here."

Wisk's tour bypassed a small office crammed with staff across the hall and headed for the surprisingly well-appointed sports facilities. "Not only for boys. We do as much for girls. We've been doing that since before Title IX."

Progressive back in the day. Maybe observing Ward Braddock's bad behavior had helped Wisk see the light.

"I woke up to how we treated women early in the game. I read *The Feminine Mystique* not long after it came out. You know, Betty Friedan had quite a revolutionary view of a woman's role in the early '60s."

I nodded. Wisk didn't care. He simply wanted me to know about his long history of advocacy for women. I sped up to match his pace as we strolled past indoor basketball courts and then to the outdoor tennis courts. We watched little kids taking swimming lessons in the outdoor pool and came back in to see the older kids doing laps in the indoor pool. As we toured the facility, children, parents, and staff greeted Wisk reverentially. I felt like I was walking with the Godfather—the preppy Godfather.

"You know," he said proudly, "what you see here is only the tip of the iceberg. We go out in the community with services—running errands for the elderly, delivering nourishment for the sick, and providing tutors to the disadvantaged." He paused to greet a young mother and pat her son on the head. "I am happy to contribute in my own small way to this city with its proud, and sometimes not so proud history. Many people never venture off the Boardwalk and out of the casinos. They don't see the real Atlantic City." He guided me back to his office. "What else can I tell you about our town?"

"What was it like when the Democrats came in 1964?"

This time he didn't miss a beat. "You are too young to remember the elegant hotels that used to line the Boardwalk. The Traymore, the Chalfonte-Haddon Hall. I see that convention as a last hurrah for those hotels, although they were well past their prime by 1964." A touch of bitterness infused his voice. "The press did not miss the opportunity to highlight their decline."

"I saw some of those articles." I made an abrupt change of topic. "Did you know Charles Speakes who worked for Congressman Braddock?"

Wisk's eyes ran through a series of emotions: surprise, fear, confusion, sadness. "Why do you ask?"

"His name came up in my investigation, you know, research."

I was surprised that Wisk accepted my explanation. He appeared sad, not suspicious. "He was my mentor. A wonderful fellow. A tragic story. You learned how he died?"

I nodded.

"It's difficult for me to talk about Charles." Apparently, he thought that was a sufficient answer.

I didn't. "You worked with him?"

"Yes." He didn't want to go on, but my silence forced the issue. "Great guy but not made for politics. He found that out the hard way. When I first worked for Charles, I had no doubt that he had taken to political life like a fish to water. Tough. Decisive. Committed. But I believe that he had a vulnerable, sensitive side that led him to end his life in the way he did. Where did you say his name came up?"

"In an article I read." I pretended to check my notes. "I saw that he worked for Ward Braddock, too."

"Why would you want to know about that?" He sounded more curious than suspicious.

"I'm looking for an approach for the article—an article I'm writing. Readers would connect to the idea of your disillusionment with political life leading to such good." I extended my arms to indicate I meant Absecon Hope. "I thought I could contrast your success with Speakes's situation. Maybe."

"I thought you were writing a book?" Now he sounded suspicious.

"I am. But an author with a book to promote is always looking for interesting hooks to build articles around." That was lame. I had to do a better job crafting my cover stories.

Wisk stopped buying my story and I could see why. I wouldn't have bought it either. If the story was bad, my delivery was worse.

"Charles's family doesn't need to be reminded of what happened. Martha has moved on. She was widowed just this year after a long, happy second marriage. Nonetheless, I am sure that Charles's passing is still a sensitive issue for her. He has living children. The younger one never even knew him. Anne was born after her father died. I don't think she or Charles Jr. would want their father remembered for the way he died."

I pretended that I didn't notice his annoyance. "Perhaps I could honor him for the work he did."

"You're forgetting that we both ended up disillusioned. Charles was closer to the action. The level of political work that I did was in no way inspiring. But the convention itself was quite interesting."

It was my own fault that I then had to listen to twenty-five minutes on the excitement of the Democratic Convention. The battles of the Mississippi delegates. The tragedy of the Kennedy family. The triumph of Lyndon Baines Johnson. There was, however, one interesting fact about Wisk's account. For all his details about the speeches and the meetings and the parties, Wisk never mentioned the reason he was there—to work for Ward Braddock. I had to bring it up.

"I heard a story about your boss from that convention."

Wisk kept his tone light. "The Senator was quite a character in those days."

"I heard a waitress threw a drink in his face at the Bella Napoli."

He looked shocked and sounded flustered. "I remember that night. Who ... why would you ask about that?"

"I've heard anecdotes about the convention. It was a different time. Politicians weren't constantly under the microscope."

Wisk's insincere smile made him resemble the politician he had been more than the social worker he was. "You are right. It was a very different time. I'm embarrassed to say that it took quite a few incidents for me to notice how unsavory my boss's behavior actually was."

"Was that night at Bella Napoli one of those incidents?"

He shrugged. "Perhaps. There were so many. I'm not criticizing Ward Braddock. As I told you, it was the time. He was no different from a lot of guys—grown men in responsible positions who thought life was one big fraternity party. But times changed. I'm sure he has, too."

My grandfather used to talk about the bum's rush. That is what Anton Wisk gave me next. I found myself out on the sidewalk shaking his hand and smiling at his blatantly insincere invitation to drop by again. As he closed the door, he added, "Good luck with your book."

I had a feeling he didn't mean it.

Chapter 15

Johnny's cautions about my relationship were swirling in my head. So I had more than my investigative needs in mind when I suggested to Andy that we visit the Pub Club for a romantic evening of music with Marco Angelini.

"It's after seven already. I thought we could stay here on the beach until the moonrise. Then, we could have an early night." Those words might have sounded romantic, but I knew the truth. Number one, Andy hadn't checked the time of the moonrise. And two, Andy wasn't so much interested in getting to bed early as he was in getting to *sleep* early.

"We can catch the early show."

He wasn't convinced.

"You can relax, have a couple drinks. I'll be the designated driver."

"I'll have to put on pants." He sighed.

"It *is* Saturday night."

He let out an even longer sigh.

"I know it will be exhausting." I let out a matching sigh. "Lift left leg. Pull. Lift right leg. Pull harder."

"And don't forget the zipper. You forgot about the zipper. I can't go out without closing the zipper." He threw his hands out to indicate he doubted he had the strength.

"Wear sweatpants."

"I'll still need to put on a shirt."

"I'll button it for you. But if you want to stay home, I can go by myself." I meant it. I wasn't being manipulative.

"Okay. I'll go," he relented. "Why are we going anyway?" He suspected there was more to the story than I'd revealed.

I filled him in on what Myra Morris had told me. "I need to ask Marco Angelini about Betty's disappearance."

"You understand that this isn't a paying gig, don't you? You're only doing Johnny a favor."

"We owe it to Betty to find out what happened to her."

He sounded exasperated. "We never met Betty, and *you* barely know Johnny."

"Would it kill you to sit through a set of love songs?"

"I don't know. I've never heard this guy sing."

"Trust me, Andy. No matter how bad he is, the music is not going to kill you."

"It's on you if it does," he mumbled.

Johnny would not have approved that I wasn't going full Angie Dickinson—that is, in the style of the Rat Pack's favorite glamour girl. I was, however, wearing mascara, high-heeled sandals, and a cotton sundress that showed a little cleavage. That's about as Angie Dickinson as I get.

Andy noticed. "Why are you all dolled up? We're not going to be out late, are we?" When I assured him we would not, he didn't even try to hide his relief. "I'm sorry I'm so out of it." With dramatic motions, he held the back of his hand against his forehead. "Do you think I have some rare disease?"

I was beginning to wonder. I just hoped it wasn't early-onset seven-year-itch. "Let's go. I'll drive."

When we arrived at the Pub Club I couldn't help noticing that Andy's mood had improved slightly—though he was still making the argument that if good music could have a positive effect on health, bad music could do the opposite. I dismissed his claims.

Judging by appearances, the Pub Club had passed its prime sometime in the last century. Finding a seat wasn't hard unless you hoped for one that didn't wobble. The few tables that were occupied were filled with drinkers roughly the same age as the performer. The small crowd and my suspicions that there were some tough customers made me think that the Pub Club wasn't getting most of its revenue from its food and entertainment offerings.

When Marco Angelini finished his opening number, a considerably more than adequate interpretation of how Frank Sinatra might have sung "All the Way," I realized that whatever else the audience members were, they were fans. The small group of people produced an impressive amount of applause.

When the clapping died down, I leaned over and whispered into Andy's ear. "I've never seen Buddy Boyle, but do you notice anything odd about Marco Angelini?"

"He parts his hair just above his left ear."

"Don't be mean," I answered before checking to find that Andy was simply stating the truth.

"I bet you think Marco is Johnny's father, based on some superficial physical similarities. And you think that may suggest he had a motive to murder Betty."

"Correct."

"If that were true, I might conclude that Buddy the cuckold husband did the crime."

Andy had made a good point.

"More importantly," he pursued it, "even *you* would find the Marco-as-dad theory implausible if you knew Buddy from more than just an old photo or two. Johnny and Buddy have the same face. Johnny's resemblance to Marco is superficial—his hairstyle, admittedly with a higher part, his tan, and his way of dressing, including those huge gold cufflinks."

Marco fingered those cufflinks as he launched into "Fly Me to the Moon." He snapped his fingers and affected the casual Sinatra stance, a style that was the height of hip fifty years before. The audience viewed the performance as kind of hip right then. I began to buy in. Andy did, too. He applauded loudly. "He's not bad," he raised his voice to speak over the applause. "Actually, I feel better being out. I feel good."

When Marco pointed to a tiny piece of wood that functioned as a dance floor, Andy turned to me. "Let's go."

I thought we looked graceful dancing to the timeless music, but we only got in one dance before Marco Angelini took a break. "Oh, no." Andy appeared surprisingly dismayed and amazingly rejuvenated.

I welcomed the intermission. I hadn't come here for a good time. Well, not *only* for a good time. I had work to do. Andy and I were waiting by the stage to meet Marco when he stepped off.

"Mr. Angelini." I took the lead.

"Yes, sweetheart, what can I do for you?" He mopped the sweat from his forehead with a white linen handkerchief.

"We're friends of Johnny Boyle. My name is Meg Daniels, and this is my boyfriend, Andy Beck."

"Boyfriend? A girl your age. Why doesn't he marry you?"

"I ... we ... that isn't something we talk about."

"Why not?" Marco protested.

Andy threw back his head and laughed, then leaned in to whisper in my ear. "He is old-fashioned. Very old-fashioned. Be nice." Andy turned to Marco and slapped him on the back. "I promise you can sing at our wedding, but, before I pop the big question to Meg, she has some questions for you. We'd love it if you would let us buy you a drink."

The offer piqued Marco's interest.

Marco drank whiskey with ice. Just like Johnny. And, I bet, just like Frank. "When I am drinking, I still miss my Camels." I was willing to wager that Sinatra smoked Camels.

Marco devoted most of his intermission to describing how he'd seen the Rat Pack perform at the 500 Club. I had almost forgotten why we'd come until Andy fixed a somber expression on his face and sat forward in his chair. "Marco, I know you're fond of Johnny. Meg has a little time on her hands while I work, and she's using it to do a favor for him. She thought you might be able to help her find out what happened to Betty Boyle."

"If only you could." Marco grabbed my hand and squeezed it tightly. "Buddy says what's done is done, but the kid, Johnny." He looked deep into my eyes. "Not knowing has eaten at him his entire life. I tell Buddy, the kid needs to know, but Buddy, he always says to let it go." He clasped his hands together and looked to heaven. "Thank you. Thank you. Thank you. Someone needs to look at this. God knows the cops didn't."

"They thought she ran away?" I suggested.

"For the most part. Some of them thought Buddy did her in." He seemed hesitant to go on. "They didn't want to ruffle any feathers by asking too many questions."

"Whose feathers?"

"Might have been one of them politicians. I admit that I was a Goldwater man even though Frank backed Kennedy. There are things you have to decide for yourself. And, in the end, Kennedy dissed Frank, so I don't regret my vote at all. Not that I wished what happened to that man on him. JFK, that is."

I cleared my throat. Not subtle but effective. Marco got back on topic.

"Anyway, being a Republican, maybe I hoped to find a criminal type among all those thousands of Dems who poured into Atlantic City. I figured that one of those out-of-towners did it, but not the cops. They were sure that if Betty didn't run off, Buddy popped her."

"But you didn't buy either of those solutions," I probed.

"Betty wouldn't have left Buddy, and she wouldn't have abandoned her baby. She was a lovely girl. Sweet. Pretty inside as well as out. I wish that I had met her first. Not that it would have mattered." He shrugged. "Betty only had eyes for Buddy. She could have done better. I mean better than Buddy back then. In those, days he wasn't much, but Betty ... she believed in him."

"You've been really good to Johnny." I smiled at Marco.

"Buddy is my friend. He had a hard time the first couple of years after … after it happened. I helped Buddy with the kid, and even a little bit with his business, until he pulled himself together. The kid and I got to be friends. He asked to take over my act, but where am I going? There's room for both of us. He wanted to be an Italian crooner, so he calls himself Angelini. Not legally. It's a stage name. I'm very flattered. You hear him sing? He's quite the performer, isn't he?"

Marco's pride seemed almost paternal.

"He's a good boy," he continued. "Like a son to me. I never had a boy. Three beautiful girls but no son. No grandsons. Only granddaughters. So, I enjoyed watching Johnny grow up. Now, I'm watching him grow old—alone. Maybe he can't find a wife until he knows what happened to his mother."

"Can you think of anyone who might have some information, anyone Betty might have seen during the last hours of her life?" I asked. "Did you see her?"

He shook his head. "The last time I saw her was during the convention. One afternoon on the Boardwalk."

* * *

Marco Angelini walked by Convention Hall to see what was going on, and there she was, wearing a wide grin as she pushed Johnny in his stroller. Marco thought Betty looked even more beautiful since the baby arrived. More natural. Motherhood suited her. With her hair puffed out just a little, she put to shame the other girls, with their oversized bouffant hairdos sprayed into a shape that gale winds off the Atlantic could not have disrupted.

She'd been so excited about the convention because she believed she was interested in politics. Marco knew better. Betty wasn't interested in politics. She was interested in politicians. Not seriously. She had a crush on those Kennedy boys, that was all. No different from the girls who screamed for those four kids from England. Crushes pass. Her interest in politics would probably end when the convention did.

In the meantime, Betty wanted Johnny to see it all—like the kid would remember. She was smiling. A real smile. Not like the girls who came up to him after a set. Betty's smile came from deep inside her. From her heart. Her happiness both cheered and depressed him. He wished that smile could have been for him.

He saw that she was approaching the protestors on the part of the Boardwalk that had been, since Sunday, known as JFK Plaza. Marco knew about this gang of intruders. Their story filled the headlines when the papers should have been full of happy stories. Troublemakers. He wished the protestors would go away. Go home. Worried, he watched to make sure that Betty got by them without incident.

He couldn't believe it. Betty didn't pass by. She stopped and waved into the sea of black faces. What was she doing? A hand waved back. Not even a white hand from one of the sympathizers. A black hand. A hand from Mississippi? Betty could not know one of the Negroes from Mississippi. How could she?

A Negro woman picked her way through the crowd of protestors and gave Betty a big hug. A hug! Then the woman leaned down and talked to Johnny. The baby smiled. What did he know? White. Black. Skin color means nothing to a kid, but his mother should know the dangers of mingling with these people.

He felt tempted to rush over and drag her away, but that might make the situation worse. He didn't want to be the one who ignited the powder keg. He stayed put and sent her mental messages: *Betty, get out of there. Betty, get out of there.* Apparently, he wasn't very good at mental telepathy. Betty pulled a bag out of her pocketbook, and the colored woman looked inside. She smiled.

He couldn't see what it was Betty had brought, but she'd brought enough for everyone. The bag passed through the crowd, and each of the protestors reached a hand in and came out holding a small item. Candy. He watched the protestors unwrap them. Betty had bought salt water taffy for the protestors. Just the kind of sweet thing Betty would do. Betty was always sweet. As sweet as she was naïve. She chatted for a few moments and then, with a warm smile on her face, she pushed Johnny south on the Boardwalk. Marco stepped in front of her.

"Betty, you should be careful. Not everyone likes what those Negroes are doing." He knelt down. "Hi, Johnny boy."

Johnny smiled and gurgled. Marco liked to think the kid recognized him, but he knew the kid was just a happy baby.

"Have you heard their story?" Betty appeared defensive.

"I heard that three fans of civil rights for colored people got their heads handed to them down in Mississippi. That's all I need to know. People want Negroes to stay in their place."

"Stay in their place? What does that mean, Marco? They had their votes stolen. They told me about it."

Marco rose. He gazed down at Betty. "I'm sure the situation is not that simple. These people are troublemakers."

Betty didn't hide her anger. "Yesterday, that creep who lives downstairs warned me to stay away. Now you. I expected it of him, but you, Marco—that I would not have expected." She shook her head as she pushed the stroller away.

"Betty, wait. I'm sorry. I'm worried. You don't understand these issues."

She stopped and stepped close. She kept one hand on the stroller and jabbed the other one in the air to punctuate her point. "I understand that those people from Mississippi deserve the same rights I have."

He didn't mean to get her riled and didn't understand why she was. "How does what goes on in Mississippi have anything to do with you?"

Betty didn't even speak. She just pursed her lips, shook her head, and moved forward.

He was speaking to her back when he called after her. "Please be careful, Betty. Promise me you'll be careful."

* * *

"Do you think someone targeted her because of her involvement with the protestors?"

"I didn't notice anyone paying attention to her, but she must have talked to those protestors before. They knew her. Someone might have noticed.

Back in those days, they had a term for people who got too friendly with the Negroes. We don't use words like that anymore, but a lot of people didn't approve of whites mixing with blacks."

"Did you mention this to the cops?"

"The cops didn't come to me. I went to see them with Buddy. I answered whatever they asked. I don't remember them asking about those protestors. Later they came back and asked some questions, mostly about Buddy but also about Betty's friends, people she worked with."

"I talked to her old roommate Myra."

"That Myra was a pistol back in the day. I used to run into her around town." He chuckled. "Not my type necessarily, but I made a run for her anyway. Didn't succeed. Buddy won that night. Lucky man. Myra was quite the looker."

"Are there other friends of Betty's I should talk to?" I tried to bring Marco back to my concerns.

He shrugged. "At that point, Betty's life consisted of home and work. She didn't have time for girlfriends."

"Did you know anyone she worked with?"

"Only Abbott and Costello."

I needed clarification on that one.

"She used to talk about these two waitresses she worked with—Lucy Abbott and Wanda Costello. Lucy was a regular, but Wanda came for the summer. Both of them were young and single and having a great time. Not that Betty felt any jealousy. She said she loved going home at night to her family, and I believed her."

I wrote the names down. "Lucy Abbott and Wanda Costello."

"At least I think Costello's name was Wanda. I know Abbott's name was Lucy. She kind of reminded me of Lucille Ball. Lucy was tiny but she had a lot of curly red hair, just like the actress." He shrugged. "Of course, I haven't seen those two in fifty years. They probably married, changed their names, maybe they died. Seems to be a lot of that going around these days."

Chapter 16

Let's hear your latest theory." Andy had barely settled into the passenger seat of our rental car before he spoke.

"I have a couple, and as soon as I maneuver my way out of this parking lot, I will tell you."

Once on the street, I started my speculations while pretending not to notice that Andy was checking out my driving and glancing in the side mirror every few seconds. "Marco fell in love with Betty. She rejected him. He hurt her. Maybe it was an accident. He couldn't admit what he did, so he hid the body. That is why he is so nice to Johnny."

"Is there one piece of evidence to support this claim?"

"Not a one."

"Is that your only theory?"

"Maybe Johnny calls himself Angelini because Marco is his father. Maybe Marco wanted Betty to leave Buddy and got angry when she wouldn't."

"As I've already said, you'll discard that theory as soon as you see Buddy in person. In the meantime, your evidence?"

"None. But I have those two names from Marco, Lucy Abbott and Wanda Costello. They both worked with Betty. Might not be easy to find—fairly common surnames and they might have gotten married. It's a long shot but I'd like to track them down and see what they have to say."

"And you think they might tell you something that incriminates Marco?"

"Actually, no. I believe he is a truly wonderful man." My patience finally broke. "Would you please stop checking the mirror? I'm watching."

"Then you noticed the black SUV behind you."

"What?" I sat up and checked my rear-view mirror.

"He's been behind you since we left the Pub Club."

I waved off his concerns. "We're not taking a tricky route."

"So make a left at the next light."

I did as Andy instructed. The car followed. I drove two blocks.

"Make a right."

The car followed. I drove one block and then made a right. The black SUV made the same turn.

"Who is it?"

Andy shrugged. "If you jam on your brakes, he'll hit you and we'll find out."

"Have another idea?"

"Go straight through the intersection and pull over."

I did as he suggested, crossed Atlantic Avenue, and pulled over to the curb. We both kept our eyes on the mirrors as the driver approached the intersection, made a left, and drove away.

"See. Coincidence," I gloated. "There are a lot of one-way streets, maybe he couldn't help but follow our car."

Andy strained to see that the car had continued away from us. "My bet is that he was following you."

"What do you mean, *me*? What about you?"

"I'm not working a case. Who would follow me?" He dismissed the thought.

I presented alternate theories. "It could have been someone who targets tourists and saw us come out of the Pub Club. That isn't unheard of. We have a rental car."

"Maybe."

"Maybe we just took his route home. Once, I thought a guy was following me so I made a series of crazy turns and ended up in a cul-de-sac. Where he drove into his garage. It can happen."

"Maybe."

"He did drive away."

"Sure." Andy stopped pushing his point. "Let's go."

I pulled away from the curb and watched my rear-view mirror all the way back to the hotel. As far as I could see, we were traveling alone. Andy must have agreed. He was asleep.

Chapter 17

There was a time, a few weeks earlier, when I was thrilled with our room's view of the sun rising over the Atlantic Ocean. The thrill was gone. I managed to pull my body to a sitting position on the side of the bed where I stared toward the beach below with unfocused eyes. When my vision cleared, the dots bouncing along the water's edge turned out to be joggers. I had always planned on being one of those people who leapt out of bed and charged into the day with a five-mile run. I became, however, a person who dragged herself out of bed and stumbled into the mini-bar for a morning Coke. I grabbed a piece of salt water taffy as I passed the box.

When I returned to the bed, I noticed more runners were taking a morning jog along the beach. Inspired, I chewed my candy as quickly as I could, stood up, and checked the clock. 8:11. While humming "Maniac," I pulled my legs up and down in an exaggerated run inspired by Jennifer Beals in *Flashdance.* When I got bored, I checked the clock. 8:11. I kept running and waited until the boredom became overwhelming to check again. 8:11. I got back into bed telling myself I could repeat the exercise sixty more times before the end of the day. Not that I would, but I could.

I was testing one of James's new-to-me flavors, piña colada, and reading the news online when the bellman arrived at 9 AM with a carton. In it, I found the faded green case of an old turntable, a bunch of 45 singles, and a note. *My mama's music.*

I feared the entire hotel would go black when I plugged the record player into the wall socket, but the power stayed on even after I pushed the lever and saw the turntable start to spin. Nice work, RCA Victor. I pulled out the first record and read the familiar title. I popped a plastic center into the record and dropped it onto the spindle with Betty's favorite side up. I lifted the needle and tried to get it at the beginning of the groove. Once again the strains of "Johnny Angel" filled the room, but this time with all the flaws and rawness of the original vinyl. I was hearing the song exactly as Betty had.

It would be easy to dismiss "Johnny Angel" as sickeningly sweet and cloyingly sentimental. Largely, because the song is both of those things. But Betty's choice of music had to say something about a naïve young girl hoping to meet her Johnny Angel and then finding that the love of her life was a six-month-old cherub named Johnny.

I flipped through the other choices. I was surprised that Betty wasn't into Elvis, but then again my personal knowledge of the music of Betty's teenaged years was limited pretty much to Elvis. Then, I noticed a cylinder that slipped on the spindle. I piled the entire stack of records on top and pushed the lever. A concert of Betty Boyle's favorite tunes began.

While Fabian, Frankie Avalon, and Bobby Rydell sang, I went back online to locate Lucy Abbott and Wanda Costello. I never found a Wanda Costello but I identified two Lucy Abbotts. I thought it was a long shot that either of them had worked as a waitress under the same name fifty years earlier, but I had no other leads.

With time to spare before I had to meet Andy downstairs, I saw no harm in gathering dirt—make that information—on Ward Braddock. A search for his aide, Charles Speakes, retrieved the *New York Times* article about his suicide and a memorial from what would have been his fiftieth reunion at Princeton. Nothing predicted the sad end for the honors graduate, who went on to Yale Law before starting a family and a career as a political advisor.

Anton Wisk would have been dismayed that he had given me enough information to find Martha Speakes—although she was no longer Martha Speakes. She was Martha Winthrop, widow of Robert Winthrop of Bernardsville, who was stepfather to Charles Speakes Jr. and Anne Speakes Bingham. I jotted down her address, just in case. In case of what, I wasn't sure.

I was already at the table when Andy came into the Café Monet. "What are you humming?"

"It's called 'Sukiyaki.' Very big in the early sixties."

"Sing a few bars. Maybe I know it."

"I can't."

"Don't be modest. Your voice isn't that bad." He patted my hand.

"Thank you, Andy, for the compliment, but I really can't. The lyrics are in Japanese."

"Oh, okay. May I?" Andy slipped my notebook from under my pen and read my morning's notes. "Have you noticed that you are spending your time investigating Ward Braddock, not the possible murder of Betty Boyle?"

"It *was* murder, and he did it."

"You don't like him, and from what I hear nobody else does either. But being a creep does not make someone a killer." Andy's tone suggested that he might have mentioned this to me on other occasions. Perhaps on *hundreds* of other occasions. "Look, go to the library to do research or whatever, but please don't go running off to talk to anyone on your own. If you can wait another few days, I might have time to function as your bodyguard. I don't mean to be an alarmist, but I do think that SUV was following us last night."

"Really?" I didn't hide my excitement. "That must mean I'm on to something."

"That means that someone is on to you. Promise me you'll be careful."

"I'll be fine." An evasive answer, but Andy was too wrapped up in his French fries to notice.

By the time we finished eating, I'd forgotten Andy's warning not to go on interviews alone. Okay, maybe I didn't forget. Maybe *ignored* would be a better word. I was going to see two seventy-year-old women, one of whom might turn out to be the Lucy Abbott who worked with Betty Boyle in the mid-1960s. I wasn't worried.

I dialed Myra Morris's number to see if she could provide any clues about Lucy Abbott's identity. When she didn't answer, I left a message. "Mrs. Morris, this is Meg Daniels. I found out the names of two women who worked with Betty Boyle. I don't know if you knew Lucy Abbott or Wanda Costello who worked at Bella Napoli." I left my cell number. "No need to call back unless you have some information." I went to end the call but stopped. "I have no news about Buddy Boyle's health but will be sure to let you know when I do."

I had to decide which of the two Lucy Abbotts to go see first. According to my search results at SearchBug.com, one of them lived alone. Since it seemed more likely that this Lucy Abbott would be listed under her maiden name, I headed for the address in Longport.

As I drove south, the urban atmosphere of Atlantic City gave way to the increasingly suburban feel of Ventnor, Margate, and, finally, Longport at the tip of Absecon Island. The uninitiated might be surprised that the trip took me past a three-stories-tall wooden elephant. I considered it an omen. A good omen. The elephant's name was Lucy.

Most houses at the end of Longport where Lucy Abbott lived could be transported cross-country and settled comfortably in any posh L.A. neighborhood populated by rock stars and movie moguls. As I drove slowly down the street, I checked the house numbers and soon realized that Lucy Abbott did not live in one of the behemoths but in one of the few vestiges of Longport's past that had avoided demolition. Her home, adorned with bright blooms crowded into compact flowerbeds on the tiny lawn and large pots on the spacious porch, was large but not when compared with neighboring residences. Smaller pots guided a visitor to the front door. I felt the tension drain out of my body. This Lucy Abbott wanted company.

I knocked on the bright red door. My heart fell when a woman answered. She was the right age and height, but I didn't believe she could ever have been a redhead. Her skin and eyes were dark and went well with her pitch-black hair.

"I'm sorry to bother you. My name is Meg Daniels, and I am trying to locate the Lucy Abbott who used to work at the Bella Napoli."

"Why?"

I felt encouraged. Maybe I'd been wrong about the hair color.

"I'm doing some research on the Democratic National Convention in 1964 and, specifically, about an incident that happened at the Bella Napoli during that time."

"What incident?"

"A woman threw a drink in the face of Ward Braddock. He was a state senator back then."

"I know about the Braddocks. Good for her."

"Were you there?"

"Where?"

"At Bella Napoli when the woman threw the drink in Braddock's face."

"No, I didn't live here in those days."

"So you weren't working at the Bella Napoli in 1964?"

"No, I didn't even move to New Jersey until 1985. I just don't trust that Paulsen Braddock who's running for governor."

"But you are Lucy Abbott?"

"I kept the name Abbott after I divorced Carl Abbott over twenty years ago. He was a jerk. You know him?"

"Sorry." I was, but not about never meeting her ex. "I've never had the pleasure."

"Take my word for it, honey, knowing Carl was no pleasure, although I've got to admit that living on his money has been." She winked.

I had the feeling I could soon be learning a lot more about Carl if I didn't get out of there fast. "Well, thank you for your time." I turned to leave.

"Would you care to come in for something cold to drink?"

I thanked the wrong Lucy Abbott but declined her offer. I had another Lucy Abbott to see.

Based on my online search, the second Lucy Abbott seemed a less likely candidate. This Lucy lived one town north in Margate. Her listing included "Deborah Abbott, aged 30 to 34," who I assumed was her daughter. I didn't hold out much hope that this Abbott would have retained her maiden name; more likely she'd divorced another jerk named Abbott. For all I knew the same Carl.

The town of Margate thoughtfully put their streets in alphabetical order, so I had no problem finding the Abbott house mid-alphabet, back on the inlet off the bay. The small driveway was crowded with what appeared to be arriving visitors. Greeting them was a tiny woman with red hair. Not natural. Now. But five decades ago? She had pale white skin that would have made a great match for bright red curls.

The hostess welcoming her guests was the right age. She was the right height. Even her weight looked right, which was pretty amazing considering half a century had passed since she was the young woman Marco described. I saw no need to interrupt her party. If Lucy Abbott had been here for the last fifty years, she would be here one more day.

"See you tomorrow, Lucy," I mumbled as I drove away.

Once on Atlantic Avenue, the route from Margate to Atlantic City doesn't involve a lot of turns. Actually, none. Nonetheless I kept my eyes on the rear-view mirror. My heart skipped a beat when I noticed an oversized black SUV in the mirror. I waited for it to turn. It didn't. I ignored that ninety percent of the cars on the road did not turn. I could barely make out the driver's form and could provide no description other than it appeared to be a human being wearing big sunglasses and a white cap.

Ahead of me the light turned yellow. I hit the gas and went through as it changed to red. The SUV followed. My heart began to race. I drove slowly, but the car didn't pass. I told myself there was no reason to panic. I would call Andy and ask him to meet me at the hotel entrance where I'd drop the car with the valet. While I dug for my phone, I kept an eye on the rear-view mirror. The vehicle continued to follow me, a little too closely. Just as I found my phone, the SUV's blinker went on and it did what the signal indicated. It made a right turn. The phone fell from my hand. The thud as it hit the console made me realize how seriously I had taken the threat.

When I spotted an empty parking space, I pulled in. I needed a few moments to compose myself. I was still in that spot when the black SUV slowly passed by me. I knew it was the same vehicle; I'd memorized the New Jersey plate number.

Had I fallen into some sort of trap? Dread paralyzed me as the car started to parallel park in the space in front of me. I knew I should move. Flee. Call for help. Do something. *Anything*. But, all I could do was wait. Motionless. Defenseless. Frozen by fear.

The door opened. A jeaned leg came out. A skinny jeaned leg. That made sense once I saw that it belonged to a five-foot-two woman who was in excellent shape. She smiled at me as she stepped back to retrieve her baby from its car seat. As I flashed a strained grin in response, I heard a weird laugh and realized that it had come from my own mouth.

"Whew!" Even after I realized I was not being threatened by a mysterious stranger, several minutes passed before I could move. When I could, I felt around the floor for my phone.

U r making me paranoid, I texted to Andy.

How?

Think everyone following me.

Even guy in red shirt?

Then, after giving me just enough time to glance around, he added, *Don't look.*

But I had and found a man in a red shirt standing by a Chrysler convertible. I decided to get out of town. Off the island. Out of the county. Perhaps a nice trip to Bernardsville would smoke out anyone who might be trying to follow me.

I sent Andy a text. *Will be late to beach.*

U ok? He responded immediately.

Ok. Just busy.

I simply didn't mention where I would be busy.

Chapter 18

I didn't plan my trip to Bernardsville, one of many beautiful north Jersey towns that serve as New York bedroom communities. I just started driving north. Then I remembered the rental car had a GPS, and it led me directly to the Winthrop home, a gracious Victorian on a gracious tree-lined street that, I soon found, was overseen by a gracious hostess.

When Martha Winthrop, formerly Speakes, opened the door, I saw that she was white-haired, petite, and neatly dressed in a suit she must have paid a lot of money for sometime in the 1980s. Her hairdo had been designed twenty years before that but maintained within the past few days. I felt as if I had interrupted Queen Elizabeth at home.

Mrs. Winthrop greeted me with a smile that was, need I say, gracious. I delivered a speech I had composed in the car, describing myself as a historian looking for some information about Ward Braddock. A cloud passed over the woman's face at the mention of the name.

"You are a fan of his?" She asked without letting her tone suggest the correct answer.

"Actually, no."

Right answer. Mrs. Winthrop invited me in.

The décor was classic. Although I recognized a few antiques, I couldn't put a time-stamp on the style. I could, however, assign a price tag to the quality. Mrs. Winthrop had the best of everything.

She led me past a graceful staircase to a large drawing room, all green and pink, with high ceilings and glimmering hardwood floors covered with carpets that even I could identify as pricey. As I slipped onto the silk sofa, I realized I thought of the space as a drawing room. It was too elegant to be deemed a mere living room.

"You're an industrious girl, working on a Sunday." Mrs. Winthrop did not approve. I could tell.

I kept the lie simple. "Yes, I do sometimes and take off during the week."

She accepted my explanation. "Why are you writing about Ward Braddock?" Mrs. Winthrop perched on the edge of a Hepplewhite chair that somehow appeared tasteful even though painted in shades of pink and green.

"I'm actually writing about the Democratic Convention in Atlantic City in 1964—he's just a part of the story."

That piqued her interest. "Do you know what happened there?" Hers was not a rhetorical question. She wanted to know.

"That's what I'm trying to find out. You don't?"

She shook her head. "I know something happened. When he returned from Atlantic City, Charles ..." She interrupted herself. "You *are* here because Braddock's aide, Charles Speakes, was my first husband, right?"

I nodded.

"I assumed so. Charles would not say what had happened, but he was a changed man. At that point, he would not even admit that anything unusual transpired, but I knew something was wrong the moment he walked in the door. The Charles I knew was gone. He never came back."

"Would you mind telling me a little about him?"

"I don't know why anyone should care." Her tone wasn't defensive. Just curious.

I didn't have a good reason that fit my cover story. I said, "Background."

She nodded. "I know this sounds crazy, it's been so long, but sometimes I like to talk about Charles. My husband, my second husband, pretended Charles didn't exist. My daughter only knew her stepfather, and Charles Jr. doesn't remember his real father. It's as if Charles Elliott Speakes never lived at all. I never get to reminisce about him." She smiled. "He was my first love." She spoke those words with pride.

I sat while she traveled somewhere into the past. I began to worry that she wouldn't come back when a broad smile spread across her face.

"Charles never lived to become an old curmudgeon so I see him through rose-colored glasses. I met him when he was a senior at Princeton." Her pale eyes shone at the recollection. "I was a freshman at Vassar. He had to go in the service after graduation, but we were lucky that the war was over and Korea had not yet begun. His father swung a nice posting for him in Paris. We were married in a big wedding after my sophomore year. Then, Paris." Her eyes sparkled. "Girls in this day and age *tsk-tsk* the idea of leaving school to get married, but I'm sure I learned much more living in Europe than I ever would have learned in college. Those years in Paris were magical." She acted wistful in a way that would have seemed more appropriate had she been talking about the husband she lost the month before. I rationalized. Maybe that loss had put her in a sentimental mood.

"Wait here." Mrs. Winthrop wagged a finger at me and disappeared into the hallway. I stayed seated. From my chair, I studied the grand piano's display of family portraits in ornate silver frames. Martha had done well in her post-Charles life. The formal portraits showed beautiful people in elegant clothes and elaborate settings. The rest of the room did not reveal much about the family other than their financial status, which appeared to rank well above comfortable.

She returned shortly with another exquisitely framed photograph in her hands. "Robert didn't wish to be reminded of my first marriage, so I hung this in my closet where I could see it every day." She sat on a delicate settee and patted the seat beside her. "Come see."

I moved to her side and looked at a picture of a woman in a white satin gown trimmed with lace holding a spray of flowers I couldn't identify, though

I thought there might be a few orchids in the mix. Soft veiling attached to some strange lacey contraption on her head flowed down her back and wrapped around to the front of her dress. I would not have recognized Martha Winthrop as the bride in the photo. Too many years and too much sadness had driven the innocent optimism from the face of the woman who sat beside me. "Wasn't Charles handsome?"

I agreed. He was. And, as my grandmother would have said, bright-eyed and bushy-tailed.

"He had everything going for him. You can see that he was very good-looking. What you can't see is how charming, how athletic he was."

I glanced to my right and saw a schoolgirl's smile on Mrs. Winthrop's face.

"I thought I was the luckiest bride on earth." Her voice quavered. "It's hard to believe that this wide-eyed boy ended his life by swallowing cyanide." She pulled a tissue from a skirt pocket and dabbed at her eyes. "I don't dwell on that incident. I prefer to think about the happy times." And so she did, recounting stories of her life with Charles traveling across post-war Europe, setting up their first home in New Jersey, and welcoming their first child. I never had to prompt her. Not even when she said, "Of course, you want to talk about the sad times, don't you?"

* * *

Martha Speakes sat in the bedroom she'd always dreamed of, in the house she'd always dreamed of, in the town she always dreamed of making her children's hometown. Charles was sitting on the side of their bed, assuming the pose he reserved for serious conversations, like career decisions or problems with the household. She hoped she hadn't done anything wrong. Today was Christmas, their baby's first. She was in a happy mood. She didn't want Charles to ruin their holiday, but, judging by the look on his face, he was about to do just that.

"Martha, you may want to leave me."

She'd never felt fear as she did at the moment. "Are you having an affair?" She'd never even considered the possibility, but that must be the reason. That was always the reason.

"No. No. I would never. Never. I've seen that behavior, and I find it repulsive."

She believed that Charles didn't approve of such hijinks. He'd seen his boss's transgressions. They'd gone to Ward Braddock's wedding only months before and Charles had made what he thought were cryptic remarks, but she'd understood. Braddock had no intention of changing his behavior, of honoring his vows. Poor young bride. She was a lovely girl, but as naïve about married life with Ward Braddock as Charles was about political life with Ward Braddock. Martha didn't mind Charles hitching his star to Braddock—that would serve their family well. She just wished he would not be a True Believer. And Charles was a True Believer in respect to Ward Braddock.

"Why would I ever want to leave you?" Martha knelt in front of her husband, but he would not let his eyes meet hers.

"I find this so hard to say, but I've done something illegal. I didn't mean to, but circumstances ... things were moving so fast."

"Something you did for Braddock?" Her fear became tinged with anger.

"On his behalf," Charles nodded. "I long ago learned he wasn't the man I thought he was when I went to work for him, and I now understand he can't change. He doesn't even try to change, want to change."

She could have told him that. "You did something illegal for Braddock?"

He nodded. She read the shame on his face.

"Do the police know?"

He shook his head.

"Well then, what's done is done. Even if the authorities find out, it's unlikely they'll go after the senator. There is nothing you can do now. We'll never speak of it again. We'll start our night over. I don't even want to know what happened. I'm going to check on the baby."

She knew she was being brisk, dismissive, but it was Christmas. Charles Jr. had been thrilled with the lights and the gifts, even if he didn't understand what was happening. It had been a perfect day and now Charles was ruining it. No, not Charles. Ward Braddock. She'd never liked the man. Never trusted him. But Charles did, simply because they were members of the same dining club at Princeton. Brotherhood. She didn't understand Charles's devotion, but it had provided them with a nice home and a brilliant future. She had learned to put her personal feelings about Braddock aside.

"Martha, I'm going to the police."

His words stopped her in her tracks. She couldn't believe it. She turned.

He raised his eyes to meet hers. "I cannot live with what I've done. I am going to the police."

"No, you're not." She'd never spoken to her husband like that before; she'd never had to. He'd always been sensible and responsible, but this behavior was crazy.

"Please, sit down." He held his hand out to her. "I want to tell you what happened. To explain."

"I don't want to know, Charles. Ever. I do not want to know. Whatever you did is known only to you and Ward Braddock and that's how it should remain." She reconsidered. "Does anyone else know?"

He shook his head. "Not really."

"What does that mean?" She'd never heard her tone so harsh.

"Anton Wisk knows something happened, but he doesn't know the entire story. And, nothing that transpired is his fault. I am responsible for the entire thing." He ran his fingers through his hair.

The effect made him look ridiculous. Well, why not? He *was* being ridiculous.

"I thought I was doing my job. It was a reflex. A horrible, unforgivable reflex."

She sat on the bed beside him and wrapped his hands in hers. "Charles, whatever happened cannot be undone. There is no value in going to the police. We have a wonderful life. We will continue to have a wonderful life. I planned on giving you your biggest gift before bed tonight, but now … Charles, we're going to have another child. Next summer." She waited for his expression of joy. In vain.

Instead, he wailed. She'd never seen him cry. She'd never even seen his eyes mist over. She didn't like the emotional side of this man, the man she chose to marry, the man to whom she had entrusted her future and that of her children. When he calmed his tears, he was mumbling, "What have I done to us?"

"You haven't done anything to us—yet. Going to the police would be doing something to us, to me, to our children." Visions forced themselves into her head. She saw herself, Martha Gordon Speakes of the Greenwich Gordons, the best-dressed passenger on a prison bus, dragging her young son and an infant to visit their father in a dingy visitor's room filled with people whom she never expected to encounter in life. *People like us don't do that*, she thought. *I won't do that. I will not give up my life because Charles is having some momentary crisis of conscience.*

She tried a soft approach. "Please, Charles, think this over. Reconsider. For the sake of our family, for young Charles and the baby."

When he laid his hand on the tiny protrusion of her stomach, she thought she'd won but she hadn't. They argued until New Year's, when she decided to take another approach. "I'm going to visit my parents in Palm Beach. To give you time to think, to experience what it will be like for you without us."

Charles drove her to the airport on January 2.

"I hope you will come to your senses, Charles. We are your family. Do you really want to live without us?"

* * *

"Those were my last words to him. I wouldn't take his calls. I would tell whoever answered to find out if he had called to say he changed his mind. Every time, his answer was the same. 'No.'" She shook her head. "I came home from Florida on January 24 and found him dead. Police said suicide. I thought that by threatening to take his family away I drove him to it." She straightened her back. I watched her grow feisty. "But I didn't see it that way as time went on. I came to question if he had actually committed suicide even though the police told me there was no doubt. Yes, he was upset. Yes, he had done something that he considered horrible. However," she waved a crooked finger at me, "he would not have done that to the children."

"Maybe he thought ..." I didn't have to finish.

"Maybe he thought it was better for them if he killed himself?" She shook her head. "Children love their father no matter what he does. To be honest, at the time, I thought it was better for me even though suicide was shameful. We tried to keep it quiet, but some young reporter wrote the truth. People surprised me; they rallied round and offered sympathy. They might not have done that if they'd understood his motivation, whatever it might have been. As far as I know, no malfeasance ever came to light, and I think I would know if it had. I've never had to face the shame of his crime, whatever it was, although I had to live with the knowledge that he had a horrible secret."

"If it wasn't suicide, then what?"

"If I knew what it was Charles did in Atlantic City that upset him so, maybe I could answer that question."

"Did you ever talk to Ward Braddock about Charles's death?"

"He hovered around me at the funeral, full of questions and platitudes. Because I blamed him, I can't imagine what I said to him, but there was no dramatic scene so I guess I managed to control my hostility."

"Did he offer any insight into what Charles may have done?"

Martha shook her head, a tight, small gesture. "I wasn't about to ask. If he knew, he wasn't going to tell me."

"And Anton Wisk?"

"He came to the funeral but barely spoke to me. When he did, I couldn't even hear what he had to say. Maybe I was afraid to hear it." She shook her head. "I don't know. Until my daughter was born and I was forced to function for her sake, I was in a daze."

I feared she might have gone into another one. We sat for a full minute before she spoke again.

"The children never had to face the shame of what their father did, but they did have to live with the idea that their father chose to leave them. Looking back on it, Charles and I could have worked something out. Charles would have done his time. We could have moved, started over. I would have lost a lot that seemed so important at the time. But I still would have had my family." Tears welled in her eyes. She held her wedding portrait to her heart. After all these years, Martha still loved Charles Speakes. "In those days, everyone didn't get to marry for love, but I did. I truly did, but I didn't know that. Then."

My face must have told her that her statement confused me.

"I loved my life. I loved what it said about me. I had done the right thing, found the right husband, bought the right house. I couldn't imagine losing that. I didn't realize how much I loved Charles, the man." Her voice quavered. "Whatever he did, he was not a bad person."

I wasn't officially a detective. When conversations got emotional, as this one had, I couldn't ask probing questions. I reverted to platitudes. I asked for no more information about her first husband. I learned that Charles was superficial, pretentious, and probably a little self-satisfied, but he was a dedicated husband, father, and employee. I felt certain it was that last role that had gotten him into trouble. I just couldn't be sure what that trouble was. I could, however, make a guess, one that suited my theory.

Martha Winthrop walked me to the door.

"Mrs. Winthrop, I appreciate your talking to me but I have to ask, Why did you tell me all this?"

She didn't require any time to answer. "Because in close to fifty years, you are the only person who ever asked."

I understood, but why had she spoken so freely? I didn't pose that question but she provided another reason for her open manner.

"Ms. Daniels, I hope you find out what happened. I need to know. I'm no spring chicken, and you may be my last chance to hear the truth. You will tell me if you find out more in the course of your research, won't you?"

I said, "Of course," but I wondered. If the news was bad, would I be able to deliver it.

I had other concerns about Mrs. Winthrop as well. It was none of my business, but I couldn't help offering my opinion. "Mrs. Winthrop, you're alone in this big house with these expensive things. Do you think it's wise to open the door to a stranger and invite her in? I mean, I appreciate your time, but you don't know me."

"Oh, don't you worry about me. I'm a good judge of character, and, more importantly, I'm a good shot." Her hand reached into her jacket pocket and reappeared holding a pistol that was as petite and elegant as the woman who wielded it. "Don't be concerned. I'm not interested in shooting you. Especially not on an Aubusson carpet. But I could if I had to."

I thought I'd better leave.

Chapter 19

I arrived almost an hour late to meet Andy at the beach. "I was getting ready to leave." He opened one eye to greet me. "The sun is going down."

"Sorry. Rush hour."

"Rush hour? Where were you?"

I'd have to fess up eventually. In the meantime, I focused on my trip to Longport and Margate. I went on the offensive. "Do you realize I found a man in a red shirt behind me when you sent me that text?"

"Atlantic City is full of Phillies fans. You can't spit without hitting a man in a red shirt. You really are getting paranoid." He raised a finger to support his point. "However, just because today's episode turned out to be a false alarm doesn't mean that the incident with the car the other night was. I thought you said you weren't going on interviews alone."

"Actually, you said that."

"I won't ask you not to talk to Lucy Abbott, but promise you'll keep an eye on the rear-view mirror. I'd rather that you act paranoid."

Than what? He didn't say. He didn't need to.

"Then I drove to Bernardsville to talk to Charles Speakes's wife, or rather his widow."

"Charles Speakes?" There was no reason he would recognize the name.

"An aide to Ward Braddock who killed himself the winter after the convention."

Suddenly alert, Andy opened his eyes and propped himself up on his elbow. "Maggie, sweetie, honey ..."

When Andy's pet name for me, Maggie, headed a list of endearments, I suspected whatever followed might not be good. It wasn't.

"Don't you think you were way out of bounds talking to her?" His tone confirmed what he thought.

"She could have known what happened, but back in 1964, when her husband told her he'd done something horrible, she didn't want to hear about it." I added, "Or that he was planning to go to the police about it."

"Maggie, honey. You shouldn't be running around digging into Ward Braddock's past. For one thing, you are not a trained or licensed investigator." He fell back and closed his eyes.

"Neither was the original Maggie."

"She was a cat." He mustered some exasperation. "She couldn't help herself. You need to take care of yourself."

I detected real concern in Andy's voice but some hypocrisy in his words. "Licensing was never a problem when you needed me to do dirty work for you," I reminded him.

He chuckled. "Your lack of a license did come in handy sometimes. But still, I worry."

"I'm a historian."

He opened one eye and studied me.

"Historians ask questions."

He continued to stare.

"Without a license."

Andy had no response to that. He did, however, have a thought about my investigation. "You think this guy Speakes would have risked destroying his political future by killing a woman just because she threw a drink in his boss's face?"

"No, I think Braddock did it, and Speakes covered it up. He protected his boss."

"Think about how many illegal activities can go on at a political convention. There are a million things Speakes might have done that he couldn't live with. And there's no way to know if he wanted to go to the authorities to be a good citizen or to cure a guilty conscience or to bring someone else down or to get to the cops before they got to him."

I didn't want to accept that Charles Speakes might have been an ordinary white-collar criminal whose offense had nothing to do with Betty Boyle. "I'll think about it." I changed the subject and asked a question even though I was fairly sure I knew the answer. "So, what do you want to do for dinner?"

Back in the room, I ordered room service while Andy showered. Then we sat in bed and watched cable news. He was cutting a steak and I was chewing shrimp when I let out a yelp.

"Are you okay?"

I pointed at the television screen with one hand and covered my mouth with the other. "It's baby Braddock."

Andy hit the remote to raise the sound. Paulsen Braddock sat in the guest commentator's chair on a popular cable news show attacking the policies of the current governor of New Jersey, policies that were part of a national trend. Braddock opposed them. Given my hostility toward his father, I hated to admit that I agreed with a lot of what young Braddock had to say.

"I hate to break it to you, Maggie, but he comes off as pretty reasonable." This time Andy used his pet name for me to soften the blow.

"I know."

"Maybe he's nothing like his father," he offered.

"I read that despite capitalizing on his father's name, he was really raised by his mother after she divorced Ward. He wasn't born until three years after Betty died. Do you realize that Braddock did what he did to Betty two months before he got married?"

"Allegedly."

I snorted. "It's a lot easier to understand why a woman divorced Ward Braddock than it is to see why she married him in the first place."

Andy waved his fork at me and smiled. For the first time in a long while, I saw his green eyes sparkle. "The one good thing about Ward Braddock is that he makes all other men look good. Even me." His expression grew serious. "I know I haven't been a lot of fun this trip, but I'll make it up to you. I promise." But first he had to finish his dinner. Or try. He dozed off before he finished dessert. I removed the tray gently so I didn't wake him—although I don't think that would have been easy. A violent thunderstorm with lightning that turned night into day didn't disturb Andy's sleep. He was out cold.

Chapter 20

When I heard my cell phone shimmying across the bedside table, my hand chased it across the hard surface. I caught it easily, but when I opened my eyes the light from the screen blinded me. I checked the time. 2:08. I flung my arm behind me expecting it to land on an empty spot, but my hand landed across Andy's stomach. He grunted and rolled away but didn't wake up. If Andy was here, who else would be sending me a message in the middle of the night? I squinted to see the name on the screen. The answer was Johnny Boyle.

Awake?

My response was brief. *Now.*

Meet me at Café Monet?

I typed my response, *5 minutes.* Luckily, I could find my way to the Café Monet in my sleep, because I wasn't quite awake as I stumbled into the casino, followed my nose toward the smoking section, turned left toward the high rollers, and then made a right when I heard the roar from the crap table. Despite eyes that were functioning at less than full capacity, I spotted Johnny easily. This time he wasn't the only customer wearing a tuxedo, he was the only customer, period.

"I worried that I might be interrupting a little romance, but …" He could see from my appearance that wasn't the case. I didn't mention that he could call any time lately and that would not be the case.

"Don't critique my wardrobe. It's the middle of the night, and I got here in under ten minutes."

He tried to force the disapproval from his face. Unsuccessfully. "I didn't say anything. I just think you have a pretty face."

Pretty face? I knew what that meant. You have a pretty face, it's a shame you don't stay in shape. You have a pretty face, you'd look much better if you fixed your hair. You have a pretty face, why don't you put on some makeup. I wondered which one Johnny would go with.

He went with hair and makeup. "This windblown, sun-kissed look—the cropped pants, the loose shirt, the flip-flops—that's all fine on the beach, but a man enjoys seeing his woman done up like a lady."

He meant a Rat Packer enjoys seeing a woman done up like Angie Dickinson.

"These are my dress flip-flops. What's up? Are you okay?"

He was nursing a cup of coffee and looking serious. A plastic bag sat beside the saucer. He slid it across the table to me. I could see blue through the clear plastic. I looked to him for an explanation.

"My mama's diary."

Now? Now he tells me his mother kept a diary? Now, five days into the investigation? *Now*, in the middle of the night?

"Papa gave me this when I turned eighteen. I knew about her from what he told me, but that …" He nodded at the package. "That really let me know my mama."

I nodded and let him talk.

"I must have read it dozens of times—again this week, before I decided to give it to you." He shrugged. "I don't see anything but I thought you might see a clue. No one else has ever read that. My father broke the lock to open it. He gave it to me. And now I am giving it to you."

No cops? If Buddy knew this existed when Betty first disappeared, shouldn't he have given it to the police? Johnny answered the question I didn't ask.

"Papa didn't give it to the police. Her diary showed how happy she was, but he didn't want strangers knowing her private thoughts."

If I'd been Buddy, I would have given the book to the cops as an incentive to intensify the investigation. Not only that, but to clear myself. I didn't mention either idea. I nodded.

"I am letting you read this so that you will really know my mama. You'll like her."

Again, I only nodded.

Johnny was growing emotional and realized I could see his feelings rising to the surface. He looked away. His sad expression reflected in the water between the fake lily pads was the only thing authentic in that pond.

"I may be a little obsessed right now. I'm not always this focused on the past. I mean, my mama's death is always in the back of my mind, but meeting you, getting you involved, it's brought all the emotion back full force."

And yet again, I nodded. This time, however, I also spoke. "Johnny, I feel as if I already know your mother. She seems like a wonderful woman. Woman! What am I saying? She was only a girl. She was robbed of so much. I'm honored to read her diary. I want to learn more about her."

I also wanted to get back to sleep, but across the table Johnny's eyes filled with tears. I sat with him while he ate his dinner and reminisced about the woman he could not remember.

Chapter 21

When I awoke, Andy was gone and the plastic bag with the blue book inside was on my bedside table. Apparently, meeting Johnny in the middle of the night had not been a dream.

My spirit was anxious to read Betty Boyle's actual words, but my flesh was weak. It took me five minutes to get the energy to stumble to the mini-bar and pull out my morning Coke. I decided to forego my sixty-second workout. I wiped the condensation off the Coke can, washed my hands, and waited for them to dry completely.

I reached into the clear bag. The gold script on the pale blue hardened plastic cover was chipped and fading. *My Diary.* A tab with a discolored brass lock hung from the side. Scratch marks recalled the night Buddy had forced the lock. I opened the book with reverence—and fear. Not of what I might find out, but of what I might damage. I couldn't have been more careful if Johnny had handed me a Gutenberg Bible.

I settled in to get to know Betty Boyle in her own words and her own surprisingly legible, even elegant handwriting.

February 14, 1964
Dear Diary,

What a happy Valentine's Day! Last year I had no valentine, but this year I have two wonderful men to love. Buddy is a wonderful husband and father, and Johnny is an angel. The Johnny Angel I dreamed of when I sang along with Shelley Fabares. Maybe I knew there was a Johnny Angel in my future. Even then.

You are my Valentine gift. I told Buddy I wanted a book to record Johnny's life. Someday when he is grown up and married, I can sit with his wife and his children and show them what an angel their daddy was. I want to record every detail so I can remember all the days of his life. So, dear diary, you and I will be together for a long time.

"A long time." Already, Betty's writings tugged at my heartstrings. Before the diary was seven months old, Betty would be gone.

Betty's daily entries—she rarely missed a day—were mostly about Johnny and his firsts. Reading through them, I became convinced that Johnny was, in fact, a baby. And that is what made Betty's descriptions so appealing. She did not paint her son as a super baby. She was thrilled to describe an ordinary child, marking the normal milestones, achieving the prescribed firsts. Again, the heartstrings. Betty got to write about so few firsts. She missed Johnny's first step, his first word, and every first that followed. That possibility never occurred to the optimistic young mother who wrote so much about her future.

June 6, 1964

I take Johnny for walks on the Boardwalk. I try to remember the sound of his stroller's wheels on the wood and the feel of the ocean breeze on my face. I want to remember every detail.

I look at the carefree graduates visiting on a class trip and think they have their whole life ahead of them. But I don't feel at all jealous. I am happy with what I have. They do make me think of my future—really, my family's. My family. I love writing that, saying that. I love Atlantic City, but I want Johnny to see the world. I figured out a way to make that happen. I am going to be a travel agent. People will always travel, and they will always need travel agents. With the new expressway to Philadelphia, people will be able to get to that airport even faster, and I hear talk of expanding our own airport. I saw ads for a travel agent school and someday I will go. I know that a lot of people frown on mothers of young children working, but Buddy works so hard and doesn't make much money. So I will earn our travel money. I can be a travel agent at home and still be a great mother. I want to go to Paris. And Rome. (Travel agents sometimes take free trips in order to study places.)

June 8, 1964

Here is my list of how I want my life to be in 1974:

Johnny a happy ten-year-old, doing well in school.

His sister, seven years old. Mary Louise after my mother. Or his brother, who I want to name after Buddy, James Patrick.

Buddy working a steady job.

Me working as a travel agent.

Me taking Johnny, the baby, and Buddy on our first free trip as a travel agent. Disneyland!

June 10, 1964

Buddy is so sweet. I told him that I wanted to be a travel agent someday. He said he was sorry we did not have money for vacations, but he promised that he would drive us to the World's Fair in New York before it ends. I want to take a picture of Johnny with that big globe. He is such a good baby. He is always smiling. I talked to him all day today, and he looked at me and listened so carefully. I want to teach him everything I know. More than what I know. I have to read more, learn more so I can teach him.

June 15, 1964

Being a mother isn't always easy. Johnny was cranky today and all I could think about was how to make him happy but I couldn't. I have to learn that I will not always be able to make him happy. Life can be so hard. I want his life to be easy. No, not easy but not painful. I don't want him to struggle the way Buddy and I do. We struggle but we are happy. I can't explain what I am feeling but I am feeling so much. All good.

June 22, 1964

I am watching Buddy playing with Johnny on a blanket on the floor. Johnny is so like his father. I am very lucky.

June 26, 1964

Buddy is home during the day so I got my old job back for lunchtime at the Bella Napoli. They were so nice to take me back. I might even get extra work during the convention. (Democrats come in August.) I miss being with Johnny so much but it is nice that he is getting to know his father.

July 1, 1964

Today when I put some clothes away in Johnny's drawer, I found a bracelet in the corner. Myra's. I don't think she should be angry because I married Buddy. She liked him, but she didn't love him. She went on and on about how she did not want to settle for someone like him. She wanted more out of life. More to Myra means money. But I felt like she was mad that I dated Buddy. I don't how why she would be. They only had a few dates. She was my best friend. I want my friend back. I want her to meet Johnny.

July 13, 1964

It is our anniversary. One year married. I am so lucky. We don't have much money—especially after Buddy takes me to the Knife & Fork tonight—but we have love and we have Johnny. My parents are keeping Johnny overnight. I hope he'll be okay. I've never been away from him for so long.

July 14, 1964

My father and mother are crazy about Johnny. And to think how upset they were when they heard a baby was on the way! How time changes things. When I went to get Johnny this morning, I don't think they wanted to give him back. Now they seem to be over their disappointment at the timing of my wedding. They have forgiven Buddy. My father used to tell him over and over how he had dreamed of walking his little girl down the aisle in a beautiful white dress. He told Buddy how disappointed he was at the news that his daughter eloped to Elkton, Maryland. Until Johnny. Now my father never mentions a fancy wedding. Now I think he can only see the good news that is Johnny.

Johnny was so excited to see me when I picked him up. My mother said he went to bed fine and didn't whine or cry but he was kind of quiet. I bet he worried. Now he knows that if I go away for a night, I will come back. I will always come back. Always come home.

July 16, 1964

Goldwater was nominated in San Francisco last night. I can't wait until the Democrats come to Atlantic City. I am going to take Johnny to see everything.

July 20, 1964

Larry downstairs complained that Johnny cries too much. It's only because he's teething. I guess that will be harder on

Larry than on us. I wish Larry would be nice about it. He was a baby once.

July 24, 1964

Buddy is the best husband in the world. He is going to change his schedule so I can work some events when the Democratic Convention is here next month. I am soooooo excited! Although I also feel sad. I am sorry that President Kennedy couldn't be here. I would have loved to see him in person. My friend Lucy at work says she did once. But it will still be fun to see all the politicians close up, people I only see in the newspaper and on TV. I hope Jackie Kennedy comes. I know Bobby will. Teddy is in the hospital because of his plane crash. I can't imagine having such bad luck like that family does. We are so lucky.

August 1, 1964

Buddy bought me an Instamatic camera so I can take pictures of Johnny and me at the convention. He gave me a dozen rolls of film. I already took five rolls (60 pictures) of Johnny just being Johnny. I can't afford to have the film developed yet but I'll save the rolls for when I have the money. I keep them in a plastic box so if a storm ever floods the island again, like it did in 1962, it won't wreck all the pictures of him. I want a history of his life. I want so much for Johnny. Maybe he can be president.

August 22, 1964

I don't think I'll be writing much next week. The Democrats are coming to town. Jackie Kennedy. Bobby Kennedy. President Johnson is having his birthday party here. I want to see as much as I can. I signed up to work every night. During the day, I want Johnny to see as much as he can. I will take pictures. It will be so much fun to show Johnny the pictures when he studies this election in History class one day. I will have so much to tell him!

Yep, Betty Boyle sure knew how to tug at the heartstrings. I brushed a tear off my cheek. Betty had dreams, and someone had stolen them from her.

If she was in fear of anyone, Betty didn't confide it to her diary. Her writings did not provide any insight into her disappearance. What they *did* provide was proof that Betty loved her life. She could see a bright future for her son and family. I couldn't believe that anyone or anything lured her away from that life in the five days between her last diary entry and her death.

I slipped the "Johnny Angel" record onto the turntable one more time and sang along in the shower.

Chapter 22

As I wove my way through the fake trees and the real flowers to join Andy at our regular table in the Café Monet, I felt motivated. "One thing is clear ..." I was talking before my body hit the chair. "Betty did not run away. She loved her life. There is not a trace of frustration in her diary." I read several passages from her diary aloud.

"Maybe she lied." Andy offered another opinion.

"To her diary?"

"You said she was writing in it to tell Johnny about his childhood. What was she going to record for posterity? 'If this little creep doesn't stop crying and go to sleep, I'm going to carry him to the ocean and set him adrift in a basket.'"

"Don't be ridiculous."

Andy wasn't finished. "'Johnny isn't the prettiest baby on the planet, or even on the block. Nonetheless, I walk him down the street just as if I were proud of him.'"

"Andy. Stop."

But he didn't. "'I am beginning to fear that Johnny will turn out like his father—and the stories I could tell you about *that* jerk!'"

I held up my hand to indicate that I'd heard enough. "I choose to believe that Betty poured her heart out ..." I pointed skyward, to the fake Giverny sky, with an elaborate gesture, "Nay, poured her *joy* out, in her diary."

"Is that all you did this morning, read Betty's diary?"

"No, I got in a workout."

He did not ask me to quantify my exercise time, and I didn't offer. I couldn't get my mind off of Betty Boyle. Her writings might not have offered much information, but they did provide inspiration. "Today is the day I break this thing wide open," I said confidently. "I've found the right Lucy Abbott, and I'm certain she holds some key piece of information that will solve the mystery."

Andy smiled, wished me luck, and tried to hide his belief that my investigation didn't stand a chance. His skepticism couldn't bring me down and his cautions couldn't slow me down. As I stood to go he said, "I know Lucy Abbott is in her seventies, Meg, but please—"

"I know, I know. Be careful and keep my eyes on the rear-view mirror."

As promised, I checked my mirrors faithfully as I made the drive to Margate, all the while singing a medley of Betty Boyle's favorite hits.

My mood dropped when I took a good look at Lucy Abbott's house. Not that it wasn't nice. It was. Not as impressive as some of the renovated houses on the street but very attractive. But that was the root of my sadness. All of Betty Boyle's contemporaries had gone on to enjoy a lot of what life had to offer. Lucy Abbott got to live in a large, tastefully shingled, well-maintained house, nicely positioned on an inlet in Margate. More importantly, Lucy Abbott got to live.

I walked up the driveway, past an Audi sedan and along the side of the house to what appeared to be, if not exactly the front door, the main entrance. I rang the bell and waited. I rang again and waited. No answer. The previous night's storm had broken the heat and humidity and left behind a beautiful morning to be outside. Maybe Lucy Abbott thought so too. I walked toward the water and found a patio overlooking the bay but saw no one enjoying the view. As I turned back toward the main entrance, I got a good look inside the living room through a sliding glass door. That was when I saw the red curls on the floor. Moving closer I could see the hair belonged to a petite female dressed in a bright green jogging suit, face up, not moving. Lucy Abbott? Whoever it was, she needed help.

I grabbed the handle on the slider and yanked hard, but it didn't budge. I slammed the palms of both hands on the glass to summon anyone else who might be in the house. It never dawned on me that I was looking at anything other than a woman who had fallen or passed out. "Hello!" I yelled. "Anybody home?" I pounded on the door with my fist.

When no one answered, I ran back to the main entrance to bang and yell some more. Still no response. I dug into my handbag and searched for my cell phone. Of course, my hand couldn't find it. Dumping the bag's contents on the cement path, I heard the phone clatter onto the ground. I grabbed it and dialed 911.

"Someone needs help." I gave the address. A soothing voice assured me that assistance was on the way, then the voice ran through a series of questions.

"No, I can't get in.

"Yes, the door is locked." I tried the handle for the first time. "No, it isn't." I pushed the door open. "I'm in."

I started toward the front room but stopped on the voice's command. "I don't know. I called but no one answered.

"I'll check." I called "hello" a few more times.

"No answer.

"Okay, I will." I walked slowly to the front room calling out again with each step.

"If they are, they are not answering."

I moved toward the woman on the floor. I believed I was looking at the same person I had seen yesterday, but I couldn't be sure. Her face was contorted. I didn't see pain. I didn't see fear. All I saw was surprise. The dispatcher plied me with questions that in retrospect I realized were designed as much to keep me calm as to gain information.

"She's on her back.

"No, she isn't breathing.

"She's cold. She's *very* cold.

"I can't be completely certain who she is but the house belongs to a Lucy Abbott.

"No, I don't know her.

"She looks like a senior citizen. Lucy Abbott is about seventy."

The 911 operator didn't ask, but I added one more comment. "She looks very surprised."

I'm sure I appeared catatonic when the EMTs found me sitting on the floor beside the body. There was nothing I could do. There was nothing they could do. When the police arrived, they had plenty to do.

Chapter 23

I suspected the last clue to Betty Boyle's fate was going to the grave with Lucy Abbott. The day that had seemed so promising at the start had turned out as badly as the weather. But the low-hanging gray clouds moving across the sky must have looked cheerful compared to my expression.

"If only I had talked to her yesterday." The waves, usually so soothing, did nothing to raise my spirits. The low light in our rendezvous spot in the dunes did not seem so much romantic as gloomy.

Apparently not to Andy. He wrapped an arm around me, and I rested my head on his shoulder. Enjoying the warmth of his embrace, I wondered if I should find a dead body every day. That thought was quickly vanquished. I never wanted to be that close to such a tragedy again.

"If you had actually met her yesterday, today you would have concluded that talking to you drove her to suicide," Andy said. "Or, worse, that someone murdered her because she talked to you."

"Her death was a suicide. She left a note."

"Have you learned nothing from hanging around with me? At least, from hanging around with me and watching *Law and Order* reruns?" He tightened his grip.

"I know. Suicide notes can be faked, but I tend to believe those written by seventy-two-year-old women with health problems."

"Is that what the note said?"

"I didn't get to see it. They found it on her computer."

I leaned away and checked Andy's face. As I expected, he had raised an eyebrow.

"I know. I know. A septuagenarian composing a suicide note on her computer. But, the cops were also talking about her Facebook account and email." I snuggled back into Andy's shoulder. "It makes sense."

My head bounced as Andy shrugged.

"The police who came to the house didn't think the note was a fake. I listened when one cop read it to the other. The note said life was getting too hard."

"But it didn't say why?"

I shook my head. "Not the part I heard. She said something about a daughter, that she should focus on her own family."

"So how did you explain being there, anyway?"

"I told the truth. I said I was interested in the 1964 Democratic National Convention and looking for eyewitnesses. I just didn't say eyewitnesses to what."

"And they didn't ask?"

"Correct."

"They detained you for quite a while."

"They *interviewed* me for quite a while," I corrected Andy. "By the way, I let them look through my text messages. They wanted to know where my son went to school."

My head bounced as, again, Andy shrugged. "I'm not insulted. While you are implying my text messages indicate immaturity, I view them as reflections of youthful exuberance." He removed his arms from around me and pulled his shirt on. "I did catch a little glare for a few minutes, but it's getting chilly out here."

I waited for him to complain that he'd missed the best sun, but his usual self-pity was apparently overridden by an interest in Lucy Abbott's death. "What else did the cops say?"

"They didn't *say* anything. They asked. They had to make sure I wasn't a petty thief who killed the old woman in the course of a robbery. And they ruled that out." I frowned. "At least initially. We'd better hope the autopsy confirms suicide."

"Do they know the cause of death?"

"There was residue on her lips, so I think the assumption is she consumed something." I shook my head. It was such a sad situation.

He pulled me close again. "Maybe you should take a break, Meg. I can see this is tearing you up."

"I want to get to the bottom of it, Andy. I'm going to see if Buddy Boyle will talk to me."

He didn't try to dissuade me, I guess because he wasn't worried. Neither of us saw Buddy Boyle as a suspect.

We didn't swim that night. Instead, we sat side by side on a beach towel and watched waves break on the shore as dark clouds moved in, finally blocking the last vestige of blue sky. At least *I* was watching. After a few moments, I realized Andy had dozed off. When a light drizzle covered us with a cold sheen, I woke him to say it was time to go inside.

Chapter 24

As soon as I was wide awake, which was shortly after I finished my morning Coke, I ordered a copy of every newspaper from the hotel gift shop and then started my workout. When the bellman did not arrive after one minute, I stopped jogging in place, grabbed a couple of pieces of salt water taffy, and settled onto the bed with my laptop for what turned out to be another unsuccessful search for information on Lucy Abbott's death. I followed up with an unsuccessful search for Wanda Costello, including an attempt to find her on Facebook, and, when that failed, in the obituaries. Nothing.

The newspapers that the bellman dropped off proved no more satisfying. I didn't expect to find anything in the Philadelphia paper, even in the New Jersey pages, but I pored over the *Press of Atlantic City* looking for news of Lucy Abbott's death. I found none. Likewise, the *Downbeach Current* with its heavy coverage of the towns that shared Absecon Island with Atlantic City offered no news of anybody's death and only a summary of the police log, but not for the time period I wanted.

The first thing I asked Andy when I arrived at the Café Monet was if he thought the lack of coverage was peculiar. He did not. "Maybe her family wanted to keep it quiet. Or there might be something in the next edition of the local paper—it's a weekly."

He quickly moved on to other topics.

"So what else did you do this morning?"

"I worked out." My tone asked, What do you *think* I did?

"Sounds as if you're getting pretty serious about it."

"Well, it isn't as if I go to the gym; I do a little routine in the room." I didn't mention how little. "I have to build up over time."

Andy stopped with his fork in the air. "Exactly how much time have you been putting in? Say, this morning?"

I sometimes find it annoying how well this man knows me. I decided to say sixty seconds. A single digit like "one" combined with any word, especially "minute," sounded so unimpressive.

He smiled as broadly as I'd seen him do in at least a week, and I realized it was probably a relief for him to talk about something besides the Betty Boyle case. For the past week, I'd been obsessed with it.

I didn't know what my next step should be and didn't trust my judgment to make the right decision. I headed for the hotel spa and a manicure and pedicure. The manicurist agreed that I was in no way responsible for Lucy's death. Of course, to protect my case, I had to hold back a lot of the salient facts, actually *all* of the salient facts. I don't really think it mattered. She didn't appear to speak much English.

I waited until I was sure my nails had dried before I caught up with Johnny at the counter in the Botticelli Buffet. As he munched on something big and greasy, I made my case. "Johnny, I don't think I can move ahead with this investigation unless I talk to your father. I know he is reluctant to revisit the past, but if he won't talk to me, I'm going to have to call it quits."

Johnny chewed fast and swallowed. "Okay, but let me think about how we do this." After a moment, he had a plan. "I could take you in and then go outside to do a little gardening. Maybe if he's alone with you, he will tell you something." He paused. "Can you be subtle?"

Can I be subtle? To be perfectly honest, I've always felt a little challenged in that area, but I could try.

"Let me think about this. I'll get back to you," he said.

I said goodbye and took my new nails to the beach. I tried to read but found that my eyes kept drifting to admire my manicure and my mind kept returning to Betty Boyle. I felt the need to do something for her, for her son. Not that the beach wasn't lovely. It was. There was a nice breeze and a lot of sun, but sitting on the sand did not appeal. I sent Andy a text. *Bored.*

He shot back a reply. *Where?*

Beach.

No sympathy.

I got his point. I had sun. I had surf. I had a good book. At least I heard it was good. I couldn't focus. I texted Andy again. *Taking car.*

I planned to stop by Myra Morris's to gauge her reaction to Lucy Abbott's death. I didn't expect much of one. After all, I didn't even know if she had ever met the woman. I was grasping at straws.

As I parked in front of Myra's big house in Brigantine, I was surprised to see Johnny coming down the driveway. Well, not exactly Johnny. The man who kissed Myra awkwardly on the cheek before heading for a black SUV parked in front of my car was a shorter, skinnier version of Johnny with lighter hair and more of it. When I got a closer look at the man, I could see that he was about fifty, about the same age as Johnny. I leaned back in my seat to take a deep breath. Wow. It all seemed so obvious. How could Buddy not know that Myra had his child?

I recalled the portrait hanging in Myra Morris's living room. Just a young Myra, a handsome husband in bad glasses, and two daughters. Why was the son here now but not in the family picture from the '70s?

Part of me wanted to skulk away and pretend I didn't see Myra's visitor, but the investigator in me needed to know more. Okay, so technically in the eyes of the state of New Jersey, I am not an investigator; let's say the *busybody* in me wanted to know.

Myra looked shocked to find me standing on her front steps when she opened the door three minutes later.

"I hope you don't mind my dropping by. I haven't seen Buddy yet but I had an update, a question really, about Betty Boyle."

"Of course." Myra seemed both annoyed and nervous.

I understood her annoyance. If I were in her place, I would be afraid that dropping by was becoming a regular thing with me. I also had a theory about her nervousness. I had to ask. "Myra, the man I saw leaving—he got into a big black SUV."

She stared at me.

"He looks familiar."

She forced a smile. "He's from up north." I detected a slight quiver in her voice.

Apparently, my expression asked for more information because she continued. "Are you familiar with Basking Ridge?"

"I do have some friends there, but I don't think that's where I've seen him." I waited for Myra to elaborate, but she didn't say a word. If she was nervous, I was hysterical. I'd never asked about such personal matters, and I wasn't sure I had the right. Or the guts. But I went for it.

"This may sound weird, Myra, but your visitor bears a remarkable resemblance to Johnny Boyle."

She let out a deep sigh and massaged her forehead. Finally she let out an even deeper sigh and relaxed her body. "Don't be coy, Ms. Daniels."

I still felt afraid to ask my question. I sputtered.

She took the lead. "You'd better come inside." She led me into the living room—I suspect because she needed to sit down—wasting no time in getting to the point or the silver box of cigarettes on her coffee table. "So you know I dated Buddy Boyle some fifty years ago. You know he dumped me. You know I took a long trip out of town after we broke up. Now, you run into a man around fifty years old in my driveway who is the spitting image of Buddy's son ..." She paused to light her cigarette. "I'd have to think you were a moron not to figure this one out." As she spoke, the fear disappeared from her voice. "I guess I should appreciate your attempt at discretion." But she didn't. Her tone was mocking.

"Does Buddy know?" I asked.

"No, I didn't tell him when it happened. I just dropped out of sight." She took a deep drag on her cigarette. "If he and Betty hadn't been so hung up on each other, they might have been suspicious. But they could only think about their love, their baby. My son was taken from me the day he was born."

She must have heard the bitterness in her own voice. "Was I bitter?" Her eyes met mine. "You bet I was. At first. Then I realized that marrying Buddy wouldn't get me anywhere that I aspired to go. I was still months away from my twentieth birthday. I didn't need a baby. While I was away, I met people, learned things, and came up with a vision of a better life for myself."

"Did you keep in touch with your son?"

She shook her head. "That wasn't an option back then. It was as if it never happened, as if he had never existed. The nuns at the home, a place for unwed mothers, promised me he was going to a decent and loving family, and I went back to my old life."

"So how? When?"

"You're making me smoke ahead of schedule." She paused to inhale deeply. "My son only came into my life five years ago. I'll tell you I wasn't thrilled about it. My husband knew I wasn't a virgin when we got married." She studied my face. I'm not sure what she found but it must have conveyed shock. "I know that's a bizarre concept to your generation, but it could be a very real problem with some men in my time. My husband had no problem with my history—but having a child? That was a different issue. I had never told him."

I couldn't imagine living with a secret like that. Actually, I can't imagine living with *any* secret. When I have a problem, I stop strangers on the street to run the situation by them.

"Brantley—his adoptive parents named him Brantley ..." she sighed, "came to find me but not because he wanted to find his real mother. He had a son with a medical condition that might have been genetic and he needed information. I lied and said I didn't know how to find his father. If I had to, if his son had gotten worse, I would have told him about Buddy but, luckily, whatever they needed, they found in my medical history."

"And he stayed in your life," I confirmed.

"Yes. Getting to know Brantley—he stops by several times a week—was a pleasant surprise." Her comment seemed sincere. "And I do mean surprise. In my day, you never expected to see your baby again, and that was fine with me. I had always feared that he might try to find me and I did not want to be found. I had a family. I didn't need a stranger disrupting my life. And then he showed up at my front door, and, seeing my son, in that very first instant, brought so many emotions to the surface." I saw those emotions rise to the surface again. "I guess a psychiatrist would tell me I'd been suppressing my feelings all along." She tried to laugh. The noise resembled a snort more than a chuckle.

"My husband has been wonderful." She ground out her cigarette. "My children think Brantley's mother was an old friend of mine. That's what I told them."

"Did you consider telling Buddy?"

"You mean five years ago?"

"Ever."

She shook her head and laughed. I detected a touch of the bitterness that she claimed had faded away.

* * *

Myra didn't want to work late at the bar, but that old lech of a manager insisted. She was annoyed. The crowd was thin, and she wouldn't make any tips. Then she would have to walk home on a night that felt cold for spring. Worst of all, she didn't feel good. Probably premenstrual. She hoped that was the problem. She couldn't think of anything she'd eaten that might have upset her stomach, but she was really queasy. She hoped it wasn't the flu. She couldn't afford to miss work.

That night, climbing the single set of steps to the apartment required a great effort. She leaned against the wall as she unlocked the door. Inside, the lights were still on, but Betty's bedroom door was closed. Myra was relieved that her roommate had gone to bed. She wasn't in the mood for Betty's babbling. Sometimes her positive outlook wore Myra out. She was happy to turn out the lights and call it a night. When she approached the lamp near the window, she saw a man's jacket thrown over the seat of the ladder-back chair. Apparently little Miss Goody-Two-Shoes was getting some action. For once, Myra wasn't jealous. She wasn't in the mood for romance.

She was awakened. Whether the nausea or the whispering or both awoke her, she wasn't sure. She needed to get to the bathroom but the noise in the hallway suggested Betty was ushering her guest to the front door. Myra sat on the side of the bed waiting to hear the door open and close. What she heard was low murmuring and giggling. She moved to the door. If this guy didn't leave soon, she would have to dash by him in her nightgown. And that was when she heard his voice. She couldn't quite make out the words, but the voice was familiar. She told herself that it could not be Buddy. It wasn't his jacket. The similarity of the two voices had to be a coincidence. She put it out of her mind.

When Myra got up the next morning, Betty's door stood wide open and she was nowhere to be found. That was unusual but not unheard of. There was no coffee in the percolator, which also marked the morning as different, but Myra didn't care. Her churning stomach didn't want any coffee.

Buddy called around 10 AM and asked if he could come by.

"Can you give me until ten-thirty?" she asked. "I worked late, I haven't been feeling good, and I'm just getting up." She didn't add that she needed some time to make herself presentable.

Even though she didn't feel good, Myra took the trouble to apply makeup and pull on a tight red sweater over tighter black pants, the garments highlighting her best assets. She opened the door as soon she heard his knock and knew. The jacket. Buddy was wearing the jacket. He looked nervous, and she understood why. Guilt. No wonder Betty disappeared early, before she had to face Myra that morning.

"Can I come in?"

"Why not?" She stepped back and waved him inside.

He held his head down as he made his way to the old sofa, the sofa on which they'd first kissed. She doubted that he was thinking about how soft her lips were at that moment.

At least he didn't beat around the bush. The words came rushing out of his mouth. "Myra, I asked to come over so I could talk to you. You are a wonderful girl, and we've had a lot of fun together."

"But?"

"Something happened. Something I need to tell you about." And he did. Without hesitation. "You were always telling me about Betty. I came over to see you last night after work and she invited me in to wait."

Wait. That was a polite word for what they did.

"I know it might strike you as silly that I am telling you this so soon, but I want to be absolutely truthful about this."

She felt as if the air had been knocked out of her, but she kept her face impassive. The tide in her churning stomach was rising.

"We talked and talked and talked, and it was so different from … our evening together was so different from any time I'd spent with a girl."

Myra wished he would at least try to hide his delight at finding such a wonderful woman.

"And, one thing led to another, and we moved into her room. But," he threw up his hands in a defensive move, "I am telling you, nothing happened. I mean nothing that doesn't take place between home plate and first base."

Yeah, that made her feel better. Buddy was dumping her for a girl who didn't even put out. Myra fought to remain calm, to keep her breathing even. In her stomach, liquid sloshed from side to side.

"That was Betty's rule. She said that you are her friend, and nothing could happen until I talked it over with you."

Myra felt her heart racing and could do nothing to stop it.

"I told her I would see you this morning. I told her that you and I had a really wonderful time together, but there was nothing special between us. That's how you feel, right?"

What did he expect her to say? *Sure, I'm just a good-time girl. A babe. A broad. A whore. But Betty? Now, that girl is a keeper. I'm so happy for you, Buddy.*

"I am sorry, Myra. Although, if it weren't for you, I would never have met Betty."

She took a deep breath, feeling she was about to lose the fight with her nausea. "Buddy, please go. No matter who you end up with, it isn't going to be me. So it might as well be Betty. Go ahead. Good luck. Now, I'm not feeling that good. It has nothing to do with you or this situation, but you need to go."

"But Betty is outside. She wants to come in."

"Her name is on the lease. She can come and go as she pleases."

Myra left Buddy in the living room and ran to the bathroom. Even after she'd vomited and her stomach began to calm down, the fight continued—this time with her emotions. She sat on the linoleum floor determined not to cry. What did it matter anyway? Buddy was far from the man of her dreams, but the humiliation hurt so much. She vowed she would be out of that apartment by sunset.

Ignoring Betty's attempts at reconciliation made her feel better. She kept a tight rein on her emotions and managed to remain civil while she packed and got out of that place for good. She was in her old bedroom at her mother's house by 5 PM.

Only then did she cry.

* * *

"Of course, you've figured out that I hadn't eaten a bad clam or caught the flu. And I wasn't premenstrual either." She shook her head. "You figured it out, but Betty and Buddy never did. If there was one talent I had back then, it was putting up a good front."

I didn't know what to say.

"If those two had half a brain between them, they would have worked it out. When a teenaged girl disappeared for six months or so in those days, everyone understood. They just never admitted they knew. But Betty and Buddy were so into each other, they never gave it a thought."

"You must have been heartbroken." The sadness in my voice was genuine.

She shook her head. "I was angry. I was embarrassed. But I wasn't sad. At least not about Buddy. Sure, I found Buddy sexy, which counts for a lot when you're nineteen." She removed another cigarette from the silver box on the coffee table and lit it with the matching silver lighter. This time she took care to exhale over her shoulder as if that would spare me from the fumes. It was a generous but futile gesture.

She shrugged. "I assumed that I would be the one to end things with Buddy when the fun stopped. I didn't want to marry him. He wasn't going anywhere. Back in my day women didn't have the opportunity to work at whatever you do."

I thought she was looking at me expectantly so I started to explain, "Now, I'm the VIP concierge at the Artistical property in the Bahamas but before ..." She didn't care. This conversation wasn't about me.

"Yeah, well the only way I could get ahead was to get a rich husband. Do you think I could have gotten all this for myself? Maybe if I were twenty years younger, but not in 1964. I actually owe Betty a debt of gratitude. If she hadn't been involved with Buddy, I might have resolved my problem by marrying him."

"Apparently Buddy has done pretty well for himself." Was I conveying information or defending Betty's choice? I wasn't sure.

"A miracle. I don't understand it. I wasn't interested in Buddy for his brains, if you get my drift. He didn't appear to have much in that department, but I am happy for him." She leaned back and took a long drag on her cigarette. "I feel that I dodged a bullet by not marrying him, yet I am emotionally bound to him forever by our son. I was shocked by the extent of my feelings when you told me he was dying." She sat, fingering her cigarette nervously. I didn't speak. She wasn't finished. At last, again after inhaling deeply and exhaling slowly, she spoke. "And what about Brantley? How do I tell him I lied? That I know who his father is? That he might have a last chance to meet him?"

"You can tell him that I brought you information about Buddy."

"That would be a half-truth, the same as a lie." She shook her head in wonderment. "So much deceit. Some half-truths. Some omissions. Some, just plain lies. I need truth in my life, but how? How do I make things right?"

Chapter 25

Andy got to the beach just after I did and within five minutes had heard the true story of Myra Morris's life.

"She seems convinced that Buddy was never even suspicious about her pregnancy," I said. My tone said I didn't believe it.

"It wasn't in his best interest to be suspicious," Andy said with empathy. "He was in a really tough situation."

I was not in a sympathetic mood.

"So now that you've uncovered a stronger motive, you're back to thinking Myra killed Betty?"

I shook my head. "Murder takes more than motive. I can't see how she disposed of the body. Unless she had an accomplice."

"Good luck tracking *that* person down after fifty years." Andy smashed the small mountain he'd built out of sand and started construction on a new one.

"I'm still convinced Ward Braddock killed Betty. I have no proof, of course, and I have to face the fact that even if Lucy Abbott knew what happened, it's unlikely she left any evidence behind. I'd like to attend her memorial service, assuming it's in Margate."

"You didn't actually know her."

"It just feels wrong to find a body and walk away."

It felt all right to Andy.

"It isn't as if I can check an etiquette book. I doubt even Emily Post in her heyday addressed this situation."

"She could have told you what to wear, at least, and I bet you don't have anything appropriate." He tried a practical approach to dissuading me.

"A black dress and mourning veil will not be necessary."

He yawned. "Let's go check your closet." I had come to accept that Andy would do anything to get back to the room, and I knew what he would do once he got there. He made an announcement. "I'm going to take a little nap. Wake me for dinner."

When room service finally arrived, he said he was too tired to eat.

"Andy, you've been getting at least eleven hours of sleep every night."

"I'm working hard."

"I know you are, but do you think you should see a doctor about this excessive sleeping? Maybe you're depressed."

"I don't get depressed—I've always been an upbeat person. Now I'm just *tired* and upbeat."

I took a deep breath before addressing my real fear about his recent sleeping habits. "Is it me, Andy? Are you trying to avoid me?"

He rolled over and I saw a stricken look on his face. "No, no—that's not it at all. Seeing you is the only bright spot in my day!"

There was real affection in his eyes and tenderness in his touch.

"I'm sorry I haven't been more fun, not to mention romantic," he said, stroking my cheek. "I wouldn't have lasted a day on this job if you weren't here with me."

We stared into each other's eyes, and I waited for that little gleam to appear in his. Instead I saw the outsides of his eyelids.

The mood and Andy were gone.

Chapter 26

I found a death notice in the next day's *Press of Atlantic City* and texted Andy. *No lunch. Funeral.*

His entire reply consisted of one letter: *K.*

I figured no further response was required or expected from me. I put on my nicest dress, actually my only dress, and headed to Margate for the celebration of Lucy Abbott's life.

The deceased's entire family consisted of one daughter, who I suspected was the spitting image of her tiny, red-haired mother some thirty years earlier. Deborah Abbott was standing with an equally petite man in the back of the church, greeting a noisy crowd of mourners. When I introduced myself, she hugged me warmly, as if I had done something to help her mother in her last moments. "I am so glad she was not alone when she passed."

I did not protest that her mother had been alone. What did it matter to me if the grieving daughter thought I'd arrived in time to provide some solace to her dying mother? Apparently that misinformation made her feel better on a day when there couldn't be too much that would.

"Please, stay for the service and come to my mother's house afterward. You know where it is."

That I couldn't deny. No doubt there were a lot of addresses I'd forget over time, but Lucy Abbott's was not likely to be one of them.

I picked my way through the crowd and found a seat near the rear of the church. Lucy Abbott was present in a gold urn sitting on a table in front of the altar and in the conversations I overheard. When I think of the elderly taking their own lives, I envision lonely people a lot older than Lucy, isolated in rundown apartments, without friends and family, unable to come up with a reason to live. If the attendance at her funeral was any indication, Lucy Abbott did not fit that stereotype. I'd seen her greeting guests at her house the day before she died. I'd met her daughter. And, now I saw the church filled with her friends. I couldn't square her social life with suicide.

Neither could her daughter.

Standing at the end of her mother's dock after a ceremony marked by more laughter than tears, Deborah turned her back on the crowd of mourners and stared across the inlet. "I don't know why she did it. And why now? I'm pregnant, and Ben and I are getting married. She should have been thrilled. She was a single mom so she felt relieved that I wouldn't have that 'row to hoe.'" She sniffed and smiled. "Her words."

"I didn't realize ..."

"I wasn't born until my mother was almost forty. I'm a product of the sexual revolution and medical technology. When I was born, single women using sperm donors was a new concept. My mother claimed she didn't know my father's identity, but even if she did, she wouldn't have let the information out. She knew how to keep a secret." Tears welled in the young woman's eyes. "So maybe her motive to kill herself was one of those secrets." She could not stop shaking her head. "Now, I realize that she asked for the week off to arrange it all. To think that she was talking to me about mundane things and all the time ..." Tears flowed down her already tear-stained cheeks.

"I'm sure there was nothing you could have done," I mumbled. Then I just stood there, silent and awkward. I felt as if I should touch her, but I barely knew her. "I should let you talk to your mother's friends."

"Friends? All they do is judge her." She glanced over her shoulder. "See the one holding court over there? She told me how disappointed she was in my mother, that she should have been braver." She sneered. "That woman never had to do a thing for herself. She married a rich man. My mother worked as a waitress for years before she got a job in an office. She saved her money, had me, and made a wonderful home for me. And she did it all on her own."

"I don't suppose Wanda Costello is here today?"

"Wanda Costello? I don't recognize the name."

I didn't think she would but saw no harm in trying. "She may have married and become Wanda something else."

"No, I never heard of a Wanda. How do you know her?"

"It's complicated." My discomfort with my own deceit was growing. I had to be straightforward. "This is not the time, but could I call you to talk about a woman your mother worked with named Betty Boyle? I'm guessing you've heard the name?"

"Betty Boyle? I don't think so. You can call, but I don't see what good it would do. Why do you ask?"

"Your mother might have been one of the last people to see Betty alive. She disappeared in 1964, during the Democratic Convention. Your mother never mentioned her?"

"No, and I'm sure I'd remember a story like that—although, as I said, my mother really knew how to keep a secret."

And then I thought, what the heck, go for it. "Did she ever mention a man named Ward Braddock?"

Deborah shook her head. "The name sounds familiar, but I don't recall anything specific. If I think of anything, I'll call you."

"Thank you. I'm staying at the Artistical. I should let you go."

I turned to leave, and that's when I saw him. Anton Wisk. I felt as if I'd been caught in all my lies. Maybe not lies. Misrepresentations. That sounded better, but call them what you will, I was still caught. With my head down, I peeked in Wisk's direction. He was walking toward us but hadn't noticed me. I turned around to look across the water, showing him only my back, but it was an unnecessary subterfuge. As he brushed by me to hug Deborah Abbott, he didn't even glance my way.

"Deborah, Deborah … I'm so terribly sorry. We are going to miss your mother so much at the center, after all these years."

Seizing my opportunity to disappear, I walked away from the hugging pair and scurried to the door. Outside, I fumbled with the keys as I tried to get into my rental vehicle. I didn't turn around to see if anyone was watching or following me, or even glance sideways as I slipped into the car.

I fumbled with the key again as I tried to get it in the ignition. When the car started I let out a sigh of relief, but as I pulled out onto the street, my heart was pounding. I didn't know exactly what I was afraid of, but I had to admit, what I was feeling was fear.

Chapter 27

I parked the rental car and sent a text to Andy. *Lucy took secret to grave. Anton Wisk took self to funeral. News @ 7.* I'd just pressed Send when Johnny called me. "Still want to talk to my papa?"

"Absolutely."

"Wait under the portico and I'll pick you up."

"How will I know your car?"

He chuckled. "You'll know."

I did. When a vintage Cadillac with big fins drove up, I was not surprised to find Johnny inside. I would not have been surprised to find Frank Sinatra inside. And, in a way I did. His voice streamed from a sound system that was far from vintage.

"Sorry." Johnny flipped off the music. "I do like other music, but listening to Frank is part of my job. I see professional listening as my professional reading. You must do professional reading."

"Right." If you counted perusing *People* magazine for information on the celebs I'd be serving.

"You look nice today, very ..." he struggled to find a word and came up with "neat."

"I had an appointment this morning." I didn't bother telling him I'd met with a corpse. I wasn't about to tell him anything until I had the whole story.

On the short ride down Atlantic and then Ventnor Avenue, Johnny talked about how much he liked working at the Artistical. I was relieved that he had not made one reference to my love life by the time he swung the car to the right, past a sign that told me we were entering Marven Gardens—known to Monopoly players worldwide as "Marvin" Gardens. No matter how you spelled it, the neighborhood was lovely, with charming houses and well-manicured lawns. It saddened me to think Betty Boyle hadn't lived to know her bartender husband would do well enough to buy a large home with grass to cut, hedges to trim, and a backyard where their son could play. I thought about how happy the doting mother would have been raising her son in a neighborhood with winding streets that suggested a time when, at least in the fantasies of many Americans, life was easier. Beaver Cleaver could easily have grown up in Marven Gardens.

Johnny pulled into the driveway of an elegant two-story stucco structure that recalled old Hollywood—at least pictures I'd seen of old Hollywood. He led me to a back door that opened into a large, very orange kitchen that screamed *Brady Bunch.* I didn't have time to take in the details. Buddy Boyle's head emerged from the harvest gold refrigerator. I recognized him not only from his face, which remained relatively unchanged from the old family photo Johnny carried, but from the stark resemblance he bore to his son. Andy had been right. Any resemblance Johnny bore to Marco Angelini was superficial. Although Johnny had not gotten his sparkling blue eyes from Buddy, the two Boyle men shared the same bone structure, eye shape, and body type.

Buddy appeared to have far more than twenty years on his son. His illness had stripped his body of any excess weight and left his face gaunt and drawn.

"Hey, Papa, you must be feeling better." Johnny gave his father's shoulder a gentle squeeze. "Did you eat anything today?" Turning to me he said, "My papa doesn't come into the kitchen very often."

"I just came out for a glass of Gatorade," Buddy said. "I got a shipment today."

"Well I'm glad you are up and about and looking so handsome. We have a visitor. Meg, this is my father, Buddy Boyle. Papa, Meg Daniels. I told you about her."

"Yes, and I told you I didn't want to see her. So, knowing I will be polite, you brought her here against my wishes." Buddy's words were harsh but his tone was not angry. Maybe he was too sick to project anger and cranky was all he had the strength for.

"I should go." I backed toward the door past a box of supplies labeled with the name and logo of Anton Wisk's organization. I'd be cranky, too, if I qualified for donations from Absecon Hope.

"I didn't mean you should scram, miss. No, my son knows me. I will be polite. I know you mean well. I know Johnny means well. Me? I say what is done is done. Let the matter rest. Just because I feel that way, it doesn't mean I can't be a good host. If you're a friend of my Johnny's, you're a friend of mine. Please come into the front room."

Buddy led me down a hallway that had been decorated, undoubtedly by men, with an admirable collection of posters. Phillies. Eagles. And most of all Frank, at his jauntiest, seemingly asking anyone passing by to come fly with him. I detected no sign of a female touch until we entered the living room. There, I discovered several decorative items that only a woman—a *'60s* woman—could love: a porcelain lamp decorated with pink flowers and colorful but cheap prints of foreign locales in ornate yet equally inexpensive frames. Prominently displayed on a wood veneer coffee table was a framed version of what I'd come to think of as the defining photo of Betty, Buddy, and baby Johnny, together at his christening.

Buddy lowered himself into a black leather sofa that matched the unabashedly masculine style of the postered hallway as well as the chair he pointed out for me.

"I don't see any point in digging into Betty's death," Buddy said. "Johnny fantasizes that his mother is living somewhere, like one of those soap opera people with amnesia." He shook his head. "I've been home a lot since I got sick. Now I even have my shows … you know, shows on TV that I have to catch every day. I'm no better than that Mrs. Wasserman you met—the whack-job me and Betty lived next door to back then. Masked bandits could have stormed into that dame's house and snatched her kids during one of her shows. She wouldn't have missed them until the news came on." His voice turned soft. "I wonder how she's doing now that they are taking those programs off." He sounded genuinely concerned.

"Did Betty watch soap operas?"

"She was no lady of leisure like Lorraine Wasserman. Betty was an 18-carat mother. *Attentive* is what people said. Took good care of Johnny. Always. Made dinner for me unless she was working nights, which she did that week. You know, the last week." He seemed lost in thought. "I wish she didn't have to work at all. If she didn't have to work …" His voice trailed off.

I imagined that Buddy regretted that he hadn't been a better provider when Betty was alive. "It's a shame she didn't live to enjoy all this."

"Yeah, if she had lived, we wouldn't … we would have had a different life."

"When did you give up hope?" *Or* did *you give up hope?* I thought. "They never found her body."

"She's dead. I know. A husband knows. We were happy, newlyweds, brand new parents. She wasn't going to run away. Even if she hated me, and she did not, she would never, ever have left her baby. For days I thought I could find her and help her. The next morning, I went everywhere I thought she could be, starting with her parents' place. She wasn't there, and she wasn't at the hospital, either. When the owners showed up to open the restaurant, I was at the door waiting. I talked to them and to the employees as they arrived, but no one had seen her after she left work. I searched under the Boardwalk, under the piers. I looked in every alley and every gutter, thinking maybe she fell and was lying somewhere, hurt and unable to move or call for help. I carried her picture and stopped strangers on the street to ask if they had seen her.

"At that point I had to go back to her parents." He paused and shook his head remembering. "That was hard, but I needed their help. Her father and

I went to the cops. All they did was tell me that Betty would call. Betty's mother watched the baby. Her father walked with me. For days. Finally, the police took a report, but …" He paused. I didn't think his deep breathing was so much about fighting the physical pain of the present as about the mental pain of the past. "I could tell they thought I'd done something to Betty. My Betty. The love of my life. Betty and I always called the baby Johnny Angel, but she was the one. Betty was the angel."

Despite the years that had passed, I read fresh pain on his face.

"If she didn't come home, she was dead. I think I knew that right away. I might have fought believing it, but I knew. I wanted to accept other explanations. It's pretty sad when you're hoping your bride ran off to Scramsville with some loser. Any story that meant she was okay …" His rueful laugh sounded more like a snort. "Uncovering the truth about what happened to her now is not going to bring Betty back."

He switched gears in an instant. "Want something to drink? I don't have much other than the Gatorade that the local community center sends over."

"Absecon Hope?" I wasn't really asking, just confirming.

Buddy nodded. "They do fine work there. Help the kids, the poor, the sick. That's me. Almost seems they knew I was sick again before I did." Again the rueful snort. "They sent me the same stuff the first time: awful-tasting crackers, Ensure, Gatorade." He poured himself a glass of the bright yellow-green liquid. "Sure you don't want some?"

I was sure.

"Anyway, Betty was such a sweet and kind girl. So excited about the convention. So anxious to take the baby everywhere." He fought tears. "I told her, 'Betty, the boy won't remember,' but she said she would take pictures to help him remember. Did you see those pictures?"

I nodded.

"I gave her that camera." Buddy's proud smile faded. "After I did, I wondered if I made a mistake. She was hanging around that convention, taking pictures and talking to strangers. I was always a little nervous about the protestors. Did you know she gave them candy? Salt water taffy. Not many people would have done that. Some folks didn't like that. Back then, we had a name for white people who got involved with the Negroes."

His tone suggested that if he were speaking to someone from back then, he might still be using the name.

"Those people weren't popular. I tried to talk to Betty, but she thought she was right and everyone would see the light. I don't know why. We had a guy who lived downstairs who probably would have been happier living in Mississippi and hanging with the Ku Klux Klan. After Betty was gone, he made some remark to me that maybe she ran off with one of those black friends of hers. Of course, he didn't say black."

"So he'd seen her with the protestors?"

Buddy shrugged. "I didn't ask. All I cared about was what happened after Thursday night, but he must have seen her around town. How else could he know she was sympathetic to the protestors?" He took a long drink of Gatorade. His lips pursed and his eyes closed. Pain was etched on his face. "You know, this doesn't sound nice these days, but I felt afraid Betty might be headed in that direction myself. You know to be a ..." He couldn't come up with a word that would be acceptable in the 21st century.

So, I did. "Civil rights activist?"

"Yeah. That. But the way she acted, I guess that was the excitement of the convention. Like I said, I didn't have nothing against nobody—except maybe Canucks—but I was worried about her."

I had to ask. "Did I hear you say you had a problem with Canadians?"

"Rotten tippers. They'd give you a penny to say you did a good job. I didn't need their opinion. I needed money. I had a family to support."

"Oh." I had no comment. I got back on topic. "What else was Betty doing during the convention?"

"Just working the events and checking out what was going on around town. She loved JFK, but he was dead by then. I didn't think he was all that great a president, although he did keep those Russki missiles out of Cuba. I couldn't convince Betty that he wasn't perfect. Then he died and became a goddamn saint. So I let her name our kid after him. No harm done. John is a nice name, and I didn't want no junior. Anyway, Betty was disappointed

Kennedy didn't live to come to Atlantic City. With him dead, I felt surprised that she was still excited about the convention, but she was. I stayed home with the baby at night so she could work some special events. Not for the money—I had to change my shift to cover for her—but because she wanted to be part of it. If I had only known."

The thought of Betty's death still brought tears to Buddy's eyes. "Look." Clearing his throat required great effort. "I know you think you're doing Johnny a favor, but you're not. It was so long ago. Even if you found someone who knew Betty, no one could possibly remember a thing. Who have you talked to?"

I told him all about my visit with Myra Morris. Well, not everything. I stuck to the basics and hoped my face didn't give away that there was more.

"I'm glad things worked out for Myra. I hope I didn't hurt her. She wasn't nuts about me or nothing, but we'd spent some time together. I didn't think anything of it at the time, but it must have meant something to her, back in the day."

He shrugged again, but this time the gaunt shoulder barely moved. "Myra was a looker and a lot of fun, but she wasn't Betty. Myra was pretty outside, but inside? Not really. She could be hard. Right away, after Betty and I got together, I apologized to Myra. I thought explaining made everything okay. I should have been kinder." His eyes brightened. "Wanna know how I met Betty? I came to the apartment they shared looking for Myra. But Myra wasn't home. Betty was. Need I say more?"

I saw love in his eyes as he revisited the moment from fifty years ago. "I took one look at Betty and that was it. But it wasn't only about how pretty she was, although she was very pretty. She had the most extraordinary blue eyes. You can see them right there on Johnny. Lucky boy. Eyes as blue as Ol' Blue Eyes' himself. Didn't get my dull green eyes."

Since I have green eyes myself, I could have taken offense but I didn't. Buddy was right—at least about his dull eyes.

"Betty was a really good person, and the best thing that ever happened to me. I didn't deserve her but she loved me." Looking embarrassed, he changed the subject. "Who else did you talk to?"

"I looked into an incident involving Ward Braddock."

"You didn't talk to him, did you?" I heard genuine fear in his voice.

"Yes, I did."

"Keep away from that man, he's no good," Buddy said with surprising force. "His entire family is no good. He thinks that damn son of his is going places, but he ain't going nowhere. Believe you me. You can't live a life like those people do and get away with it forever." He paused. "If Betty had ever told me what he did to her, I would have killed him."

"How did you find out?"

"Years later, Lucy Abbott finally told me. I wish Betty had told me. I would have killed the bastard then and there."

"Did you know Lucy died this week?"

He appeared agitated. "How did she die?"

"It's being called a suicide."

"Suicide? That's very sad. I didn't know her well, other than to say hello. She came to see me in 1968—the day Bobby Kennedy was shot."

* * *

Buddy Boyle thought his living room must look shabby to Lucy, but she thought it looked nice. At least that's what she said. "Betty did the place up nice." She walked to a mahogany end table that Betty had refinished after picking it from the garbage over on Florida Street. Lucy touched the picture of Betty and Buddy with their son on his christening day. Buddy loved the photo because it reminded him of the night his young wife lovingly trimmed its edges to fit into a frame she'd splurged on at Lit Brothers department store. A frame from Woolworth's was not good enough for her baby.

"This your boy?"

Buddy nodded.

"Of course it is. He looks like his daddy, but I see Betty in his smile and his eyes. She loved that little boy so much. Is he here?"

"He's with Betty's parents. He stays there when I'm at work. I work nights; in fact I'm due in soon." He glanced at his wrist and realized he hadn't put on his watch. He made a show of reaching for it and buckling it onto his wrist, the final touch of dressing. Lucy didn't notice, or take the hint.

"Lucy, is there something I can do for you?" He'd only met the woman twice before in his life, when he'd gone to meet Betty to walk her home from work and once when he went there to find her.

"I've been thinking about Betty with Bobby Kennedy being shot and all. She was so excited she saw him. I was the one who covered for her so she could duck out. It was just hours before she ..." Lucy fought to find a verb but came up empty. It didn't matter. They both knew what she meant.

She gave up waiting for an invitation to sit and dropped into a settee Betty's mother had given the couple as a housewarming gift. "I have something on my conscience that I can't stand no more, Buddy."

He froze. "Do you know where Betty is?"

She shook her head. "No, but I did see something that night ... that last night."

Afraid that any word he breathed might change her mind about confessing what she'd seen, he didn't speak.

"Betty and I were walking out together after work," she resumed. "Out the back door and down that alley to Pacific."

He nodded. He knew the setup.

"Anyway, I reached for the compact I keep in my purse and couldn't find it. I figured I left it in the ladies room so I went back to look. I found it," she said as if he would care. "When I came back down the alley, I saw Betty standing with a man by the back door of a limo. When I passed them, I could see he was holding her arm. It looked like maybe he was trying to get her into the car and she wasn't cooperating." She stopped.

What the hell was she stopping for? "Did you recognize him?"

"I saw his picture in the paper. He's a pretty big deal."

"Does he have a name?"

"Braddock. Ward Braddock."

Buddy felt his anger rise. "Why did you wait so long to tell me this?"

"I didn't know if Betty would want me saying nothing. I thought maybe they were having a thing, and for awhile after she went missing, I wondered if maybe she'd gone off to be with him. I mean, I'm sure you're a nice guy and all—but Ward Braddock? A girl don't get a chance like that every day." She continued nervously, her words spilling out in a long, rapid run-on sentence. "I didn't know Betty all that good, Buddy, I didn't know how she lived, and, besides, I was afraid to get involved because the Braddocks are an important family and the guy I was seeing at the time didn't want me to go anywhere near the police." She paused for a breath. "I had a lot of reasons to keep my mouth shut."

"I wish you'd told me the day I came to see you, Lucy. It could have helped the investigation. We might even have found Betty."

"Maybe if I'd known about the earlier incident I would have, Buddy. I didn't know nothing about that at the time. I swear."

"What earlier incident?"

"You know—a couple days earlier. The party at Bella Napoli?" Seeing only confusion in Buddy's eyes, she added, "Didn't Betty tell you what happened? Or the cops, at least? I can't believe you don't know about that night."

"You better tell me about it," Buddy sputtered. "Now."

Lucy recounted what she'd heard about Betty's encounter with Ward Braddock the night of the party. "I wasn't there," she said in conclusion, "but after Betty went missing, I heard about it from another waitress. A lot of people knew, but I guess none of them told you."

Buddy could barely suppress the rage he felt toward Ward Braddock. Yet the strongest emotion he experienced was sadness. "Why didn't Betty tell me about it? I would have taken care of Braddock."

There was a pause and Lucy said reluctantly, "I think that's maybe why she didn't say nothing to you."

"But the cops. Why wasn't I told?"

"That's no surprise. They never challenged the big-shot from the start."

Buddy felt like he'd just gone ten rounds with Muhammad Ali. As he collapsed back onto a chair, he gave Lucy a hard look. "Whether you knew about what happened at that party or not, when you saw Braddock holding Betty against her will, you should have said something."

Lucy shrugged. "I saw her pull away a bit, but she seemed to know him so I wondered if she was just being a tease."

"So much that he was practically dragging her into his car?" *What was wrong with this woman?* Buddy thought. "You didn't even stop to ask if she was okay?"

"She wasn't screaming or nothing, and I didn't see her get in the car."

"But you said she was resisting."

Lucy stood up. "Look at me. How could I help?"

"Even a tiny woman can yell for help. You could have tried."

"I didn't know what was going on. I was afraid to get involved."

* * *

"Buddy, I don't understand. Didn't the police do anything with this information?"

"I didn't go to the cops. It was four years after Betty disappeared. The police looked at me back in 1964, and I didn't want any more trouble with them." He clutched his stomach and squirmed. "I'd like to talk to you some more, but I'm not feeling too good."

I could tell by the discomfort on his face that he wasn't lying. I called to Johnny to help his father and waited in his car trading texts with Andy.

Buddy knows about WB, I texted.

Wilford Brimley?

Not funny.

Warner Brothers?

Still not funny.

World Bank?

Stop. Going back to see Anton Wisk.

Not w/o me.

I saw no point in arguing via text message. I typed: *Talk @ 7.*

Chapter 28

I started talking before Andy had time to settle on the beach beside me. "Lucy Abbott may have been the last person to see Betty Boyle alive. Other than the responsible party, of course."

He yawned as he settled. "Sorry, it's not that I'm not interested."

"I know. Office work." A mollusk would have gotten the picture by now.

"So who is your main suspect this evening?" He stretched out on his back and folded his arms behind his head.

"It has always, well, almost always, been Ward Braddock. And now I'm sure. Well, maybe not *completely* sure." I continued despite his closed eyes. "In 1968, Lucy told Buddy she'd seen Betty with Ward Braddock the night she disappeared."

"And the police did nothing?"

"*Buddy* did nothing."

"*Nothing?*"

"Remember, the cops had accused him, put him on the defensive. And the Braddocks were powerful. Even four years later, Buddy was still afraid."

"But to do *nothing?*" Andy opened his eyes and stared into the graying sky. "Nothing at all?"

I didn't understand either. "I'll try to get Johnny to arrange for me to see his father again, but considering Buddy started to feel worse while I was there, Johnny may not be thrilled with the idea. Anyway, I got what I wanted—proof that Braddock was with Betty on August 27. Something he's always denied."

"It's only hearsay," Andy corrected me. "And being seen with Betty is not the same as murdering her." He made eye contact for the first time since he'd arrived.

My stare asked him, 'Are you kidding me?' I thought the verdict was in.

"What about your other suspects?" He wasn't ready to settle on Braddock just yet. "What about Myra Morris?"

"Logistically improbable." I had dismissed Myra as a suspect.

"Donovan?"

"Motive isn't strong enough. He couldn't kill everyone who didn't share his political views."

"A political argument could have gotten out of hand," Andy countered.

"It's possible." I had to agree.

"You believe Lucy Abbott was one of the last people to see Betty alive. I'd think that would at least earn her a spot on your suspect list."

"But she had no motive."

"That we know of. Maybe she was stealing from the restaurant and Betty caught her. From what you say about Betty, she wasn't the type to go along or keep quiet."

"Lucy was tiny. I have the same issue with her that I have with Myra. How could she have disposed of the body?"

"You're assuming Betty was incapacitated and then her body was moved, but no one ever located a crime scene. Maybe she was taken somewhere under false pretenses and then killed. Lucy could have lured her somewhere."

"But why?"

"I don't know, but if you decide to run off and ask someone, tell me first. I'm serious. I'll be your bodyguard. Just in case."

Chapter 29

My morning plan, made after my sixty-second *Flashdance* workout, was a visit to Absecon Hope. Since I was going to an agency that provided social services, to meet an elderly man who had devoted his life to helping the underdog, I did not think I needed a bodyguard.

I texted Andy. *Going to Absecon Hope.*

Andy replied. *Not w/o me.*

I responded. *Can't wait.*

Andy didn't make me wait. The room phone rang. "Be right there. Told them personal emergency." He was beginning to talk like his text messages.

"You appeared awfully happy about that emergency." I said when he arrived at our room seven minutes later.

"So, they can fire me." He appeared unconcerned. No, make that hopeful. "This is your gig. You do all the talking. I'll have your back." He zipped his lips.

When Anton Wisk peered through the wire-mesh glass on his office door and spotted us on the other side, he pretended he was happy to see me again and to meet Andy, but he wasn't. We pretended not to notice, made ourselves comfortable in the visitor chairs, and stared at him across his desk.

"I saw you at Lucy Abbott's house yesterday." I forced a smile.

He appeared perplexed. "Yes, of course I was there. What a tragedy. I was sorry to have missed the service but we had a small emergency here."

"I didn't realize you knew Lucy."

"Likewise."

"How did she come to work at Absecon Hope?"

"Very simple, really. There were jobs. She applied. We hired her. That was a long time ago. Decades ago. In fact, she was with us from the day we opened, way back in the fall of '68. I'm a little confused. What does this have to do with the book you're writing?"

"I'm curious because you both had a connection to Betty Boyle."

"Betty Boyle?"

"The waitress I told you about on my last visit—the one who threw a drink at Ward Braddock during the convention festivities? Tuesday night at the Bella Napoli?"

"Oh."

I found his forced look of confusion a little over the top. "You must remember the police talking to Braddock about Betty's disappearance two nights later. You were with him at the time of the questioning."

There was no crack in Wisk's bewildered façade.

"As it turns out," I continued. "Lucy Abbott saw Betty Boyle with your boss the night she disappeared."

"Really?"

"She never mentioned it?"

"Missing waitresses and Ward Braddock's personal life are not frequent topics of conversation here at Absecon Hope. We're very focused on the important work we do every day, making sure the sick are cared for, the young are educated, and the hungry are fed."

"It just seems like such an odd coincidence."

Wisk screwed up his face as if to ask, "How so?" He was going to make me explain.

"That a coworker of Betty Boyle's who saw her with your boss the night she went missing ends up in your employ a few years later."

"I find that a *remarkable* coincidence." Andy offered some support.

Wisk glanced nervously at him, probably trying to figure out what purpose he served at this meeting. Andy flashed a strained grin, insincere but extremely polite.

"It's quite a reach to conclude that because I paid my respects to a coworker who knew Betty Boyle that I am somehow involved in her disappearance. I believe that's what you are implying."

I didn't deny my intention. I laid my cards on the table. "Mr. Wisk, you're a good man—that's obvious from everything you've accomplished here. How can you live with whatever secret you are keeping? How can you live with the guilt?"

Wisk turned his pleading eyes to Andy, as if he thought he might side with him. "There is no guilt!"

I followed a tactic Andy had taught me and said nothing. Andy kept his promise and followed suit.

After a short pause, Wisk, who had not been trained by Andy in the art of coercion by silence, continued. "There was the *appearance* of guilt. That's all. And, in the political world, that's all it takes to ruin a career."

I didn't prompt him to continue. The silence did.

"I don't know how Ward found Lucy, or if Lucy found Ward, but you are right that she'd seen Ward with Betty Boyle the night she disappeared. Even though it was four years later, Ward knew if that came out, it could be damaging, even though he'd done nothing wrong. It was the kind of attention he didn't need. So it was in his interest to help Lucy, and he asked me to give her a job. He'd been extremely generous in funding the center, so naturally I agreed. It worked out well for everyone."

"Except Betty Boyle."

"It was too late for Betty Boyle. What happened to her wasn't Ward's fault, but it looked bad. When Lucy saw Ward talking with Betty by the limo, he was just apologizing for his earlier rude behavior and encouraging her to get in so they could talk." He paused for a moment. "Betty *did* get in, but I promise you, she did get out."

* * *

Anton Wisk couldn't understand why Ward just couldn't get over it. He *wouldn't* get over it. He was still spewing obscenities at the little snip who threw a drink at him. *Who did she think she was? Didn't she know who he was?* Event after event, party after party, he went over the details of the incident time and time again. Now back on his cabin cruiser, hidden away by his staff because he was too drunk to be seen at the Boardwalk festivities, the politician remained obsessed.

Ever the dutiful aide, Charles Speakes tried to reason with him, to make him understand how inappropriate his behavior had been, but Ward was convinced that a Braddock could behave any way he pleased, especially to "a bitch waitress." As Ward saw it, the waitress and others in her social stratum had but one mission in life: to serve families like his—"the families that made America great."

"Your family did make this country great," Charles said, sliding his chair forward in an effort to keep Ward in his. The ploy didn't work.

Ward stood up, brushed by his assistant, and nearly went down in the process.

"Whoa, boy." Charles got his boss settled back into his chair.

"My family was here building America while hers was stomping grapes in Italy," Ward slurred. "Or is she a potato digger? Let's go find out and explain the facts of life in the United States of America to the bitch."

"Ward, it's late. We're doing fine right here." Charles's tone was intended to soothe.

"Come on, boys, let's go for a ride." Ward regained his balance.

Anton reached out to steady his boss as he staggered toward the stairs. Ward's breath and pores exuded an ugly stench of alcohol.

Ward patted Anton on the chest. "Anton, you're with me, right? You'll help me straighten the tramp out before we leave this city, right?"

Charles moved between the senator and the exit. "That's a bad idea, Ward. A very bad idea. Anyway, we've already agreed that your night is over."

"Hey, who's paying you? If I say we go for a ride, we go for a ride."

Charles stared hard at his boss. "Think of your future, Ward. You're the heir to a political dynasty. Right now the party is letting Johnson have his turn, and, when that's over, you'll have just hit forty with a term in the Senate under your belt. Then you make your move. The country that feels it got shortchanged when JFK was killed will be ready to elect another charismatic young president."

Ward became momentarily distracted. He began to hum "Hail to the Chief." Charles marched him back toward his seat.

For a moment Anton thought Charles had won the war, but Ward still had a battle in him. His handsome face contorted into an ugly mask. "That little bitch threw a drink in the face of the future president—that's like treason! Isn't that treason, Anton? You're a lawyer. So tell me. Didn't that little bitch commit treason?" He didn't wait for an answer. He headed for the deck.

Charles tried to stop him, but Ward was bigger and stronger, and, Anton suspected, when push actually came to shove, Charles would always defer to Ward's name and position. He couldn't quite bring himself to knock his boss to the floor. After all, Ward was the rising star Charles had hitched his wagon to, the one person who could give him the life and career he'd always wanted.

"Let's go say hello to the milkmaid," Ward spat. "She should be getting off work just about now." He stumbled.

"We don't know that." Charles made a good point.

"If we have to, we'll wait." Ward tried to get to the deck again.

"You sent the driver home." Charles sounded relieved to have a strong argument.

It wasn't strong enough to stop Ward. As he ascended the steps he called behind him, "Chauffeur didn't take the car. Anton will drive."

Anton doubted Ward would make it off the boat, as drunk as he was. But he was wrong. After a lifetime spent on family yachts and sport boats, the senator had great sea legs even when plastered. He made it all the way to the car, his nervous aides trailing behind him.

Charles advised Anton to utilize every time-waster possible while he worked to distract their boss. Anton complied, taking the longest route, driving well below the speed limit, and stopping at yellow lights. As it turned out, his delaying tactics only guaranteed the limo's arrival at Bella Napoli at just the wrong moment.

"I see her!" Ward slurred gleefully, slapping his knee. "She's in that alley!"

Looking to his right, Anton saw a pretty young woman in a neat white uniform and black apron step out of the dimly lit alley that ran alongside the restaurant. She was moving fast, pocketbook in hand, no doubt headed for home after a day's work.

"Stop the car!" the senator shouted.

Anton pulled to the curb then watched in the side-view mirror as the girl came up the sidewalk toward the rear of the limo.

The back door flew open. Ward struggled to climb out of the car. He could barely stand.

Anton closed the driver's side window to block the noise from the Boardwalk parade and lowered the passenger side window so he could hear what was going on. As he looked into the back of the limo, Charles caught his eye and held up a finger as if to say, watch and wait. He'd slid over to the passenger side where his boss was draped drunkenly across the door frame. If his boss made one wrong move, he could pull him back into the car.

"Remember me?" Ward asked the girl as she came alongside the limo.

"I remember you," she said, staring straight ahead as she tried to walk past. The senator reached out and grabbed her arm, stopping her. Charles stiffened but did not make his move.

"I came to apologize," Ward said, trying to strike a sincere note but slurring his words badly.

Her look was tense, but she didn't cower. "There's no need to apologize," she said, trying unsuccessfully to shake off his grip.

In the mirror, Anton spotted a waitress in identical attire walking along the sidewalk toward the car. He saw her appraise the scene with a quick glance before hurrying past.

"I insist you give me a chance to apologize." Ward's tone was almost chivalrous but Anton heard trouble in the word "insist."

"People make mistakes," the girl said. "It's okay." Her tone was dismissive and insincere, but Anton hoped his drunk boss would buy it. Apparently he didn't.

"I don't make mistakes," the senator said haughtily as he pulled her closer. She tried to break free of his grip again, this time more forcefully, but he held fast. Looking past him into the back seat, she shot Charles an imploring look.

"Let her go, Ward," Charles said. "You've had your say."

Ward ignored him. The waitress spoke in a worried but not panicked tone. "Okay, you apologized. Now let me go."

Ward responded with a snort as he tightened his hold on her arm.

"I'm sure you don't want to make a scene," she said, trying her best to remain calm. "If you don't let me go right now you'll leave me no choice but to—"

"You impudent little bitch." Ward glared down at her. "You have no choice in the matter. You're going to get in my car and hear my apology."

The young woman looked truly fearful now, as she began struggling in earnest against her captor. He could hear Charles repeating, "Let her go, Ward, let her go," but the words were falling on deaf ears. Looking around him nervously, Anton wished the girl would just get in the car, out of plain sight, and give Ward a few minutes to tell her off and be done with it.

The girl screamed, shrilly, and just as quickly a hand covered her mouth, stifling her cries. From Anton's perspective, it appeared she was pushing Ward into the limo, but he quickly realized that Charles was actually pulling the two of them inside. Good idea, he thought as he performed another visual survey of the neighborhood.

There was traffic moving by quickly but no pedestrians were on the block. He hoped the girl's scream had gone unheard, and he hoped that at this late hour there were no diners left at the restaurant's front tables—at least not bored ones who'd rather watch the street than gaze into the eyes of their dates. He half expected to see the door fly open and some hero rush out to defend the waitress's honor. Nothing. Nobody. Anton could hardly believe Ward's luck. Maybe he could win the presidency after all.

Anton heard the rear door close and turned to see Ward tangled up with the waitress in the back seat. He had dropped all pretenses of apologizing and spewed expletives at the struggling woman. Charles murmured reassuring words to the girl as he tried to restrain his boss. Ward managed to wrestle himself free as he fought to keep his hand over the waitress's mouth. Anton recoiled whenever a truncated scream escaped her lips. He turned up the radio and raised the window between the two compartments. He told himself he was giving his boss some privacy but the truth was he was afraid of what he might see, what he might hear. What alarmed him most was the fear that he would be considered a party to whatever happened back there. What if for once, his boss was unable to worm his way out of the situation?

As the music blared and the limo rocked, Anton faced straight ahead waiting for orders. He yanked off his tie, loosened his collar, and leaned back into the headrest. He closed his eyes, not so much to rest as to shut out the world. He jumped when Charles pulled open the driver's door. Charles was wild-eyed, frantic. Blood trickled down his forehead into one eye.

"Turn off the damn music!"

As Anton complied he could hear Charles's words though he did not fully comprehend them.

"It's over, Anton. Get Ward out of here. Fast. I'll try to talk to the girl, but this time he's really done it. It's over."

* * *

"Later, Charles told me he'd been trying to defuse the situation and keep Ward and the girl separated, and I never doubted that," Wisk said. "At some point during the struggle, Ward landed such a powerful shot to the side of his head that he lost consciousness. He didn't know how long he'd been out, but when he came to Ward was on top of the waitress and her clothes were disheveled. Charles was very frightened. He thought Ward had raped the woman."

I grew excited. This must have been the act that had filled Speakes with such guilt. My question was, had he covered up for a rapist or for a murderer? I found it difficult not to prompt Wisk but I forced myself to sit in silence.

"I didn't even realize the girl was out of the car until Charles banged on the window. I could see her in the side mirror, slumped on a bench near the front of the restaurant. As I was pulling away, I saw a woman walking down the street in our direction. Charles must have seen her too, because I could see in my rear-view mirror that he crossed the street. I assumed to get out of sight."

"The other woman you saw—was it Lucy Abbott?"

Wisk considered his answer, then quickly shook his head. "No, this was someone else."

"Did you recognize her?"

Again, he shook his head. "I didn't know anyone in Atlantic City back then. All I remember is a young woman in a gaudy red, white, and blue dress—it was a common theme that week."

"Did she approach Betty?"

"Not that I could see. She was heading toward her but I left."

"Sure, I understand." I wanted to appear sympathetic, though sympathy was far from the emotion I was feeling. "Did Charles tell you what happened after that?"

Wisk nodded. "When I went back."

"After you dropped Braddock at the boat?"

"No, I'd gotten about halfway to the marina when Ward began waving something in the rear-view mirror. It was the waitress's handbag, and he was laughing about it, calling it a cheap piece of junk. I knew I'd have to take it back, but the last thing I wanted was another public scene with him so I kept on toward the boat. I would have dropped him there and gone back, but then I heard him snoring and could see he was out cold. Orders or no orders, I decided to turn around and drop the purse near the restaurant before he came to."

"I see," I prompted him. "And … ?"

"When I got back, the only person in sight was Charles, waving me down. I'd never seen him so jumpy. He took a look at Ward in the back seat and climbed in the front with me. We drove to the boat. On the way, he told me about the heated conversation between Betty and the girl in the flag-colored dress. He was too far away to hear what it was about but it led to a physical altercation. The girl in the gaudy dress either hit or pushed the waitress." Wisk paused and formed the next sentence carefully. "The waitress fell and hit her head during an argument with the young woman."

"Where was this young woman when you got back?"

"She was long gone. Charles said she took off running down Pacific Avenue after the waitress went down. She hadn't seen him, had no idea he'd witnessed the whole thing."

"And you drove off without making any effort to check on Betty's condition? You didn't even think to alert the police?"

Wisk looked guilty. I thought for good reason. "We couldn't afford to get involved. If we had, the entire story would have come out. Ward would have been finished." He couldn't let his eyes meet mine.

"What did you do with the handbag?"

Wisk froze momentarily. "I ... I believe I handed it to Charles and he left it there, on the sidewalk."

"Weren't you concerned about fingerprints?"

"I wasn't guilty of anything. It never even occurred to me to worry about fingerprints." His tone was defensive.

"But if you believed she was seriously injured, possibly even dead, then you should have realized the cops would look at the bag as evidence. Why would you incriminate yourself like that, not to mention Braddock and Speakes?"

"Charles might have kept the bag, I'm not certain. There was so much going on that a lot of it is just a blur."

"But the reason you went back to the restaurant in the first place was to return that handbag."

He was growing increasingly annoyed and agitated. "Right, but then I heard Charles's story about the fight in the alley, and the waitress on the ground with a head injury. Do you think I was thinking about a handbag at that point?"

"Did you think she was dead?"

"It was a distinct possibility."

"But you weren't sure."

"No, I wasn't, and neither was Charles."

"Wouldn't it have been a good idea to leave the handbag with her, so she could be identified at the hospital, if for no other reason?"

He hung his head and shook it slowly. "These are completely appropriate thoughts, Ms. Daniels, but I do not recall having any of them at the time. I'd never been involved in anything remotely like this. I was in a state of shock—I didn't know what to do."

"Other than follow Charles Speakes's orders."

He didn't reply.

"Did Charles make any effort to confront the young woman who attacked Betty?"

"As I said, he was out of sight, observing—he didn't want to be seen. And she didn't waste any time after knocking the waitress down. She just took off running."

"And Charles never checked to see if Betty was dead or alive? Seems to me he'd want to know, given the likely criminal charges if she survived."

"It was like a nightmare. He probably didn't know what he was doing."

"But you've said that Charles *always* knew what to do." I tried to sound confused not confrontational.

"Charles was a good man, not a perfect one."

"If he'd helped her as any good man would, she would have owed him—it might have given him some leverage with her. Didn't that occur to him?"

"I don't know. I wasn't inside Charles's head, and I never dreamt how it would all end." Wisk looked to me and then to Andy but found no sympathy, just unforgiving stares. "It's been fifty years, Ms. Daniels, and I'm still haunted by that night. I wish to God I'd done more than simply follow orders."

"Do you think Charles Speakes's failure to help Betty Boyle was the root of his depression?" After all, the man was dead within six months of the incident.

"I can only tell you that it has been the root of mine."

Chapter 30

Andy and I had only the ride back to the Artistical to discuss Anton Wisk's story. Andy was due back in his dungeon.

I felt certain Wisk was not telling the whole truth.

"I agree," Andy said "On the other hand, I'm inclined to buy his story about the girl in the red, white, and blue dress. Well, maybe not all the details."

"Myra Morris mentioned a red, white, and blue dress she was wearing during the convention."

He stopped at a red light and turned to face me. "I imagine quite a few women were wrapped in the flag that week."

"But Myra had motive."

He didn't argue, but he did make me promise I wouldn't visit Myra again. "Let's talk things over before we take any action."

I nodded.

"Seriously, Meg—I'm begging you. If you feel the need to act, call me. No one else. I think you're onto something. I'm just not sure what it is."

The light changed and he turned his attention back to the traffic on Atlantic Avenue.

Back at the hotel, Andy returned to work and I spent the afternoon transcribing my notes, trying to prove or disprove various hypotheses and listening to Betty Boyle's collection of 45s. When an up-tempo song came on I didn't exactly leap to my feet, but I did get up to pursue my *Flashdance* exercise program on three separate occasions. It seemed like a good idea considering the amount of salt water taffy I'd been consuming.

At 7 PM, I carried my papers to the beach where Andy and I reviewed them. Well, I reviewed them. Andy lay on his back with his eyes closed and listened to me go over them. By the time dusk fell we still hadn't decided on our next step. We continued to speculate over our room service dinner until Andy fell asleep before dessert. I went into the bathroom, managed ten seconds of *Flashdance*, then followed his lead.

I didn't want Myra to be the killer, but as I drifted off to sleep that night "she did it" was my last thought.

The clock said 3 AM when I sat bolt upright. I slipped off the bed, felt my way across the room to the file on the table, and carried it to the bathroom. I closed the door before hitting the light. I lowered the lid on the toilet seat, sat down, and waited for my eyes to adjust to the light. As soon as I could focus I dug through the file looking for the program from the convention.

I heard a knock. "Will you be long?"

I opened the door to find Andy leaning across the doorjamb. He raised an arm to shield his eyes from the glare.

"I didn't mean to wake you."

"You didn't. My last beer did." He dropped his arm and spotted the papers on the floor. "What are you doing?"

"I may have found the smoking gun. Myra Morris told me that Betty saw Bobby Kennedy speak. That would have been on the closing night—the same night Betty disappeared. Myra saw Betty the night she disappeared. She must have."

"Myra was specific about the night?"

"She was specific about Bobby Kennedy. She said his speech had inspired Betty." I handed him a printout of a newspaper story from 1964.

"This article describes the ovation he received when he introduced a movie about his brother. On the last night."

"Did Bobby Kennedy speak any other time?" Andy asked.

"Not that I can find."

"I came in here for a reason," he reminded me. "Give me a minute."

I gathered my stuff and moved to the bed. I had all the lights on when Andy emerged from the bathroom, talking. "Fifty years is a long time. The memory can play tricks. Myra's reminiscences might be off." He shrugged. "But it's worth following up. I assume you plan to confront her."

"First I'll try to cajole her into telling the truth."

"Neither approach will get a good reaction at three in the morning. I guess I'll have to drive you over in the morning," he said climbing back into bed, "just in case Myra *is* a killer."

The comment stopped me in my tracks. "That's so hard to believe."

"But you do believe it."

"I do, Andy. I do."

His response was a snore.

At 8 AM, Andy dropped me about a block from the Morris house. He agreed to wait in the car but only after giving me explicit directions. "Keep your phone in your hand, with your finger on the button. If you need help, push it and say 'call Andy.' For example, *If you don't put down that knife, I will—*" he raised his voice, "*call Andy.*" He checked the signal on my phone. "It should connect."

"Got it, but I'm not afraid." That was true, although I swore I heard my heart pounding as I approached Myra Morris's front door.

"Meg?" Myra seemed surprised but not particularly happy to see me. If I were she, I wouldn't have been happy either. Even I understood that I was making a pest of myself. "Has something happened to Buddy?"

"No. I mean he is still struggling, but there is no change in his condition. I take it you have not been to see him?"

"I couldn't."

Given what I'd recently concluded, I understood what her comment meant.

"You could have called." Her tone indicated a suggestion not a reprimand.

"I had to be in Brigantine."

I stopped there. The shorter the lie the better. If the situation had been reversed, I would have written my visitor off as some sort of lonely misfit or worse and, rather than offering an invitation, would have requested a restraining order. Luckily, Myra didn't share my temperament. "Well, don't stand out there in the heat. Come in."

If the early morning heat outside was hard to take, the cold air inside was worse. Weren't people supposed to grow sensitive to cold as they aged? Apparently not in Myra's case, because her AC was going full blast. I forced myself to focus on the task at hand, not the temperature.

Myra waved me into the same chair as on my previous visits. I waited until she had settled in the wing chair before beginning.

"Buddy doesn't know, does he?"

"About the baby? No, I told you. He doesn't know."

"Not that you had his baby—that you saw Betty the night she disappeared. That you had an altercation with her."

She stared at me for a moment and made no attempt to deny it, either with her face or her words. "No one knew, or so I thought."

I expected her to ask how I found out, but she didn't. She merely shook her head. "I was such a fool." She started to talk with an urgency that suggested she, like Martha Speakes, had been waiting a half century for someone to ask. "Thursday night, I went back to that damn convention. I still thought I could meet someone respectable and find a meaningful relationship. To me, 'meaningful' meant a meal ticket. Hah! All I managed was to hook up with a drunken conventioneer from some state where it is apparently permissible to stick a hand down a lady's dress before being formally introduced. For the third night in a row, I left pretty disillusioned. That was when I ran into Betty."

* * *

Myra was on the verge of tears as she came out of the hotel onto the Boardwalk. The wooden walkway was crowded with happy people trying to get a look at the parade celebrating LBJ's birthday. She didn't want to be around happy people. As she fought her way to a down ramp and headed to Pacific Avenue, she could still feel the man's touch on her breast. The pig had pinched her nipple. She'd cried out in pain, but he only laughed when she slapped his hand away. "Don't be a prude." He mocked her. A prude. She was no prude, but she did deserve respect. She'd heard his laughter as she fled from the room.

Now, as she made her way down Pacific Avenue, she couldn't ignore the cheers of the crowd as fireworks celebrating the president's birthday lit the night sky. Hardly anyone was on Pacific Avenue, and the few who were paid no attention to her. They were focused on the show above them.

When Myra crossed the street, she couldn't believe her eyes. Down the block, a long black limo was idling. The kind of car she'd always wanted to travel in but doubted she ever would. And in the light of the street lamp, she saw Betty Boyle climbing out of the back seat. A man popped his head out of the back seat and called out to Betty—Ward Braddock! Myra felt her anger flare.

What was it with Betty? How did she manage to get everything Myra wanted? Buddy. Buddy's baby. Now, the attention of a man like Ward Braddock? Betty throws a damn drink in a senator's face, and he ends up going for her.

Myra couldn't understand what a man like Braddock would see in a girl like Betty, but then she couldn't see what a man like Buddy would see in Betty. She'd dismissed Betty as a naïve goody-two-shoes—apparently she'd underestimated her former roommate's sex appeal.

Myra realized she had only herself to blame for her situation. She'd never told Betty what happened with Buddy. After all, she'd only gone out with him a couple of times. Betty didn't even know she'd slept with him, let alone that she was carrying his child. Hell, Myra hadn't even known she was pregnant when Buddy dumped her.

So now Betty not only had Buddy and his baby, she had the big-shot Ward Braddock fawning over her. Myra didn't know why. Betty's hair and uniform were disheveled. She appeared drunk. Her back heaved like she was gasping for breath as she staggered to a bench. She dropped onto the seat, slumped forward, and buried her face in her hands. She seemed to need help but Myra wasn't about to jump in and offer it. Let her high-fallutin' friend sober her up and get her home.

But Braddock wasn't going to come through for her either. A young man in a seersucker suit got out of the limo and slammed his hand on the roof. The car sped down Pacific Avenue with Braddock inside. Myra thought the man might help Betty but when he took a step toward her, she lurched into the alley. The man didn't follow. He glanced Myra's way and then crossed the street and disappeared from sight.

Myra kept her eyes down as she approached the alley. Whatever trouble Betty had gotten herself into, she was going to have to get herself out of. Then Myra heard a loud crash. Peering into the dimly lit alley, she saw Betty on her hands and knees beside an overturned trash can. Damn Betty. She never could hold her liquor and now here she was in a pile of garbage, too drunk to get up.

"Are you okay?" Myra sounded more polite than solicitous, but not at all angry. She took satisfaction in the knowledge that she was doing the right thing.

"I'm fine." Betty stared at Convention Hall across the street. "I snuck out of work tonight to go over there and hear Bobby Kennedy. He made me believe that people can do good, that anyone can make a difference in the world. I want to make a difference."

"Sneaking out of your job and getting fired will make a difference all right. Come on, Betty. Get up." Myra extended a hand. "You're drunk."

Betty ignored her offer of help and climbed to her feet. "What do you think, Myra?" Betty moved closer. "Do you think that I'm some party girl like you who wastes her time and her money out drinking? Well, I'm not. I have a husband and a baby to get home to. I'm nothing like you."

Myra felt her fury rising. She pictured Betty going home to a man who might have been her husband, to their baby, after fighting off the attentions of a man of wealth and influence. "Go home then, Betty! Go home to your perfect little family!" She pushed Betty away from her. She was still shouting as Betty staggered backward. But she heard it. Even over her screaming, she heard the sound of Betty's head hitting the base of the brick wall when she fell.

* * *

"I will never forget that sound. When I knelt down beside her, her eyes were closed and she wasn't moving. She was making a strange puffing noise so I knew she was alive. I whispered I was going to get help but I never did. It was an accident, but I was so afraid. I just ran. I was a dumb kid. A dumb, terrified kid. I don't even know how I got home. But I did. I ran straight home and up to my room. Not that I could sleep. I sat up all night. The next morning, I walked by the spot where I'd last seen her, but she wasn't there. I stopped by her house but she wasn't there either."

Myra paused to light a cigarette. I thought today might be more than a three-cigarette day.

"I assumed someone had taken her to the hospital. Other people used that alley, too. Employees leaving the restaurant. People going home. There were houses at the back of the alley. There were thousands of people at that parade. I thought *someone* must have helped her.

"I only found out she was missing when the story came out in the newspaper. Eventually, the police came to see me. I told them I saw her Tuesday night. I never mentioned Thursday, the night she fell."

I didn't comment on her word selection. *Fell.* I guess technically she'd chosen the correct verb. Technically.

"As time passed and there was no sign of her, I wanted to think she'd developed amnesia or something. But in my heart, I felt some crazy person had found her and taken her away, maybe killed her. Nothing I could have confessed would have made any difference. Betty was gone. I didn't do that. She was alive when I left her." Her voice trailed off. "She was alive."

Alive, unconscious, and vulnerable. "And you never told the police about the Braddock limo?"

"How could I if I was never there? I kept an eye on the news, and Braddock never came forward."

"Do you think he abducted her?"

"I couldn't say, though his car didn't stick around after she got out of it." She shrugged. "What would it matter if Braddock did take Betty? Would the cops ever find out? Would they ever care? Those people were rich and powe-ful. Betty wasn't."

I knew it wasn't my job to judge Myra, but I did. What could possibly justify leaving any person, friend or not, seriously injured on a sidewalk at night in a pile of trash? No level of fear could excuse it in my mind. It occurred to me that since Betty had never been seen again, there might be a case for bringing murder charges against Myra. I didn't mention that.

"I've taken too much of your time, Myra. Thank you for sharing your story with me."

If she wondered what I was going to do with the information, she didn't ask. I hurried across the entrance hall but stopped at the door with one more question.

"I almost forgot to ask—did you happen to notice Betty's handbag?"

"Her handbag?"

"When you saw her, did she have her handbag with her?"

"I never even thought about it," she shrugged.

Chapter 31

"I haven't gotten any closer to solving this case." I sounded dejected as I finished recounting Myra Morris's story to Andy.

"Not true." He gave me a reassuring hug. "You basically got the woman to admit she assaulted and incapacitated Betty Boyle."

"There's no evidence to convict her of any crime."

"No, but if you believe her story you should let the police know about it." He leaned back on the large towel we'd spread on the beach at Brigantine. The sun shone through a filter of haze, and the heat was rising to what promised to become an oppressive level. Even the ocean appeared lethargic, sending waves to the shore at a leisurely pace. A flow of heavy humidity, not to be confused with a breeze, rolled across the beach. It was not yet 11 AM. I hoped to decide on a course of action and be in an air-conditioned room by noon.

"Why would she tell me all that?"

He stared at me over the top of his sunglasses. "You asked, she answered—telling you exactly what you wanted to know. And you're disappointed?"

"But why would she confess to me now, after all this time?"

"That's the point. She's been sitting on this for fifty years. Remember what Speakes's widow told you: *No one ever asked before.* You're not a cop. You've spent so much time in her living room, she probably mistakes you for a friend. And, clearly, she does not believe she can be charged in Betty's death."

I shook my head as if the action would make the pieces fall into place. "I've got a lot to think about."

"I'm here to help." Yes, Andy might have been happy to help, but he appeared thrilled to find an excuse to take the morning off. "Let's put the legal considerations aside and focus on what happened to Betty."

"We don't know if Myra actually killed Betty. However," I paused and pictured the night of August 27, 1964, "Myra is about five-foot-one, and even taking age-related shrinkage into consideration, she wasn't much bigger back then. So it's unlikely she could have disposed of the body by herself."

"One of your original reasons for ruling her out," he reminded me. "You said she would have needed an accomplice."

"Who would help her? The one consistent theme in her convention stories is how she failed to find companionship there. She always ended up alone."

"Did she have family in town?" he asked.

"No idea."

Andy threw out another option. "She could have gotten a passerby to help her."

"Why would a complete stranger become her partner in a capital crime? She didn't have any money."

"If we accept that she didn't move Betty, do you believe her story that Betty was alive when she left her?"

"I guess I do, though it's hard to believe some pervert got so lucky as to happen upon a defenseless woman lying in the alley in the few minutes before a decent person came by, especially with the restaurant closing up for the night. How could her coworkers have left without tripping over her?"

"Good question. Besides the late Lucy Abbott, have any of them turned up?"

"The owners and the chef are with the detectives who investigated the case—in heaven, presumably. And there's no trace of Wanda Costello, the other waitress Marco told me about."

"Well, I guess it's *possible* Betty could have been abducted by a stranger." Andy did not sound convinced. "But what a lucky break for Ward Braddock."

I thought about Andy's proposition. "Too much of a lucky break, don't you think? A woman with the power to destroy the senator's high flying political career exits his limo and is almost immediately rendered unconscious by an emotional former friend before being kidnapped by a passing pervert?"

"If we look at it from Betty's point of view, no one's luck is that bad. And if we look at it from Braddock's point of view—"

We finished the thought together. "No one's luck is that good."

Chapter 32

Andy was parked in the rental car, while I sat across from Anton Wisk in his office, my phone cradled in my hand. He did not look surprised to see me. "I knew you'd be back. Come in."

Wisk pointed to a chair in front of his desk and closed the door behind me. His shoulders were slumped, and he dragged his feet across the beaten floor as he shuffled back to his desk. When he sank into his chair, he looked old and bent, a ghost of the smiling man in the newspaper clippings that covered the wall behind him. Taking a closer look, I noticed there wasn't a single photo of Ward Braddock among them.

"I realize you are suspicious of me, Ms. Daniels, but I did not kill that young woman. And neither did Ward Braddock."

"But … ?"

He stared at me as if not comprehending.

"But there is more," I prompted.

Wisk slid even lower in his chair—so far down that I thought his chin would hit his desk. "This all happened so long ago. I thought it was over."

"But it isn't, and it isn't going away." I gripped my phone tightly in case Wisk tried to make *me* go away, permanently. "I know there is more to this story." I didn't have a clear idea of what Wisk knew, but I was certain there was something and I hoped my steady gaze told him that. Or would if he could bring himself to make eye contact.

"You're right, there is," he sighed. "I didn't tell you everything that happened after I went back to drop off the purse, when I picked up Charles."

Raising an eyebrow, I said, "Go on."

* * *

As Anton drove the limo down Pacific Avenue, he saw an arm wave from the alley. The arm was sheathed in seersucker just as Charles's had been. Anton stopped at the curb and spotted Charles—romancing a young woman. At least that is what the scene looked like, at first. Then, he realized that was what Charles wanted the scene to look like. The truth was very different.

Charles waved him out of the car, and Anton obeyed. When he got close, he realized it was the waitress from earlier and her hair was covered in a dark gooey substance. Blood. He took a step closer.

"I have no idea what you're doing back here, Anton, but I have never been more happy to see you."

Anton didn't know what to say. He said nothing.

Charles put his handkerchief over the young woman's head so it resembled one of those triangles the girls wore as head scarves. A spreading pool of liquid turned the cloth dark.

"She's drunk. Help me get her to the car."

"But, Charles, she's bleed—"

"She's *drunk*, Anton," Charles cut him off. "Check the street. We have to get her into the car."

Anton peeked around the corner of the building. He jerked his head back. "There's a couple leaving the restaurant."

"Are they coming this way? Take another look."

Anton did as he was told. That was what made him a good employee. He always did as he was told. He took one step forward onto the sidewalk and affected a casual stance. The couple strolled away in the opposite direction. He signaled Charles. "All clear," he whispered in a voice that brought back memories of childhood war games. His conscience reminded him that this was no game.

After helping Charles load the unconscious waitress into the back of the limo, Anton jumped into the driver's seat. He drove to the boat as quickly as he could without attracting the attention of the few police not involved in the activities up on the Boardwalk. Pulling up to the dock, he heard no sounds coming from the passenger compartment. He circled the front of the car and opened the back door. Charles cradled the waitress's head in his lap.

"I need help getting her out of here, Anton. I don't want to get any blood on the seat, so be careful."

"She's out cold. What happened to her?"

"She hit her head," Charles said impatiently. "She's out, but she's breathing. She'll be fine."

"Charles, what are you going to do? What if she goes to the cops?"

He'd never forget the look in Charles's eyes at that moment. There was no fear. There was no sadness. There was only determination. "She's not going to talk to the police or anyone else about tonight. I'll make sure of it. Now help me get her on board. Then we'll come back for Ward."

With all the activity at Convention Hall, there were relatively few people hanging around the marina. Those who'd remained on their vessels were too busy partying to pay any attention to two guys bringing a drunken female onto their boat.

They deposited the waitress on a bench on the aft deck. Charles instructed Anton to throw a blanket over her on the off chance that a boat passed. And if another boater dropped by? Charles would take control of the situation. Charles could do that. Take control. Always. Anton was afraid the waitress would wake up and flee, but Charles did not appear worried. At least about the girl. He was worried about Ward.

"Keep an eye on things," he told Anton as he disappeared into the forward cabin.

Anton stood on the dock so he could keep an eye on "things" he identified as Ward, the car, and the waitress—in that order. When Charles reappeared a few minutes later, Anton saw he'd traded his blood-stained suit for slacks and a polo shirt.

"Tomorrow, I'll need you to get me a new suit. Tonight, we need to get the boss on board."

Inside the limo, loud, rhythmic snoring confirmed that Ward remained in a deep, alcohol-induced sleep. Once Charles and Anton had draped his arms around their shoulders, however, he managed to keep his weight on his feet. There was no sign of anyone who might note his drunken condition as they half-dragged, half-walked him onto the boat. Sometimes Anton thought Ward Braddock was charmed. More likely, Charles Speakes was his lucky charm; the senator's good fortune came from having Charles around to protect him.

They dropped their boss, semi-conscious and mumbling incoherently, into the most comfortable seat in the cabin.

"Wipe down the limo the best you can, but don't make a show of it. We can worry about cleaning it thoroughly in the morning." Charles spoke as if he were instructing Anton to finish drafting a press release for the next day.

Anton left Ward in Charles's care and went to take care of the car. He did what he could in the car's dim lighting and spread a beach towel across the back seat, just in case anyone happened to get a close look before he could finish up.

Back on the boat, he found Charles keeping watch over Ward. He didn't know if the woman had stirred or not. The blanket was still covering her. Ward on the other hand was stirring. When he opened his eyes and tried to get up, Charles persuaded him not only to have another drink but to down it. Another followed, and Anton wondered what the hell Charles was doing.

By the third drink, even Ward was asking what they were doing sitting on the boat in the dark, knocking back his best scotch. Charles explained that they were going to take a little cruise and sleep out at sea. Ward said that sounded nice, then got a head start on the sleep portion of the outing.

Charles told Anton to start the engines and prepare to cast off. Anton didn't question him—he really didn't want to know why they were taking the boat out so late, or where they were headed. He didn't want to admit it, but he was afraid to ask. As he completed the preparations Charles joined him on the bridge.

"I'll take the wheel. You watch Ward."

"What about the girl?" Anton wanted to know.

"The girl doesn't need watching."

Anton tried not to think about what that statement meant. He went below and watched Ward as he slept. Part of the politician's success was based on the unavoidable fact that he was a handsome man; at thirty-three, he still had his youthful good looks but had begun to acquire a physical maturity that encouraged voters to trust him. Despite his boss's attractiveness, Anton found watching Ward Braddock drool while mumbling obscenities an ugly job. And a long one.

The boat traveled far out to sea. So far that Anton wondered if they'd have enough gas to make it back. Technically it wasn't his problem to worry about, but Charles had taught him that, to be successful, he had to keep his eye on every aspect of Braddock's life. He considered going above deck to ask Charles about the fuel, but decided to let it go and follow his orders to stay with Ward. Charles was Mr. Efficiency, after all—he wouldn't have made this trip without sufficient fuel on board.

Ward slept through the night with Anton watching over him.

When they got back into their slip just after dawn, Anton climbed the ladder and found Charles standing alone on the deck.

"Where's the girl?"

Charles looked at him with dead eyes. "What girl?"

* * *

"Charles never brought the waitress up again, at least in my presence, except one time. A story about her showed up in the *Atlantic City Press.*" Wisk shook his head as if amazed by the behavior of a total stranger, his younger self. "I had been keeping an eye on the news, but we didn't even know her name. It was almost a week before her picture finally showed up in the *Press*, in an article describing her as a missing person. We were sick over it."

"Did *we* include Ward?"

"Ward slept through the entire trip. He never even knew the girl was on board. When the cops came to the office, he wanted to cover up that he had seen her, that he had ... raped her in the back of the limo. He didn't know the whole story, and Charles said it was best left that way."

I waited silently for Wisk to continue. My gamble paid off.

"I tried to kid myself, but eventually the truth about what happened that night started to really eat at me. I didn't kill the girl, but I did nothing to prevent it, either. Not that I could have known what Charles would do after he loaded her into the limo—I don't think *he* even knew. I don't know what he would have done if I hadn't brought the car back. When I asked him, he said he never had to figure it out."

Another prolonged silence. I didn't say a word.

"I knew that girl needed help, and I didn't offer any. It took me awhile to admit my guilt, even to myself." His eyes met mine. "I hope you won't condemn Charles."

Didn't he worry that I might condemn him as well? Apparently not.

"His job was all about protecting Ward, and I think he was on auto-pilot that night. He was just trying to control the situation by taking the girl to the boat—there was nothing sinister about it. Later, when the reality of what had happened sunk in, I could see he was distraught. But he couldn't undo it."

"Do you think it's the reason he took his own life?"

"I only knew Charles from our professional activities. There may have been other things bothering him about which I had no knowledge. I do believe he was a decent person who made a huge mistake. That sort of thing can be tough for an honorable man to live with."

"Betty Boyle."

"What?" he said, confusion on his face.

"The woman, the waitress, she had a name, a husband, parents, and a son who had to grow up without a mother. I think if you're going to talk about her, you should know." I stood and turned my back on him. "I can see myself out."

Chapter 33

By the time I finished telling him Anton Wisk's story, Andy had driven us back to the hotel. He took the down elevator to his office and I took the up elevator to our room. We'd agreed that I would close my investigation with a memo presenting both the hard information we'd gathered, and our most likely theories as to what had happened to Betty Boyle.

Andy had suggested the document be worded in such a way as to provide me with a measure of legal protection, "Just in case."

"Just in case of what?" I'd asked.

"You never know." Not much of an answer but it seemed like advice worth following.

In the late afternoon, Andy sent me a text.

Meet in room @ 7.

Romance, at last! I thought, before it hit me that I wasn't really in the mood. Then it hit me that he wasn't either. His next message was *Anxious to read report.*

He arrived around 6:45. I kept one eye on the news while he read my memo. He shrugged. He shook his head. He threw his hands out. I guess he ran out of gestures to indicate futility, because he resorted to verbalizing his frustration.

"No one comes out looking good in this report, do they? Yet, it doesn't seem that anyone can be held accountable for what happened to Betty." The sadness in his eyes matched his sentiments. "Braddock is guilty of a lot of things, but Betty's death isn't one of them. Lucy Abbott, the only person who could link Betty to Braddock and Speakes, is dead. Speakes, the only witness to Myra's scuffle with Betty, is dead. Even if we could prove Myra assaulted Betty, even if she confessed to it in court, there's no proof the assault resulted in Betty's death."

I let out a long sigh. "Wisk's story is based on what Charles Speakes told him, if it's even true."

"Hearsay," he acknowledged. "And we only know about Betty's alleged rape by Braddock from something Speakes *might* have told Wisk. We have no living witnesses and no forensic evidence. All we have is hearsay."

I nodded my agreement. "We don't know if Speakes killed a living person or disposed of a dead body."

"If, in fact, he threw anything at all into the ocean, because we only have Wisk's word for it which is—"

Together we said, "Hearsay."

"I don't know exactly what all these parties are guilty of," he said angrily, "but I know they are *not* innocent." He walked to the window and stared at the action on the Boardwalk below.

I felt more sad than angry. "Betty walked into a nest of vipers. Cowards and criminals." I considered Lucy Abbott and Anton Wisk part of the first group. Myra Morris, Ward Braddock, and Charles Speakes fell into the latter. "All of them got to live, except Charles Speakes, who chose not to. Betty wasn't given a choice."

"Maybe they've at least suffered for it." Andy sounded hopeful.

"Wisk isn't exactly living a life of luxury," I offered.

"He loves playing the martyr." Andy was not impressed. "He changed his life, launched his do-gooder establishment, and convinced himself he's a humanitarian while sweeping a murder under the rug."

I pointed to the TV. "Look, Andy—it's candidate Braddock, promising to do what's right for the community. Just like his father."

Andy glanced over his shoulder, responded with an indefinable noise, and, again, appeared to get lost in the panorama outside our window.

The next news story covered an event community members had put together at Absecon Hope to honor Lucy Abbott. The anchor described her as the woman who died from cyanide poisoning.

"Andy."

"Yeah?" He remained distracted.

"Andy, this is important. Lucy Abbott died from cyanide poisoning."

That got his attention. "Just like Charles Speakes," he said after a moment's pause.

"Think about it. In our little circle of personalities surrounding Ward Braddock, there have been *two* suicides by cyanide poisoning."

"Let's think it through," he said. "Why would Braddock kill Lucy Abbott now?"

"Maybe because he's kept the entire mess covered up all these years, and now that his son is making his move to reclaim the Braddock family entitlement, he can't afford a scandal."

"But why would there be a scandal *now*?" Andy countered. "He'd have to have a powerful motive for acting—it's so risky."

"He might not even recognize the risk. Ward Braddock is nothing if not arrogant; he still thinks he's above it all. Either that, or he had no choice. Someone could have forced his hand."

"I think we should have another talk with Anton Wisk," Andy said. "If someone pushed Braddock into taking action, he might know who that someone is."

Chapter 34

Absecon Hope's director lived over the store, so to speak, in an apartment that looked more institutional than the center below it. Andy and I climbed the steps to a small porch and knocked on the door. Anton Wisk didn't even ask whether a friend or foe had come to call. The door swung open, wide enough that an unfriendly visitor could have pushed his way past Wisk, who relied on his seventy-something frame to block the entrance. Or at least forty percent of it.

Looking past Wisk, I could see enough to realize that while he may not have gone to prison for his part in Betty Boyle's demise, he had sentenced himself to life in a place just as drab. Monks had more luxurious digs than this guy. Unlike my previous two visits, he made no effort to play the gracious host.

"I've already told you everything I know … things I've never spoken of before," he huffed. "Please, just leave me alone."

"This has nothing to do with Betty Boyle," I said.

"Then what?" His frustration rose to the surface.

Andy responded. "We were wondering if you've had any contact with Ward Braddock lately."

"Why?" Wisk asked, then looked up and down the street behind us.

It seemed clear to me that Andy's question had hit a nerve.

"You'd better come in," he said, stepping back to provide just enough room for Andy and me to slip into his living room. Looking back on it later, I realized we'd never seen his right hand. But once we were inside and had turned to face him, we did, and there was a gun in it. The weapon wasn't so much pointed at us as pointed away from him.

Andy stepped in front of me. "Anton, you can put the gun down. We are not a threat to you."

He was being truthful. We hadn't planned on telling Wisk's story to anyone other than Johnny and Buddy Boyle. Of course, we couldn't account for what *they* might do with the information.

Wisk appeared confused.

"Put down the gun," Andy said softly.

"Oh, this ..." Wisk waved the gun.

Andy ducked. Behind him I followed his lead and closed my eyes, waiting for the shot.

"I forgot ... I mean, when I saw you were at the door, I realized I didn't need a gun. I keep it for protection. I'll put it down." With that he tossed the weapon on a folding table. It skidded along the top until it hit a wall.

"Not loaded?" Andy asked.

"Not usually, but it is tonight. I guess I should be more careful."

I admired the casualness with which Andy strolled across the room, picked up the gun, and let the magazine drop into his hand. He smiled at our host. "Do you mind? Just while we're here?"

Wisk made a dismissive gesture. "No problem."

Andy laid the gun and ammunition side by side on the beat-up metal table.

"Why are you here?" Wisk asked. "Oh, that's right—about Ward Braddock."

He didn't offer us a chair, and I didn't request one. From the looks of the available seating options, I suspected standing might be more comfortable.

"I rarely see him," Wisk continued. "One of his charities provides funding for us, but all the financial arrangements are handled through the Braddock trust." He looked uncomfortable, and I knew he was lying about something. "Why do you ask?"

I looked to Andy. "We're wondering if the senator has spoken with you about the Boyle case recently."

"But you said this isn't *about* Betty Boyle."

"It isn't. It's about Braddock's interest in the case." Andy's presentation of what I considered a pretty illogical argument turned out to be surprisingly convincing. "We'd like to know if the topic has come up recently."

"I haven't seen or talked to Ward recently."

Recently was a well-chosen word on both sides, open to conflicting interpretations.

"Ward used to attend our major events, but he hasn't in quite some time."

"So all interaction with Braddock is through the trust?" Andy turned Wisk's earlier claim into a question. "And the process is completely routine? No special dealings with the board?"

Wisk did not make eye contact with either of us or answer right away. I thought he was biding his time, trying to figure out what we knew. He must have decided we knew more than we did, because when he finally spoke he offered much more than we had even suspected.

"When I heard his son Paulsen was running for governor, I did send a request to the trust. The lot next door is for sale, and we could use a new pool here—there are some issues with our existing facilities. So I asked the trust to consider endowing a pool for Absecon Hope."

He hadn't mentioned any problems when he took me on the tour, which had included both an indoor and outdoor pool. I made a mental note of it.

He continued. "Paulsen's candidacy suggested it might be the right moment to offer Ward another opportunity to help the community. I suggested calling it the Paulsen Braddock Pool."

I would have suggested calling it the Extortion Pool but withheld my thought.

"*Another* opportunity?" I probed, wondering if there was a more complex story surrounding Braddock's support of Absecon Hope waiting to be told. I didn't expect what came next.

"The first idea to ask him for support came to me while I was in the Peace Corps. I knew Ward would never expose me. If the truth about Betty Boyle came out—her rape or her death—the worst I could get was obstruction. I saw no way that an accessory after the fact charge would stick. But Ward had a lot to lose, and it wasn't just the incident with Mrs. Boyle that could hurt him. I had other information he would not want made public. If I wanted to, shall we say, encourage him to make a contribution, he could hardly refuse. So when I got back, I made a trip to his Trenton office, reminded him about the night Betty Boyle was in his limousine, and gave him the opportunity to enhance his image by providing the seed money for Absecon Hope."

"So he remembered the details of the rape, as drunk as you said he was?" I asked.

"I assume Charles filled in the blanks. Either way, he knew."

"But you never discussed it with him before that day?" Andy queried.

"No." Wisk was adamant.

My brain hurt as Andy assumed an authoritative air, recalling the PI he had been. "Mr. Wisk, can you tell us about any conversation between the senator and Charles Speakes about the events surrounding Betty Boyle's disappearance?"

"I was not present for any discussion the two might have had about Betty Boyle." Wisk sounded very much like a lawyer.

"When did you last see Speakes?" Andy's voice was firm.

Wisk seemed flustered. "Charles came to see me on January 20, 1965. I remember the date because it was Inauguration Day for LBJ. I was living in an apartment just north of Trenton—a little place over a garage. Not that much different from where I live now, but with better furniture."

Andy cleared his throat, and Wisk got to the point.

* * *

Anton wondered who the hell was knocking. It was after ten. He was still up, though. He'd been watching the inaugural festivities and thinking how lackluster they seemed in comparison to 1961. Poor LBJ, living in the shadow of a man whose greatness derived from youth, charisma, myth, and public obsession over what might have been. No way to win that competition.

When he pulled open the door, he was shocked to find Charles Speakes shivering on the tiny porch. "Charles, come in. Sit down. You look awful!"

"I *feel* awful."

Anton went to the bar he'd modeled on the one in Ward Braddock's office and poured three fingers of scotch into a crystal tumbler, just as Ward would have. He delivered the glass to his visitor, who leaned back in the center of the couch with his arms outstretched. His shirt was open, his tie was loose. He hadn't bothered with an overcoat—an affectation appropriated from JFK.

Charles sat up and took a long drink. "Anton, I'm going to the police about what happened that night."

Anton felt his stomach heave. His first thought was for himself. He'd only been following his bosses' orders—surely the police would understand that, wouldn't they?

"I don't think that's a good idea, Charles." Anton dragged a chair from his dining room table to set it in front of his boss. "No good can come of it. You can't change what happened."

Charles would not meet his gaze. He glanced around the room with frantic eye movements, but Anton knew he wasn't seeing its carefully selected and arranged contents.

"I went into politics for all the wrong reasons," Charles said at last. He bit his lip and shook his head. "Yes, I said all the right things, talked about the inspiration of the Kennedy inaugural, and lauded the importance of public service, but the truth is, I wanted to be a big shot. I wanted the kids I grew up with to talk about me. 'Did you hear about little Charlie Speakes? Do you know where he works?' I honestly thought I was going to the White House." He appeared disgusted thinking about it now.

As Anton listened, Charles gazed into his glass but didn't take another sip. "When I met Ward Braddock, my dreams began unfolding just as I'd envisioned. I liked where the man stood on the issues, but I also saw the true picture. I knew he wasn't a good man, but I told myself he was no worse than any other politician. Sure, he was prone to an occasional indiscretion, but what did those things matter so long as they could be kept private?" He put his glass down and got up to pace the room.

Anton didn't know what to say, but he had to say something. He'd been tormented since that night as well, but the past could not be altered. What good would be accomplished if Charles went to the police? None. He had to stop him. "Charles, please, think carefully about this."

"I've done nothing but think about it since the summer, Anton. I can't believe I did what I did, and I can't live this way any longer. I'm going to the police in the morning."

"You didn't kill her."

"She was breathing, Anton."

"But that girl you saw with her … she was to blame."

"I'd like to think so. I would." Charles knelt in front of Anton, planted a hand on each of his knees, and stared into the younger man's eyes. "But it really doesn't matter what happened before I took her out of that alley and to the boat. Do you understand? She might have lived."

Anton was relieved when Charles stood and resumed pacing. The guy was making him nervous. Maybe he was just drunk. Maybe he would feel differently in the morning.

"Charles, what happened was very unfortunate. Very upsetting. To me, also. We've never discussed it. Not really, and we should. Sleep here tonight—we'll talk about it after a good night's sleep."

He didn't think Charles had even heard him. He was gazing into space with an intensity in his eyes that made Anton wonder about his sanity.

"Today, Anton, I sat and watched the inauguration on television, and I realized that, until that night on the boat, I would have done anything to put Ward Braddock on that podium. I would have lied and covered up all his little indiscretions. Minor improprieties, that's what I told myself they were. Minor improprieties." He turned and stared into Anton's eyes. "He raped that girl, Anton. I saw him. Drunk or not, he raped her. He doesn't think people like her matter. No money. No status. Politics is supposed to be about the people, Anton—not the powerful, but the powerless. About people just like that girl."

Anton relaxed. This was drunk talk. Anton had had the same idealistic notions when JFK first inspired him to go into politics. Learning the truth was painful, but he didn't think Ward Braddock was much different from anyone else who craved that kind of power. Compromises had to be made, as he reminded himself every day.

"Look, Charles, sleep it off. You'll see things differently in the morning."

"Will I see Betty Boyle back with her family in the morning?" Now Charles was angry. "Will I, Anton? Will her baby have its mother back?"

"Charles, go to sleep. Please." Anton stood and put his hands on his boss's shoulders. "Please."

Charles twisted out of his grip, picked up his drink, and downed it. "It's over, Anton. It's all over. Silence is lying, no less than if we'd opened our mouths and lied. I can't keep silent any longer. I'm going to tell the truth. Let the voters decide what to do about Braddock." He turned to the door.

Anton made a move to block him. "Don't you think you owe Ward some notice?"

"I'm not worried about damage control. From now on, I only worry about the truth." He met Anton's gaze and held it. "And Anton, I want you to know. This has nothing to do with you. If you were suspicious, fine, but you knew nothing. That's the truth. You did not see a thing, and I'm prepared to swear to it."

That might fly as a legal defense, Anton thought, but what would the scandal mean to his career? Charles was making a mistake that would haunt both of them. "Charles, you will go to jail."

"You think I don't understand that? I do, and frankly that's where I belong."

Anton was surprised by the peaceful expression that settled across Charles's face.

"You know, Anton, I believe I can have a happy life in prison. Well, not happy, exactly, but fruitful, productive. I'm sure I could help people."

"Charles, you have a wife and a child. How can you do this to them?"

"You don't understand, do you? If I don't do the right thing, what kind of role model can I be for my son? How could I live with myself knowing I have all the things in life that I stole from that girl?"

"But she wasn't like you, Charles—she wasn't even in your league. You have an education, a career. You've made something of yourself. You can make a contribution. You are truly worth something."

"Oh, my God." Charles pounded his head with both hands. "Listen to yourself! Do you hear what you are saying?" He yanked open the door and charged down the stairs.

"Charles!" Anton called after the fleeing man. "You've got to let Ward know—you owe it to him!"

It wasn't Ward's career Anton was worried about, but his own. At this moment, more than ever before, he knew they were inextricably bound.

* * *

"I never saw Charles again. He didn't come to work. I didn't ask why, and, if Ward knew, he didn't say. I held my breath, but the police never even asked to question me—I assumed Charles had changed his mind about going to them. I thought maybe he'd decided to quit his job and go away for awhile, but a few days later his wife called the office with the news. She'd been away. His body had been in the house for several days."

"Do you know if he did what you asked, if he went to see Braddock?" I asked.

"I don't know, but if he had, Ward would have bought him off. The Braddocks have deep pockets. In fact, paying people off was one of my jobs. Arranging payments that couldn't be traced."

I offered my opinion. "In this case, it didn't sound like Charles could have been paid off."

"He had a wife and a child to support, and his wife didn't want him going to the police. Money might have made him come to his senses."

I didn't agree. I suspected Charles Speakes had experienced a moral awakening that could not be reversed. Unless of course the drink had done all the talking. "Are you sure he was drunk?"

"At the time I was, but … no, I am not."

Andy cut in. "Did it ever occur to you that Braddock may have assisted in his suicide?" His tone was devoid of judgment.

Wisk retrieved a packet of tissues from his pocket and meticulously removed one to dab his eyes. When he spoke again, however, it wasn't about Charles Speakes but about himself.

"Braddock may have already tried to kill me. I thought I was being paranoid until I heard about Lucy." He shook his head. "I thought I was doing a good thing for the center, but now I wonder if my request for a donation had resurrected an issue that should have been left to die.

"One night when I came home—not that long after I contacted the trust about the money—I got an open bottle of wine out of the fridge. I took a few sips but there was something off about it, so I poured it down the drain."

My first reaction was great, no proof.

"An hour later, I developed severe nausea and cramping. I made myself throw up. I felt afraid, and I swear, the first thing I thought of was Charles. The police report said he killed himself by drinking cyanide, but, God help me, I always questioned if he actually committed suicide. Then again, he may have believed his death was the best thing for his wife and family. *Maybe.*"

Wisk sat silently. I watched as the muscles around his mouth started to twitch. His entire face contorted. His first sob was a long, slow roar of pain. Tears flooded his face. He tried to speak through his sobs but couldn't form a word. He buried his face in his hands.

I stepped forward, sat on the hard folding chair next to his, and put an arm around his shoulder. He continued to sob. Finally, when he raised his head, he held it with one hand as if it would fall forward again if he released it.

"God forgive me. As soon as Charles left, I called Ward and told him Charles was going to the cops—and not just to report the rape, but to report her murder too. That was how Ward finally found out what had happened to Betty Boyle. And next thing I knew, Charles was dead."

Chapter 35

While Wisk sobbed, Andy and I stepped aside to confer.

"I'm beginning to understand why you thought my visit to Ward Braddock was not the best idea," I whispered. "Do you think he may come after Anton to stop him from talking? Do you think he went after Lucy Abbott to keep her quiet?"

"We can't be sure, but it might be better to err on the side of caution," Andy said.

He walked back to Wisk and put a hand on the weeping man's shoulder. "Anton, we want you to come with us, for your own safety."

"I don't need to leave. I have a gun."

"Which will be useful only if you see your attacker first. You're coming with us."

"I can't," Wisk protested.

"At least for one night. Anton, if someone is trying to kill you, they'll have no trouble finding you here. You shouldn't be alone."

Wisk brushed off Andy's concerns. "I can ask a couple of our volunteers to come over."

"And put them in jeopardy? No way." Andy stood firm. "Get whatever you need. You're moving. At least for tonight."

"You can't force me to go anywhere."

"No, I can't. Not legally. But I'm not going to let you remain a sitting duck, alone all night in this complex, until we sort all this out."

A sullen Wisk disappeared into the other room and returned with a small duffel bag. Before heading for the door, he picked up the gun and ammo off the table. "I'll keep this with me just in case."

Andy thought for a moment, then shrugged. I figured he'd deal with that issue after we got Wisk out of Absecon Hope.

On the ride back to the Boardwalk, Andy called the Artistical and was told there were no rooms available. "Not even the Presidential suite?" The answer: With 35,000 conventioneers in town, no, not even the Presidential suite. If Andy wanted to stash Anton Wisk close by, it would have to be in our room.

Once in the room, Andy immediately wrested the gun from Wisk. "I'm locking this in the hotel safe overnight—you can get it back in the morning." He added, "You can't expect us to share our room with a man packing a loaded weapon."

Wisk understood, or said he did. We left him there, working hard at sulking, with strict instructions to stay put. He was watching the Animal Channel when Andy and I went in search of a quiet spot in the Artistical. No luck with that, so we ended up in Andy's office.

I stood with my eyes closed in the cool, dark room and waited for Andy to hit the light switch. "This is wonderful," I exhaled.

"That's because your eyes are closed. What are you doing?"

"Enjoying the absolute silence. You could hear a pin drop in here. I love it."

"Meg, look around."

I opened my eyes. "This is horrible."

"You didn't believe me?"

"I thought you were exaggerating, but you may be the master of understatement. How far underground are we?"

"We could probably survive a nuclear blast if the casino was Ground Zero. That's why I keep these nutritious food supplies here." He opened a refrigerator meant for a dorm room and handed me a Coke and a pack of peanut butter crackers. He chose a beer and Cheez-Its. "I don't want to leave Wisk alone too long. He might bolt." Andy pulled up a screen on the computer at his desk. "This will alert us if he opens the door. If he does, he won't get far." He hit a few keys and turned to face me. "What's our next step? I don't want to share a room with Wisk for any longer than necessary."

I took the lead. "Wisk's suspicion that Braddock killed Charles Speakes and that he killed Lucy Abbott too seem plausible. It appears as if maybe he tried to poison Wisk also. I'm thinking that after I confronted him, Braddock concluded that either Wisk or Lucy had tipped me off. They both saw him with Betty the night she disappeared, and either could offer damaging testimony. He might have taken action to protect his son's gubernatorial run."

"Or because Paulsen's success is sure to invite scrutiny." Andy glanced at his computer screen. The door to our hotel room still remained closed.

"I bet it really hit home when he saw the primary results." I considered the mixed feelings Braddock must have had: exhilaration over his son's commanding lead, and paranoia that the press was sure to come digging as the race continued and even more if he won.

"So whether it was out of concern for his son or himself, Braddock did act," Andy offered. "It's time for Wisk to go to the police with his suspicions about Lucy's death."

I second-guessed myself. "There is one problem with our theory. Yes, Ward Braddock had a huge mess on his hands because of Betty's rape, and I can see him buying Wisk's and Lucy's silence. But he's a lawyer. He is well aware that statutes of limitation run out on most charges and that hearsay on the rape is not admissible. Yet he has continued to fund Absecon Hope all these years. And all this time, he has had no career to protect. People have forgotten about him. Until his son started his run for governor, a scandal would have been a blip on the radar. And even considering his son's race, would a fifty-year-old rape accusation against Braddock really matter? Would it really be worth killing someone over?"

Andy reminded me, "Betty did end up dead."

"But Braddock didn't kill her, if we can believe Wisk, and even if Wisk is lying, there's no evidence to convict Braddock. If the public accepts Wisk's story that Speakes is the killer, all Braddock has to do is play the recovered alcoholic card and express deep regret over the actions of his staff at the time."

"I see your point, but if not Braddock, then who is behind the poison plot?"

"Oh, it's Braddock, all right, but he must have a stronger motive than covering up a rape from fifty years ago. Maybe he's worried that the police will look into Betty's disappearance because any investigation would lead to Anton Wisk, and Wisk is the only person who can link Braddock to the murder of Charles Speakes."

Andy considered my theory. "It would be awfully hard to prove that fifty years later, but if it could be proved, the charge is murder—no statute of limitations. The stakes are high for Braddock."

"High enough that he'll do whatever it takes to keep the Betty Boyle case from being reopened."

"Meaning potential witnesses must be silenced." Andy nodded.

"Andy, Buddy told me Lucy visited him in 1968 the day Bobby Kennedy was shot. Lucy contacted Braddock too at some point, and there's a good chance she told him she had been to see Buddy. When I went to see him, he mentioned that he had been receiving deliveries of snacks and beverages from Absecon Hope. He drinks the Gatorade regularly." I looked deep into Andy's eyes. "And as we know, Absecon Hope is heavily funded by ..."

"Ward Braddock."

"It's too much of a coincidence, Andy, although Buddy started getting sick *before* I stirred things up with Braddock. He even mentioned that the charity must be psychic because they seemed to know he was sick before he did."

"So you think the Gatorade may be tainted?"

"If we believe Braddock poisoned Lucy Abbott and tried to kill Anton Wisk the same way, why not Buddy? It's a good chance Braddock knows that Lucy told Buddy what she saw all those years ago. I think it's worth looking into."

Andy turned to his computer and checked the Artistical's entertainment schedule. "Johnny's working for several more hours. I don't think we should wait to see Buddy. We'll just have to hope Wisk sticks around."

Chapter 36

Buddy Boyle leaned all his weight against his front door as he opened it. His expression said he wasn't happy to see anyone. Then, he spotted Andy and his eyes twinkled.

"Andy Beck! Johnny told me you were in town. I met your girl here. How are you?" Buddy let go of the doorknob to extend a hand to Andy. Andy caught the older man as he staggered toward him.

"Rough night," Buddy said as he used Andy's arm to steady himself. "Maybe you could help me back to the couch."

"What's the problem?" I asked as Andy lowered Buddy onto the seat.

"Dizziness, headache, nausea. When I felt sick like this the first time I had cancer, I thought the treatments were the problem, but I'm not getting any treatments this time. Maybe it was the cancer that caused these symptoms the last time too."

Andy's eyes met mine over the ailing man's head.

"Buddy, we're sorry to bother you when you don't feel well, but we wanted to ask you one question. We wondered ... do you think Lucy Abbott might have told Ward Braddock that you knew what she saw the night Betty disappeared?"

"Or maybe," Andy ventured, "you contacted Ward Braddock yourself?"

Buddy didn't answer. At least, he believed he didn't answer. His eyes, however, told the story. I'd never seen anyone, including a deer standing in the middle of a dark highway, look more like a deer caught in headlights.

Andy's voice was soft and comforting. "So, you did meet him at some point?"

Buddy sighed and nodded. "A long time ago."

"After Lucy came to see you?" Andy asked.

Buddy nodded. "As I told your girl here …"

"Meg," Andy reminded him.

"Yeah, Meg. I told Meg that I didn't go to the police after Lucy told me what she saw. Thing is, I was gonna handle everything myself. Betty'd been gone for four years before Lucy came to see me. Even after all that time, I wasn't going to approach the same cops that looked at me for the murder of my own wife and tell them I thought Ward Braddock had something to do with it. The Braddocks were powerful. No one in authority would take my word over theirs. In my heart, I knew Betty was gone. I just wanted to find out how. At least that's what I told myself." He paused, but only to take a deep breath that appeared to pain him. "I went to see Braddock the day after Lucy came to see me. To his office in Trenton."

* * *

Buddy had only seen offices like Braddock's in the movies. Paneled walls. Leather furniture. Fancy paintings. Looked authentic. Looked expensive. Braddock dressed to match his surroundings. His tie probably cost more than Buddy made in a week. His suit probably cost more than he made in a month.

Braddock didn't get up, didn't offer his hand. He kept his hands folded across his stomach and greeted Buddy from the seat behind his desk. That didn't feel right to Buddy, but what did he know? He didn't visit offices like this every day. Actually, he had never visited an office like this one. He had no idea how to behave, so he stood before the desk as he had before the principal's desk so many times, so many years before.

"Mr. Boyle, what can I do for you?" Braddock asked with a phony smile.

"You know why I'm here. I should have come years ago, but I just found out that you killed my Betty."

"I'm sorry, but I … I don't understand." Braddock's forced frown, shaking head, and contrived stammer didn't fool Buddy. Braddock knew exactly what Buddy was talking about.

"Someone saw you with my wife the night she disappeared. Pulling her into your limousine. I want to know what happened."

"Mr. Boyle, I must admit I'm confused." Braddock pretended to search his memory. When he pretended to recall that night, he pretended to be apologetic. "Of course. The woman the police asked about. Her name was Boyle. How thoughtless of me. Please sit down." He pointed to a chair but Buddy didn't move. Braddock continued. "Mr. Boyle, first let me assure you that I have no knowledge of what happened to your wife. The incident when I was so rude to her occurred several days before her disappearance."

Buddy clenched his fists. "You saw her again the night she went missing. I have an eyewitness."

Braddock remained unshaken. "Oh yes, well, as I recall, after my aides told me how badly I'd behaved while under the influence, I did go to your wife's place of employment to offer an apology."

"As I recall, you killed her." Buddy realized he had taken a step toward the politician.

"Ridiculous!" Braddock sputtered. "When your wife approached my car outside the restaurant, I invited her inside to hear my apology. She was not as receptive as I had hoped and I'm afraid I may have been a little forceful in my request, but I can assure you that when Mrs. Boyle left my car and stepped back onto Pacific Avenue, she was very much alive. She would not accept my apology, but at least I'd tried. I understand that I must appear selfish for not coming forward at the time, but I had no pertinent information to add to the investigation."

Buddy glared at the man and felt his fists clench even tighter. "I could kill you. I should kill you." He took another step forward.

Braddock did not appear threatened. "Mr. Boyle, please have a seat."

"I ain't taking anything from you, not even a seat." Buddy thought over what he said and corrected himself. "Only thing I will take is an explanation of what happened to my Betty."

"Mr. Boyle, I cannot give you that. I was not a witness to whatever happened to your wife."

Buddy couldn't believe his ears. Braddock had the nerve to sound annoyed with him.

"If you wish, I can provide a witness who can testify that I was not involved in your wife's death."

"I wouldn't believe any witness you could produce. How much would you pay him?"

"I assure you that there is only *one* person who can testify what I did that night. If I were paying witnesses, don't you think I would produce more than one? The man who was with me that night is a most reliable witness. He's just come back from the Peace Corps. He will be able to verify that your wife was very much alive the last time I saw her."

Buddy could not believe how calmly, how coolly Braddock spoke. Could he possibly be telling the truth? No, the guy was playing him. People like Braddock believed they could fool anyone, everyone.

"Mr. Boyle, knowing that I did see your wife that night, you are right to question me. I am not at all offended. In fact, I admire that you are still a devoted husband to her."

Buddy knew Braddock was trying to soften him up. Well, let him try.

"I've admitted to you that your wife would not accept my apology. If I were going to lie to you, I would tell you that she and I had a wonderful talk and that everything was fine between us the last time I saw her. I can't tell you that. It would be a lie. Mrs. Boyle was still angry when she got out of the limo. I think she despised me, and I guess I'd given her good reason to feel that way. I understand that now. On that night, I was still a single man. Today, I'm a married man expecting to become a father at any moment. Only now do I truly understand how objectionable my behavior was, even when I was attempting to apologize."

Buddy said nothing. He fought the creeping feeling that Braddock was telling the truth. He didn't want to believe him, couldn't let himself believe him.

"If you insist, we can go to the police and ask them to administer a polygraph test. I can assure you that I will pass with flying colors. I did not murder your wife. I did not witness the murder of your wife."

"I don't believe you."

"You don't want to believe me, Mr. Boyle. I understand that, but I can't lie and say I killed her just to make you feel better. What I can tell you is that she was on the curb just steps away from the restaurant where she worked, alive and well, the last time I saw her."

Unflappable. That was the word for it, Buddy thought. Braddock was unflappable … or he was innocent.

"When you've had time to think things over, you will realize that I bear no responsibility for your wife's fate, whatever that may be. On the other hand, you will also realize that the information you have about my behavior could be extremely damaging to me. It could easily be misconstrued. My opponents will seize upon any appearance of impropriety. I have ambitions, Mr. Boyle. They are no secret. The editorials are full of conjecture about my future. I don't think you would really want to interfere with such a bright future." Braddock smiled.

Buddy realized the message the expression conveyed was not a friendly one. He suddenly felt fear. What if Braddock *had* killed Betty? He was a powerful man. He could do the same to him.

"Perhaps we could reach some sort of agreement that might guarantee your silence."

"Money?" Did he really think money could replace Betty? Make up for the years Betty had lost? For what he'd lost? For the mother Johnny had lost? He spat at the man.

The spittle landed on a leather-bound volume on the big desk. As he plucked a monogrammed handkerchief from his pocket and carefully wiped his book clean, Braddock showed no emotion.

"I understand how that sounds, Mr. Boyle," he said evenly, "but please hear me out. I had nothing to do with Mrs. Boyle's death, assuming she has, in fact, passed. However, I behaved horribly toward her. As I said, she never did accept my apology. Not really. I feel I owe her something. I understand you have a son. I believe your wife would want you to do what is best for him."

"What would be best for my boy would be to have his mother back."

"Obviously that cannot happen. Even a man as powerful as I am cannot make that happen." Braddock sighed. "What do you do for a living, Mr. Boyle?"

"I tend bar at the Haddon Hall."

"A fine hotel, but is that what you plan to do for the rest of your working life? What kind of a life can bartending provide for your son?"

"I do okay. I make good tips." Buddy didn't feel the need to defend his work to this snob.

"I am sure you do, but it must have occurred to you that had you been in a better financial position, your wife would not have found herself in such a vulnerable position, working late, walking home alone."

Buddy never hated anyone more than he hated Braddock at that moment. Anyone other than himself, anyway. The way the man stared at him. It was like he could read his mind, see Buddy pacing the floor, blaming himself, wishing he had been more successful so that Betty could have been home with her baby, rather than walking home from the job she needed because he was a lousy provider.

"I am sure you look at your son and wonder how you are going to be able to do better by him, to keep him safe."

Buddy wanted a drink, needed a drink. He'd sobered up for this visit in order to be in top shape for his confrontation with the man he believed killed his Betty, but now he felt nothing but self-loathing. He knew who was responsible for Betty's death. He was. His inability to support his family had put her at that restaurant.

"I am a wealthy man, Mr. Boyle. I am always looking for investment opportunities. Is there something that you have always wanted to do? Something that might prove more lucrative than tending bar? Something that will help you provide your son, the son your wife loved so much, with a better life?"

* * *

Now I understood how a depressed single father with minimal business skills had turned his life around.

"You believed what he told you about Betty?" I asked. "That she was alive the last time he saw her?"

"I didn't know what to think. I hated him for how he treated her, but I couldn't be sure he was responsible for her disappearance." Wringing his hands gave the impression his doubt lingered. "And I worried, What if he *was* guilty? I couldn't prove it. He would go to the cops with his witness, and the cops would never touch him. I was sure of that. Why would he volunteer to take a lie detector test if he killed her? I bet the cops wouldn't even make him take it. They might even start looking at me again. I was scared, and not just of the cops."

He took a deep breath before continuing. "I saw it like this: I go to the cops because I believe Ward Braddock killed Betty. He convinces the cops he's innocent. But the story he wants to stay hidden is out. Even if it doesn't get out, I have tried to ruin the career of a very powerful man. Who's to say he won't retaliate? He could hurt Johnny." Buddy gazed into space and shook his head. "I was so confused."

He leaned his head back and closed his eyes. Andy and I waited for him to continue.

"I came to see that it suited my purposes to believe him. All night, I sat up drinking and thinking over what he'd said. He told me not to come to his office again, so the next night I met him at his summer house in Spring Lake—a nicer house than any regular house I'd ever been in. Giving me money wouldn't hurt him a bit, I figured, but it could help Johnny."

He paused again for several deep breaths then said, "I can explain things away by saying I was drunk when we did the deal. I was. But even after I sobered up, I didn't know what else I could do. Braddock made it possible for me to give Johnny things a bartender could never provide. He convinced me that Betty would want me to do what was best for the boy."

Buddy defended himself against unmade accusations.

"Betty was gone. She was never coming back. The son she loved more than anything on this earth was saddled with a depressed, alcoholic father. The cops would never have believed me about Braddock, even if I had proof, and I knew it.

"Braddock offered me a way out of the hole I dug for my family. I killed Betty by failing to provide. I wasn't going to ruin her son's life the same way."

I didn't agree but I hadn't walked in his shoes.

"Do you understand what I did for that boy? I gave him everything. I sent him to the best schools. Private prep school. The top-rated law school. It's not my fault that he ended up singing in bars. I did the right thing. I raised him well."

He was not trying to convince me. He was trying to convince himself. Still. Fifty years later.

Buddy paused as he fought through a coughing spell. "I realize some people see Johnny as a failure. Bad job. No family. That might be my fault. Not because I made him think the Rat Pack life was cool, although I did. Not because I thought he should find a girl that looked like Ava Gardner, although I did. My failure was that I never proved to him that his mother didn't leave him." His eyes misted over. "A boy relates to women based on his relationship with his mother, and I think Johnny says to himself, My mother did not love me enough to stay, so why would *any* woman love me enough to stay? You know what I mean?"

I knew.

Andy interrupted Buddy's analysis of Johnny's love life. "Buddy, Meg is worried that Braddock has a motive to hurt you because of what you know. From what you've told us tonight, I think she may be right. Now that his son is running for governor, he's eager to avoid any breath of scandal. So you need to tell us if you had any *recent* contact with Braddock."

Again, Buddy's eyes answered first. "I just didn't think it was fair that his son should be so happy and successful when my son had to grow up without a mother. I went to see him in early June after Paulsen won the primary, back to the same house in Spring Lake, the one I visited in 1968. I was angry. I told him I intended to go to his son and tell him everything—all about our *arrangement*." He put his head down and held it in both hands. "I know I shouldn't have threatened him and I know I took his money all those years ago, when deep in my heart I knew he killed my Betty. Anyway, he told me he would tell his son himself. I didn't know what to do. I left."

Andy's eyes met mine. I shook my head. I didn't think this was the moment to explain everything I had discovered. From a legal viewpoint, Ward Braddock had not murdered Betty Boyle. From a moral perspective, the view was not so clear.

Andy comforted Buddy. "You did the best you knew how. But listen, Buddy, right now we're going to take you to the emergency room," I told Buddy gently. "We'll tell Johnny where you are."

I searched the kitchen cabinets until I found a trash bag. I retrieved the bottle of Gatorade from the refrigerator and put it in the bag. Andy helped Buddy to his feet.

"Come on," I said. "Let's get you better and then we'll talk some more."

Chapter 37

Andy dropped me at the Artistical on the way to the hospital, with a promise he would call as soon as he had an update on Buddy.

"If you're right that Gatorade from the Absecon Center was being poisoned," Andy whispered as he glanced at Buddy sleeping in the back seat, "I'm beginning to think our roommate Mr. Wisk may not be the innocent potential victim we thought we were protecting. He very well may be doing Braddock's dirty work, although that wouldn't preclude Braddock's trying to get rid of him—he might eliminate him for just that reason." He fixed me with a serious look. "Don't say a word, Meg—no, don't even *think* a word about that possibility in Wisk's presence until we're sure what we're dealing with. You have a tendency to confront suspects and get yourself in a little trouble."

"One time, Andy. I did that *one* time. A long time ago. The other minor jams weren't my fault. In fact, if my boyfriend hadn't been a PI none of those incidents ever would have happened."

He continued to stare at me.

"Okay, okay. Maybe I went a little rogue. I just wanted to help."

Still he stared.

"Okay, I promise. No confrontation. My lips are sealed."

At the hotel bar, I found Johnny singing "In the Wee Small Hours of the Morning," his velvet tones worthy of Ol' Blue Eyes himself. When he finished, I applauded loudly, partially to make up for the indifference of the audience. His smile shone big and bright as he moved into "This Will Be the Start of Something Big"—his closer ever since he learned that the song was Frank's closer. Literally. It was the last song Sinatra ever performed before a live audience.

After his set, Johnny strode toward me with a Sinatra swagger. He leaned down to kiss me, but I spoke before his lips touched my cheek. "First of all, Buddy will be fine, Johnny."

"What happened?" I don't think he even realized he'd just taken a step toward the exit.

"Andy has taken him to the ER as a precaution." I explained that a question had arisen about the possible contamination of something he'd been drinking. For now, I could say no more.

"I'll get right over there." He smiled a bit uncertainly. "I guess the good news is he's finally getting some medical care."

Johnny disappeared into the casino, and I headed to Café Monet. I told myself that I was hungry because I'd missed dinner. Truth was I didn't want to be locked in a room with Anton Wisk. I placed a call to our room to see if he was still there. This time I lied not to myself, but to Wisk. "I'm picking up some take-out for myself. Would you like anything?"

"Where are you?" he asked.

"Café Monet. As you might imagine, they have a lot of French pastries, tarts, pies."

"Really anything is fine."

So, I asked for two Napoleons. One to go. "For a friend," I explained. The waitress didn't believe me. I could tell.

I lingered over my Napoleon for as long as I could. The sugar rush didn't make the prospect of sitting alone in a room with Wisk any more palatable. I thought I'd step out for a breath of air. Maybe many breaths. Wisk's Napoleon in one hand and phone in the other, I crossed the Boardwalk and stared across the dunes at the dark night sky to wait for Andy's call. I turned my back on the ocean, spread my arms down the rails, and watched happy vacationers enjoying the Boardwalk under the lights of the city. I felt relieved. I'd found out the truth for Johnny Boyle, I might have saved Buddy Boyle's life, and, if all my suspicions proved to be true, the authorities might even be able to prosecute Ward Braddock for the murder of Lucy Abbott and, maybe, somehow, Charles Speakes. I wasn't just feeling relieved. I was feeling cocky. I turned my face back into the breeze. And that was when I saw it, the first curvature of the moon coming over the horizon.

I walked down the walkway to the beach past the lively bar scene toward the water's edge where I dropped onto the sand. I was wishing Andy were sitting beside me to watch the moon climb into the sky when I sensed movement behind me. Hoping to see Andy, I started to turn when my head was yanked backward. A hand covered my mouth and a piece of cloth covered my nose. The smell was horrible, but I didn't have much time to recoil. The night sky faded to black.

Chapter 38

"How did you get me here?"

I didn't actually know where *here* was, but I was on a boat. More specifically, a very impressive cabin cruiser—large, classic, and beautifully maintained, with a galley that put the kitchen in my old New York apartment to shame. The caliber of the boat, however, was of less importance to me than my position within it. I was not only *inside* the cabin, I was secured to it, with my arms tied behind my back and bound to the cabin table. My fingers could trace nice, neat nautical knots. What they couldn't do was loosen them. I should have paid more attention when Andy tried to teach me about sailing.

"Sadly, Ms. Daniels, people underestimate the elderly, if they bother to think of them at all. I could have carried you off that beach all by myself that day you came to see me, but there might have been witnesses. Still, I could have done it. I carried you here from the car—although you might find a nasty lump on your shin tomorrow. Not that you'll be here tomorrow." Ward Braddock looked calm and controlled and—definitely—a little bit crazy.

I wasn't worrying about bruises or even my aching head; my concern was where I would be for the next day's sunset. I didn't ask. I had a pretty good idea that if Braddock had his way, I'd be with Luca Brasi, *sleeping with the fishes.* I didn't accept that. I didn't have a plan, but I had every confidence I would develop one. I worked at the knots but to no avail. Screaming was an option, but I suspected it would not be a productive one; since there was no gag, one was likely not necessary. Nevertheless, I screamed. At first rather weakly, but once I got the knack of it, I was screeching at the top of my lungs. Braddock didn't flinch. I continued to scream.

"You are welcome to make all the racket you wish, Ms. Daniels, but no one will hear you. Well, no one except me, and I am actually finding the noise quite annoying. So, unless you wish me to gag you, please desist." He glanced out the cabin window then turned back to face me. "One of the many things I like about being very, very rich is that you have friends who are obscenely wealthy, and they let you use the very isolated dock along their very isolated waterfront in front of their very isolated summer home that they can't even be bothered to visit."

Isolated? I searched my mind. I wasn't aware of any isolated estates at the Jersey Shore. Assuming we were still in New Jersey. How far from Atlantic City had Braddock taken me? Maybe he was lying about our location and we were not in an isolated spot. If he was lying, however, I'd be gagged. I abandoned screaming and switched to conversation.

"So, how *did* you get me off the beach?" I played for time. I needed to come up with a plan.

"I happened upon two young gentlemen—well, not exactly gentlemen—and asked them to help me get my drunken daughter to the car. They were reluctant to provide assistance at first, but I am exceedingly expert at playing the helpless old man." His eyes took on a fierceness that made me shiver. "Mark my words, I am *no* helpless old man." He paused, no doubt enjoying my fear. When I remained silent, his tone grew lighter. "I'll concede that my eyes are a bit weak in the dark, which is why we haven't left the dock yet. But at the first sign of morning light, we'll be off on our little cruise."

A cruise for which I assumed I held only a one-way ticket.

"You won't get away with killing me. There will be video showing you and two men taking me to the car." I could not get my thumb and my index finger together. Whatever his shortcomings, Braddock knew how to incapacitate a captive with a knot. I couldn't help thinking he'd done this before.

"Don't be ridiculous. Do you think I'm stupid enough to have accompanied them to the car?"

I'd been hoping.

"The video will show two strapping young men assisting you across the Boardwalk. No one will notice the bent-over senior citizen who just happens to be walking behind them. However, if the police identify them from the video, they will report that some feeble old man asked them to help get his drunken daughter to the car. I certainly do not fit the description of a feeble old man.

"You know, in a way you are lucky, Ms. Daniels ... you will never experience what it is like to be old, to be invisible, to be peripheral to a world you don't quite understand any more. Those two kids never saw me as an individual. They saw a generic old person. Do you know how I got them to move ahead of me?"

I looked away to express my disinterest, but once he got started he was not to be stopped.

"I simply talked. About my daughter, Bella. About how her mother and I were so disappointed in the way Bella turned out. About how Bella had tried to overcome her problem. With each new detail, they lengthened their lead. After all, no one under forty wants to listen to an old codger go on and on. I had already told them what car to look for and that it was unlocked."

"But they didn't bring me here, onto this boat."

"No, once you were safely in the car, I managed on my own."

"The surveillance cameras in Atlantic City will show us together at some point." I caught the tip of a rope between my index and middle finger. I yanked but it slipped from my grasp and the knot held.

"Some video may possibly show those two young men dumping you in the back seat of an old Toyota sedan. And that video might show some elderly man showing up at the car several minutes after your arrival, getting in, and driving away. And I know what you're thinking. The camera must have caught the car's license plate."

Actually, I was thinking how tough it had been being a PI's girlfriend, and how foolhardy I'd been to get involved in his cases.

Braddock continued. "It might have if somehow or other the plate hadn't gotten incredibly dirty. And the feeble old man on the video. Why, he certainly could not be mistaken for me."

When he got up, I understood why. Braddock moved with remarkable grace for a man his age. He reached for a brown bottle and a handkerchief sitting on the countertop.

Ah, he'd made a mistake, I thought. Surely the chemical would leave traces on his hands. Well, if anyone ever checked ...

I told myself to stop worrying about *evidence* of a crime—I had to *stop* the crime from happening. I wasn't going to thwart Braddock's efforts at that moment, however. No matter how hard I tried, I couldn't fight off the handkerchief pressed against my face. A spiral spun before my eyes for a very few moments and then darkness.

Chapter 39

When I came to, Braddock had moved me topside. This guy was phenomenally fit for his age. Still, I was pretty sure that if I ever got a shot at him while conscious and untied, I could take him. At this moment, however, even though I was conscious, I was still tied up. I was no longer secured to the boat, but why would I be? There was little danger I would attempt to disembark with no land in sight.

The sounds and smells wafting from the cabin suggested that Braddock was making breakfast. Never commit murder on an empty stomach, I always say. And I knew murder was his plan for the day. Despite traces of terror and depression, I felt a calm that I could neither understand nor condone. Sprawled on the bench along the stern, I had to admit that my options were limited. My emotions told me I would get myself out of this, somehow. My brain told me there was no way out. My emotions won. I would not give up. If I went down, and I meant that literally, I would go down fighting.

If I didn't make it, I knew Andy would find out what happened to me. I felt tears welling. He was devoted, but once I was gone, he would move on. He had to. If I loved him, I would want him to. I called my mind back from fantasies of Andy's new life. I had a long list of reasons to live. To spite Ward Braddock was currently Number One.

"Ah, I see you're awake." Braddock wore a wide smile along with Nantucket-red Bermuda shorts, a white golf shirt, and boat shoes that had seen some hard duty. "How nice that you can enjoy a truly gorgeous morning."

I didn't know where he was looking. Yes, the sky above us was blue, but I could see dark clouds in the west. "Can you tell me where we're going?" I asked with a calm demeanor that surprised me.

"We both know where we are going, Ms. Daniels. Why ruin such a lovely day by discussing such unpleasantness?" Even though he did not add *tsk-tsk*, I could hear the reprimand in his tone.

"You understand that if I disappear, you'll be the prime suspect. And there will be quite a list of charges. The rape of Betty Boyle. The murders of Charles Speakes and Lucy Abbott. The attempted murder of Anton Wisk and Buddy Boyle. As you well know, there's no statute of limitations on murder in New Jersey."

Braddock laughed at my claims. "You fail to take into account who I am, Ms. Daniels. Nobody in their right mind would risk coming after me without evidence piled upon evidence stacked upon evidence. Trust me, the State is not going to bring frivolous charges against the governor's father, and rest assured my son will be the next governor of New Jersey."

I took several deep breaths to suppress the hysteria that lurked right below the surface. I didn't have time to be terrified—I had to take control of my emotions. I had to win this one. By now, Andy knew I was missing and would suspect Braddock. Someone would check and discover that Braddock's boat was off its mooring, and Andy would assume I was on it. And in trouble. Wouldn't he?

"What a poor host I am. Let me offer you something to drink." Braddock poured orange juice from a plastic pitcher. The refreshing liquid taunted me through the clear cup. My head ached, my throat burned, and my lips were cracked and dry, but I couldn't give in. No way would I consume anything he offered, repeating what was no doubt Lucy Abbott's fatal mistake.

"It's not poison, Ms. Daniels. Think about it—why would I need to poison you now? A toxicology report would be problematic for me should your body ever be found, which is, admittedly, unlikely. I suspect the sharks will get you—there have been so many sightings this summer. However, should your remains wash to shore, we'll want the autopsy to support the theory that you went for a late night swim, swam out too far, were caught in the current, and couldn't get back to shore. It happens all the time, you know."

"I tied myself up and went for a swim?"

"Don't be silly. I'll remove the ropes before I toss you in."

"You aren't afraid I'll swim back to shore?"

"While unconscious? I hardly think so!"

At least I now had the entire plan. He would keep me tied up until he was ready to knock me out again with what I assumed was chloroform, then throw me overboard. It sounded like a pretty good plan to me. I just hoped it wasn't perfect.

Braddock poured himself a glass of juice and took a long sip—probably to give me a false sense of security. I still wouldn't take a drink.

Smirking, he leaned against the console with a casual elegance that I suspected was encoded in his very patrician DNA. "You know, I have a tremendous amount of respect for you, Ms. Daniels. You are the first to have figured it out. Sometimes, I thought it was so obvious what had happened, but no one looked very closely. Until you came along."

"Is that why you feel you have to take care of all the loose ends?"

He ignored my question and took another sip of his orange juice. "You know, you should never underestimate the power of a father's love. Perhaps I did not always appear to be a very good father to my son. That's because I wasn't. His mother and I divorced when he was young. I showed up for graduations, weddings, and christenings, and I posed for happy family photos, but that's about it." His tone became tinged with sadness, or maybe the emotion was bitterness. "Because my son does not want to be too closely identified with my legacy, he and his staff keep me away from campaign events, although they do trot me out for election nights and swearing-ins. People expect parents to show up at those things." His voice grew strong.

"Paulsen has led an exemplary life—none of the youthful foibles that sabotaged my political future. I will not let my own foolish mistakes ruin his career."

"Foolish mistakes like Lucy Abbott?"

"Ah, yes, the little red-haired tramp who left us recently. Conniving little bitch deserved what happened to her. I guess you know she came to see me in 1968."

* * *

Ward didn't agree with the direction Bobby Kennedy had dictated for the party, but he was still unnerved by his assassination. If the Kennedys could be taken out, any politician could face the same fate.

He was watching the funeral on television when she came to the door. He looked over her shoulder and realized she'd probably arrived in the Ford Falcon at the curb. He didn't associate with people who drove economy cars. He knew he'd never met this petite redhead before.

"You must have the wrong house," he said without giving her time to state her case.

"Ward Braddock?"

"Yes?" He searched his brain. Had he encountered her when he was drunk? Who knew the kind of people he fraternized with during those episodes? Looking at her, he felt an uneasiness in the pit of his stomach but did not let any emotion show.

"I'm looking for Ward Braddock. You look like him to me, so this must be the right house."

He didn't respond.

"I think you'll want to invite me in. I have a story to tell you. About the last night of the convention in '64. In Atlantic City. At a restaurant called Bella Napoli."

He wanted to see where she was going with this but played it cool. "I have no idea what you're talking about," he said stiffly, "but by all means come in."

He glanced up and down the street. No sign of neighbors. He hoped no one had seen her arrive. They'd think he had resorted to hookers while his wife lay forty miles away in the maternity ward. He had occasionally enjoyed the services of call girls, but not one of the professionals he'd employed in any way resembled the badly dressed creature standing in his front hall.

"I was just watching the end of the RFK ceremony. They're at Arlington now." Aside from a quick trip to see his wife and new baby, he'd spent the day watching the mass in New York and the train ride to Washington, wondering how he could create the kind of persona that would bring people to line railroad tracks to watch his body pass by.

As he led the woman to his den, he hoped the clacking of her high heels did not mean dents in his mahogany floors. He walked to the television and pushed in the knob to turn it off. "A very sad day."

"The kind of day that makes you think about life and about what you're doing with your own." Her words emerged with an unpleasant nasality, making what she viewed as a profound thought sound like a whine. "An important day."

So, something about Bobby Kennedy's death had created a social conscience in this creature. "Yes, it is. Won't you please have a seat?"

She threw herself onto an antique English Windsor chair and assumed a position he found worthy of a chimpanzee on its day off from the zoo.

"I don't understand why you've come to see me." He tried to form a pleasant expression on his face.

"I worked with Betty Boyle."

He thought he did a good job of hiding his emotions. "I am not familiar—"

"Don't pretend you don't know her. I was there the night she disappeared, and I know what happened."

"I'm sorry. I do recognize the name, but I am not sure what you're talking about."

"I think you do," the woman snapped.

He tried to remain calm in the face of her insolence. "I believe that is the name of the waitress with whom I had a minor altercation during a party at some quaint little restaurant in Atlantic City. An incident I regret greatly, especially since the police told me she had some problems after that. Did they ever resolve the matter?"

"You know they didn't."

"I must say, again, that I am afraid I do not understand your point."

"I'm not talking about the night you made an ass of yourself groping Betty at that party. I'm talking about the night she disappeared."

"As I recall, our little contretemps took place several nights earlier." For the first time he began to feel apprehensive.

"I'm not saying you killed her," she said, turning back to face him. "I'm saying you know what happened, and you owe it to her family to come forward."

"I am sorry—"

She interrupted again. "I was there, and I saw you with Betty Boyle."

"I am sure you must have seen Miss Boyle with many customers that evening."

She glared at him and spoke in a determined, confrontational tone. "Do I have to spell it out for you? You saw Mrs. Betty Boyle on two different nights that week. And I'm not talking about the night she poured a drink over your head."

"Certainly if that were true, and if this woman did meet with some misfortune, you would have gone to the police at the time. The convention was almost four years ago."

"Some misfortune!" she laughed. "Betty never came home that night or ever again and you know it."

"I recall talking to the police in 1964, but I never heard from them again. I'm very sorry to hear the situation had an unhappy resolution."

"Unhappy resolution!" she snorted. "You crack me up. I saw you with Betty the night she disappeared. When I was leaving work, you were grabbing her arm outside your car, a big black limo."

"I did not kill your Betty Boyle." That was the truth. "And I have no idea what happened to her." That was a lie. Even though he didn't do it himself, he knew the details, thanks to his staff.

"I went to see Buddy Boyle Wednesday, and I told him what I saw." Sitting back into the chair, she crossed her legs and began to swing her top foot back and forth.

Ward watched as her foot came within inches of the fragile tea table that had been in his mother's house and her mother's before that. He said nothing, aloud. Under his breath he uttered, "Barbarian."

"I thought he'd go to the police, but nothing has happened. So, I figured you and Buddy must have come to an arrangement."

The little extortionist! She must have found out that Buddy had gotten his share, and now she wanted hers.

"Who else have you discussed this with?"

"No one. I never said a word. I didn't want to get involved. I didn't think anyone would believe me, or, even if they did, that they would do anything. I knew who you were. I was afraid. But then, after Bobby Kennedy was shot, I kept thinking about what type of person he was. He would have told the truth. So I decided to tell the truth. As I said, I told Buddy Boyle."

Ward could accept that at the moment she approached Buddy Boyle, her motives were pure, but once she suspected Boyle had made a deal, her perspective changed. Had the spirit of her beloved Bobby Kennedy told her to blackmail him?

"I have no idea how Mr. Boyle reacted to the news you gave him. I can assure you, however, that I had nothing to do with Mrs. Boyle's death." He walked behind his desk and settled on the soft leather chair. "Sometimes, however, the appearance of impropriety is just as damaging as actual impropriety, and I would prefer our brief interaction that evening never come to light. I am, of course, horrified to think it may have been the last night of her life, but while I don't deny we had a conversation I can assure you she was fine when she left my car."

The woman watched him expectantly with eyes that he realized were red and swollen. Probably been crying since Wednesday. He never understood how someone could get so upset about other people's misfortune. After all, the Kennedy family might be willing to include her in one of their many tragedies, but did they ever think to invite her to their happy events? He didn't think so. Voters were such fools. He had to learn how to capitalize on that.

"I'm sorry. I didn't catch your name."

"Abbott. Lucy Abbott."

"You worked with Mrs. Boyle, so I presume you work as a waitress. Is that correct, Miss Abbott?"

"Nothing wrong with that." Her tone was defensive.

"Of course not. But it isn't what you'd call lucrative." He gave her a sly smile. "From your concern over Bobby Kennedy's death, I can see you are far more interested in social issues than in any personal gain, but I have an idea that would allow you to improve your financial situation and provide an important public service at the same time. All I'd ask in return is that you keep my brief, harmless encounter with Mrs. Boyle between us."

The woman smiled. He'd felt pretty sure he understood why she had come to see him all along. Now, he knew he was right.

* * *

"I had already set Anton Wisk up with his little altruistic endeavor, so I got him to hire her when the center opened that fall. Best paid secretary in history. We had to send her to typing class. If they had a spelling class, we would have sent her to that, too. I told her if she ever said a word, I would take care of her so she could never testify. I didn't say what I would do, but I knew she still worried that I might have killed Mrs. Boyle. And that if I killed once, I could kill again. Lucy Abbott wasn't going to say a word.

"You know, I almost forgot about the entire incident. I retain one lawyer, an old friend from Princeton, simply to handle my more delicate financial transactions. I didn't worry that anyone would talk, especially after decades went by. I thought I'd taken care of—what did you call them?—all the 'loose ends.' Apparently, I was wrong."

"Speaking of loose ends," I forced a calm, conversational tone, even though I was lying, "I guess you heard they're going to reopen Charles Speakes's case. The body is set to be exhumed."

"Why would they do that?" he stammered. "Speakes committed suicide … that was over fifty years ago." The news rattled him.

"By the same method as Lucy Abbott?" I shook my head and let out a sigh. "That was sloppy."

He brushed it off. "There's no possible connection to be made between the two deaths."

"Look around. Do you think I'm getting out of this situation? I would think you'd relish bragging about how you got away with a major cover-up for fifty years. That's an impressive feat." My intent was to play for time, but I realized I might be giving him yet another motive to kill me. Did it matter? No, I decided, one more revelation would not tip the scale.

He studied me, and I saw his expression morph from feigned innocence to unmasked recognition to pure joy.

"I suspect you're lying about the exhumation, Ms. Daniels," he said finally. "But you're right about Charles's suicide. Orchestrating it was quite a challenge."

Hoping to entice me into asking for a sip of liquid, Braddock drank his orange juice slowly and with exaggerated relish. I did not give in.

"I felt quite nervous in the days after Charles met his maker. Everyone accepted that his death was a suicide. Luckily for me, he'd become inexplicably but very visibly depressed several months before. His wife had told many friends that she couldn't understand how a man with one young child and another on the way could be so despondent. Perfect cover for me.

"For awhile, I thought young Wisk was so upset by Charles's death that he, too, might have to meet the same fate. But once he joined the Peace Corps in Africa, I figured that was it. Case closed.

"I heard from him soon enough once he returned to Atlantic City. He had a lot on me—about the incident with Betty Boyle and his suspicion about Charles. However, he felt no need to go to the police. He had a different plan, which explains how I became such a ..." he paused to clear his throat, "humanitarian."

Settling on the bench across from me, Braddock looked out at the sea before resuming. "I set up a trust to sponsor Wisk's organization, and it was smooth sailing for many years after that. Wisk worked off his guilt through his little community center, and Miss Abbott continued to earn an obscene amount of money for sheer incompetence. I rarely gave the situation a thought. I had more urgent problems."

He didn't elaborate that a hit-and-run accident ended his career and that his marriage fell apart soon after.

"I found myself forced to revisit the unfortunate events of 1964 again in June after the primary, when Mr. Boyle came to see me at my home. He said he wanted to talk to me about *my* son and *his* wife, and I have to admit that for the briefest moment I wondered if Paulsen had been foolish enough to get involved with a married woman. But Paulsen is nothing like me."

I could have sworn he looked wistful at the thought.

"I was surprised when I learned the identity of my visitor. As far as I knew, my lawyer had not heard from Boyle in years. The initial money transfer went without a hitch, and after a few false starts, I had heard Boyle got a business up and running and moved his son into a nice new house. Our only contact was, as agreed upon, related to his son's education expenses. So I was shocked to see him and appalled by his physical deterioration. Buddy Boyle has that look of people who spend their entire lifetimes smoking and drinking, though at least he used my money to buy some decent clothes. Ill-fitting, but of fairly good quality. Of course, he apparently did have cancer at some point. I guess that must have taken its toll."

Braddock appeared amused by his observations. I wouldn't have been amused even if I hadn't been consumed by hunger, fear, pain, sadness, despair, panic, and any number of other sensations, but most of all thirst. I saw that the dark clouds were moving closer, and I hoped for rain so I could catch some droplets on my tongue.

"Once I saw the expression on Boyle's face, I realized he had not come to thank me for the money, the house, his business, or his son's education. I feared the conversation would turn to Paulsen's run for governor. And, sure enough, it did. Boyle yelled at me. *He* yelled at *me.*" Braddock shook his head in disbelief. "He started going on about how for close to fifty years he'd kept his mouth shut about what happened to his wife. 'My Betty,' he called her. After fifty years." Braddock shook his head.

I felt fairly certain he could not understand that kind of devotion to anything but his own success.

"I had to explain *again* that I had not killed his wife. Once more, I reviewed the events as he knew them so that he could accept that I was not culpable. What a tiresome man. Tiresome, but tenacious. I'll give him that."

Braddock started as if shocked to suddenly recall that he had a problem at hand. Namely me. He raised the glass to my lips, but I held them tightly closed. He chuckled and returned to his story.

I was guessing he meant to sound like an everyday kind of guy, but his imitation of Buddy Boyle suggested Sylvester Stallone as Rocky Balboa. "'I raised my son without his mother. He's a good boy and he says he's happy, but I know better. No wife. No children. His mother would have been a good influence, maybe encourage him to make something of himself.' Blah. Blah. Blah. I thought Boyle would never get to the point, but finally he tells me, 'What I am saying is that you took away something from my son, so I want to take something away from yours.' Can you imagine?"

Actually, I could.

"Who the hell was *he* to threaten *my* son? After all I did for him and his little brat, he had the audacity to try to sabotage my son's career with ancient history. He said he was going to start by telling Paulsen the whole story. I remained very patient, but I was worried. I reminded him that if any information about our agreement were to go public, he would be charged with blackmail. He said he didn't care, and I believed him. That alarmed me. I told him Paulsen had done nothing wrong. My son *deserved* to be governor.

"Ultimately I lied to Boyle and told him I would tell Paulsen the truth. Not that I could guarantee what would happen, but I asked him to keep our secret until I had time to consider my options. I actually hoped he would calm down and think again about the possibility he'd face criminal charges. Either way, I wasn't about to tell Paulsen anything."

Braddock took a sip of his drink. I pretended not to care, but my lips pursed in an involuntary reflex. I eyed the sky. The clouds were dark overhead, but still no rain.

"I thought I was taking care of Boyle but then you showed up and started asking questions. I knew I now had a bigger problem. I checked out your investigation. I even followed you around a little. I'm good. You never spotted me."

"I spotted you."

"When?" He sounded like a three-year-old.

"One night you followed us from the Pub Club." I sounded no more than three and a half.

"No, I didn't do that." He retained the tone of a petulant child.

"I saw you." I didn't sound much more mature.

"You didn't. It wasn't me."

I didn't believe him.

"Well, Ms. Daniels, as much as I've enjoyed chatting with you, it's time for your little dip." He glanced at the sky. "So sad that our beautiful day has slipped away. Then again, you're not going to have to worry about the weather very much longer, are you?" He pulled out a handkerchief, doused it with liquid, and moved toward me. The waves were getting rougher, but I couldn't count on help from the sea. If I wanted to see the sun come up tomorrow, I'd have to rely on my own devices. I'd used that term so often without ever, not once, thinking what those devices might be. I had to think fast—not easy considering the terror that was overwhelming me.

As Braddock lurched toward me, I had only one shot at knocking him over. By "over," I was thinking over onto the deck, but when I yanked my legs up and slammed them into his knees, the ocean did its part. Despite a well-seasoned pair of sea legs, he pitched forward and staggered to his left. If he had let go of the bottle or the handkerchief, he might have saved himself, but the experienced yachtsman seemed convinced he could regain his balance. He couldn't. As he flipped backward over the starboard rail, I saw the amazement on his face. Ward Braddock was not used to losing.

I dropped onto my knees and crawled to the rail. I felt nothing as I watched the ranting old man float out to sea. Actually, "float" was far too gentle a word for what was happening to him. As he tried to swim back to the boat, I saw his arms flailing as he came to the crest of a wave, but instead of moving forward, he disappeared behind the high water. I saw the pattern repeat as wave after wave defeated his efforts. His bobbing head got smaller and smaller in the distance. Even after I could no longer see him, I could swear I heard him screaming that he would get me for this. I also thought I heard some rather unpleasant names that could only have been meant for me. Braddock's veneer of civility had cracked quickly when he was the one facing death.

"Watch out for the sharks—lots of sightings this year!" I called out hoping the wind carried both the message and my sarcastic tone in his direction. "Love to help, but I've got to run."

Run was not exactly the right word. Creep seemed more appropriate. The highly polished teak deck was attractive but hell on my knees as I started a painful trek to the radio mounted high above me. Cursing Braddock's knot-tying prowess I shimmied over to the spot where the side wall met the console and pushed my side against the hard wood surface. I turned my toes under and pushed. After a half dozen sharp bumps, I worked my way upward. I couldn't complain when a wave tossed the boat and I was thrown back to the deck and very nearly down the ladder into the cabin. After all, a wave had just saved my life. I simply began my climb again.

During the ten minutes it took me to get to my feet, I feared the sound of Ward Braddock clambering back on the boat. When I finally got to a standing position, I looked for him but he had drifted out of sight. I didn't spend any time mourning his loss. I threw my torso across the top of the console to make sure I didn't fall back. Didn't want to start that climb again. Hop by hop, I moved over to the ship-to-shore. Setting my chin on the base I spoke in a controlled voice.

"May Day, May Day."

I lifted my chin and waited for a response. None came. I had no idea what frequency the radio was on or even if it worked. I hadn't seen Braddock use it, but as far as I could see it was my best hope. Plan B—drifting into the shipping lanes and hoping for some keen-eyed captain to spot me before his giant vessel plowed over my small one—was a decidedly less attractive option.

I depressed the button again. "May Day, May Day." When I lifted my chin, I heard static. Again, I pushed with my chin. "May Day. Help!" Being unfamiliar with nautical protocol, I shouted the facts. "I've been kidnapped. I'm adrift on this boat. No idea what it's called. May Day! May Day!"

I released the button and heard something beautiful. A voice. A male voice that sounded twelve years old, but I didn't care. Someone knew I was out here and alive. He told me to hold the button for a full minute so they could get my location. I counted. One, one thousand. Two, one thousand. Just after fifty-eight one thousand, a wave hit the boat from the side. My chin slipped from the button and I fell to the deck with a thud.

I issued an expletive that drowned out the advice coming over the radio. I didn't understand every word, but I did hear a kind voice add, "We're on our way. Sit tight." I didn't think that would be a problem. I lay on the deck with my back pushed against the console to thwart any effort by a rogue wave to toss me overboard.

When the Coast Guard got to me in what they later said was twenty minutes but I would have estimated as two hours, I told them immediately about the man overboard. I'd already said I'd been abducted and left alone on the boat, but had not thought to specify that the kidnapper was now out drifting in the Atlantic Ocean. Two officers stayed with me as their boat took off in search of Ward Braddock. I did not wish them good luck.

Chapter 40

Andy held my hand as we sat in the ER of Atlantic City Medical Center watching a somber-faced Paulsen Braddock on the breaking news segment of the local news. The heir to the Braddock legacy thanked everyone who had expressed concern for his father's safety and asked the public to pray for his rescue—which the candidate, Andy, and I knew meant the recovery of Ward Braddock's body.

"Sans his soul, if in fact he ever had one," I added.

The details of how Ward Braddock ended up floating around in the Atlantic Ocean two miles from shore were not made clear to the public. I suspected, however, that some news outlet would eventually begin to put the pieces together and show up at my door with questions. In the meantime, I remained incommunicado.

Andy thought that was a good idea, especially given that I had arrived in the ER in what he described as "a somewhat manic frame of mind." His own frame of mind had escalated from frantic, when he returned to the hotel and found only a still-hungry Wisk, to manic, when he could find no trace of me on the security tapes in his office.

When I woke up the next morning in a hospital bed, I had gained some perspective on my recent experience. I no longer felt elated at the thought of Ward Braddock's unpleasant demise in the waters off Atlantic City. I wasn't mourning, but I did understand that there were those who were. Nonetheless I felt I had a right to be happy. After all, I was alive, and not long ago that possibility had seemed like a long shot. Still, I couldn't shake the feeling of sadness for Betty.

When I was released from the ER, Andy was waiting to take me home. Well, home to the Artistical, that is.

"I'd like to see Johnny before we leave. I want him to hear everything from me."

"Are you yourself again?"

"Yep. I'm back."

"I still don't think you should talk to any press. But just in case, can I trust you to respond appropriately to their questions?"

I held up my hand. "Scouts' honor."

"You were never a Girl Scout, so let me just run through a few test questions." He included a fill-in-the-blank: "Ward Braddock is _____."

"A husband, a father, and a grandfather. Let's hope for a happy resolution to the search for him."

He nodded approvingly and skipped any further test questions. "Okay," he said, "I'll meet you outside. You did all the work. You take the credit."

I found my way to the floor where Buddy Boyle was recuperating, no doubt comforted by the knowledge that he was in a hospital with a Frank Sinatra Wing, named so in honor of the thousands of dollars Sinatra had raised for the medical center.

It took me a moment to recognize Johnny sitting in the corridor outside his father's room. I had never seen the singer without his tuxedo. I would have expected Rat Pack gear, but he was dressed for the 21st century. Well dressed in fact. He lifted his head when I stopped beside him.

"How is he?" I asked.

"He's recovering from ethylene glycol poisoning. The doctors ran some tests, and believe it or not, there's no sign of cancer. It looks like he'll be fine, thanks to you and Andy."

"You're the one who sent us down the path."

Johnny demurred but appeared pleased by the remark.

"I found out what happened that night," I said. I didn't have to say what night. "Are you ready to hear about it?"

He nodded. We walked down the hall to a quiet spot where I told him the story of August 27, 1964.

"She was rushing out of work to get home to you," I began. I didn't sugarcoat the facts for Johnny. I explained how Braddock had assaulted his mother in a drunken rage. "She got away from him but ended up in an argument with Myra Morris. Somehow it got physical and Myra pushed your mother. She fell and struck her head. Myra left her unconscious on the sidewalk. She thought someone would find her."

"But no one did."

"Braddock's top aide did, a man named Charles Speakes." This would be the hardest part. How do you tell a man that his mother was discarded like a piece of garbage? I stumbled a bit as I tried to use the kindest words to tell Johnny the whole story. Finally, I got to the end.

"Speakes admitted to another Braddock aide that your mother was still breathing when he dropped her over. But, Johnny, I don't think she suffered. We can never be certain, but my conclusion is that she never regained consciousness from the head injury." That was small consolation, I knew.

Johnny listened with a lot of attention and a few tears. "I have so much to think about," he said when I'd finished.

"Johnny, I can't imagine how painful it must be, realizing what your mother experienced that night. But everyone I spoke to said that all she wanted to do was get home to her family. Everyone knew how much she loved you."

He nodded but couldn't speak.

"You always felt that, but now you know."

Johnny turned the topic my way. "Are you sure you're okay?"

"I'm fine. Just some rope burns and a few bruises. Andy's pulling the car around. I'm going home ... well, home to the Artistical for another week or so."

"Get going then. Don't keep your man waiting."

I kissed his cheek and headed for the elevator. Andy was waiting outside the hotel lobby. I protested that I was no invalid as he helped me into the car, but to tell the truth, I could get used to that kind of attention.

"You rest tonight while I finish up work. Tomorrow night we're going to celebrate the good that's come out of this trip. You found the truth about Betty for the people who love her."

When he asked where I wanted to go, I knew immediately.

"1964."

Andy had been thinking more of the Artistical's high-end Dali Bistro. "There were a lot of bad things going on in 1964," he reminded me.

"True," I said, "but a lot of people were trying to make the world a better place. 1964 was a turning point."

Chapter 41

The next morning after a good night's sleep I headed off to see Sylvia, the hairdresser Johnny had recommended, and asked for a modified bouffant. I wanted to have that early '60s pouf yet I didn't want to be a source of amusement. After having my nails and toenails painted a dark red shade, I visited a lobby shop where I found a little black dress to create a '60s effect and a chiffon wrap to hide my bruises. I removed my tiny diamond studs and replaced them with big rhinestone button earrings from the jewelry store in the lobby, where I also found bracelets big enough to mask my rope burns.

My last stop was the lingerie store where I bought Andy's favorite and my least favorite part of the outfit—a garter belt and stockings that I planned to stuff into a pair of black high heels I owned but seldom wore.

For his big entrance to 1964, Andy emerged from the bathroom in a conservative gray suit and struck a pose he'd obviously stolen from a Brooks Brothers catalog.

"Like the narrow tie? I found it at Goodwill on Atlantic Avenue." He lifted the tie for a closer look. "I suspect this is actually in style again."

Disappearing behind the closet door he called out, "Now for the *pièce de résistance.*" When he reemerged he was sporting a straw fedora accented with a gray and maroon ribbon. "I made the band myself," he said, his eyes sparkling in a way I had not seen in weeks.

"Let me guess—Halloween was your favorite holiday as a kid?"

"How did you know?" He looked in the mirror to straighten his tie.

I shrugged. "Lucky guess."

"It's been a long time since I've gone out in costume."

I hadn't been thinking 'costume,' I'd been thinking a look that suggested the '60s. I guess I should have been more specific, but it was too late. Andy looked pleased as punch with himself. As we studied our outfits in the mirror, I didn't think we looked silly—at least we wouldn't if Andy left the hat home.

"If you wear the hat, you won't see the hair you slicked down," I pointed out.

He put the hat on and studied the effect. Then he took it off and surveyed the damage to his hairstyle. "It's too cool to leave behind. The worst I'll get is a little hat ridge and that would be authentic." He extended his arm. "Let's go."

When Andy gave the parking ticket to the hotel valet, the man in the red jacket returned not with our mid-size rental but with a 1964 Buick LeSabre convertible. Okay, Andy had to tell me the car was a 1964 Buick LeSabre convertible. I could see it was a convertible, I could guess it was a Buick by the portholes on the side, and I could testify that it was longer than my first New York apartment was wide. However, I had to rely on Andy's word that the model year was 1964.

"I believe you. No fins, but still oversized. My grandfather would have loved the white walls. But Andy, how did you ever … ?"

"I borrowed it." He held open the door for me and caressed the red interior. "Don't damage it, or we've bought it."

I'd settled into the front seat before I remembered. "Convertibles don't work with 1964 hair."

"Use your scarf."

As I wrapped the chiffon around my bouffant and tied it under my chin, I noticed a couple waiting for their car studying us. It was obvious he admired the car. She did not appear similarly impressed with our outfits.

"This is embarrassing, but I guess it's too late to back out now." I smiled up at my date.

"Don't even think about it." He grabbed the big stick on the column, shifted the car into drive and drove to the point where Atlantic Avenue meets Pacific Avenue. It was here where, according to Betty Boyle's diary, Buddy had taken her to celebrate their first and only anniversary.

"The Knife & Fork—I've never been here," I said, wondering why. The restaurant had been an AC landmark since before the Roaring Twenties.

Andy hesitated at the curb, reluctant to turn the Buick over to the youthful valet. He begged the kid to take care with the car before relinquishing the keys. "I borrowed it, you see."

"No problem, dude," the attendant assured him.

"That's future talk for 'Sure, Daddy-O,'" Andy explained to me.

As my beau and I sipped Manhattans at the bar, never once did I catch his eyes straying to the baseball games playing out on the screens behind the bar. I construed that to mean romance was in the air. To do my part, I plucked the cherry from the glass and fondled it seductively with my tongue. "I think 1964 girls did this."

"1964 hussies, you mean." He sighed. "We should be smoking."

"Not legal."

"Now. But we're not from now."

"We are two non-smoking 1964 people. There had to be some." I slipped off the stool. "I have to powder my nose. Can you spare a girl a dollar for the powder room?"

"We don't have to be completely authentic. Besides, all I have are twenties."

And, apparently, I wasn't getting one of them.

When I returned, I found my date and the bartender wiping up the bar in front of my stool. "Your drink spilled while you were gone," Andy explained.

"Don't you mean, 'I spilled your drink while you were gone'?"

"If that's what you deduce. I can't control what you conclude."

I stared at him. "Andy, can you say that again?"

"Probably not, but it was something like, 'I can't be held responsible for what you deduce from my truthful comment.' Why am I repeating myself?"

I couldn't keep myself from thinking about Ward Braddock. "Because I deduced from Ward Braddock's statements that he killed Lucy Abbott and was trying to kill Buddy Boyle, but he never actually said those things. When he spoke about Charles Speakes, he was very specific, but when he talked about what's been happening recently, he mentioned no details."

Andy understood. "But that doesn't mean he didn't kill Lucy."

"Or that he did."

Andy seemed to be frustrated that our date was beginning to go off-course. "All that happened *this* year—in the future. We've got to get back to 1964."

But I couldn't go back. "Andy, how did Ward Braddock find me? I never told him where I was staying. He said he followed me, but where did he pick up my trail in the first place? He couldn't have tailed me from Spring Lake. He was still on the beach when I left. He never even saw my car." I was growing excited. "And, yes, I aroused his suspicions when I interviewed him, but he said ... he actually *said* I had figured it out. Why would he think I had anything figured out? How would the questions I asked him on the beach convince him of that? At that point I didn't have any *idea* what had happened."

The bartender slipped another drink in front of me. I nursed it while Andy speculated. "Your conversation in Spring Lake would not have persuaded him to risk killing you. Someone must have convinced him you were a credible threat to his son's candidacy."

"So why not follow his usual pattern and try to buy me off?" I sounded disappointed. "I wonder how much he would have offered."

Andy answered with a disparaging look.

My tone let him know I was serious. "Because someone convinced him I couldn't be bought."

"Although he might have believed you were incorruptible, he could have just as easily concluded that trying to pay you off would only create new complications. Can we talk about this tomorrow? For now, perhaps we could talk about the Beatles?"

I ignored his attempt to take the conversation back in time. "If he found me, he could have followed me when I went to see Charles Speakes's widow and Lucy Abbott."

"He might have assumed that one or both of them told you everything they knew. At least in Lucy's case, that could have been outside his comfort zone. We can sleep on this and talk about it some more tomorrow. Which one do you think is the cutest?" Andy asked.

"Cutest who?"

"Beatle. Who's your pick for the cutest Beatle?"

"Paul, of course. Everyone knows he was the cute one." I took a sip of my Manhattan. "How could I have missed this? I was so blinded by my desire to prove Braddock's guilt that I overlooked any clue that didn't support my theory."

"I was no better. I was so involved in my own problems ..." Andy's voice trailed off.

"The important thing is we're thinking about it now. How did Braddock know where to find me?"

"Who knew you were staying at the Artistical?"

"I made a lot of calls from the room. Anyone with Caller ID might have known."

"It had to be someone who knew Braddock."

We spoke in unison. "Anton Wisk."

After a moment's reflection Andy said, "Even if Wisk told Braddock you were staying at the Artistical, tracking you down that last night would not have been easy."

"I called Wisk from Café Monet to ask if he wanted a snack—it couldn't have been more than a half hour later when Braddock found me on the beach."

"So Wisk was able to give him a precise location," Andy said. "But why would he help Braddock? That was a pretty convincing story about Braddock trying to poison him."

"True or not, Braddock was Wisk's meal ticket."

"Right. And if you brought Braddock down, Wisk wouldn't have him to blackmail anymore." Andy grew animated. "So, faced with losing his funding, Wisk shares with Braddock what you've discovered, who you might tell about it, and, most importantly, where you can be found."

"Wisk could have put Lucy Abbott in danger by telling Braddock a similar story about her," I offered. "That is, if he didn't poison her himself."

"Why would Wisk want Lucy dead?"

"Well, she was extorting money from Braddock," I said. "And Braddock isn't a billionaire." I corrected my tense. "*Wasn't* a billionaire. If the well ran dry, that would have been a problem for Wisk. Plus, she was one more person who could have blown the whistle on Braddock." I puzzled over the idea for a moment. "That could explain why Wisk would target Lucy, but what about Buddy? As far as we know, he didn't have his hand in Braddock's pocket anymore."

"I'm thinking Buddy falls in the same category you did," Andy said. "If he exposed Braddock, Braddock might go to jail, and with him, any funds for Absecon Hope, let alone a large endowment for a new pool."

"So the question is, how did Wisk find out about Buddy's threat?" I took a long drink of my Manhattan as if that would help.

"If I may do some wild speculating," Andy offered, "maybe Braddock told him about it.'"

"We'll never know unless we can get Wisk to admit what happened." I smiled at Andy. "That may require some creativity."

"Okay. We cook up some tricks. Tomorrow. For tonight, Wisk thinks he's in the clear. We can talk to him when we get back to modern times. Then, if we hear anything interesting, we can go to the police."

I leaned in close to him. "Okay, handsome," I whispered seductively, or at least my version of seductively. "Let's get back to 1964."

It turned out we couldn't. Every attempt at discussions of the past led to talk of the present. Finally, Andy said, "I don't want us wasting our special night talking about Anton Wisk. Let's go take him out for a drink."

"To get him drunk?" I asked.

"To take him somewhere where he would have no expectation of privacy and we would have no expectation of meeting his many fans." He called for the check. "Let me just make a call and we can be on our way."

Chapter 42

Andy pulled up slowly in front of Absecon Hope less than forty-five minutes after we decided to visit Anton Wisk. We walked up the steps unhurriedly. No one watching would think we were on a critical mission. Andy knocked on the door lightly. No one inside would think we had come on an urgent matter.

As the door cracked open, Wisk looked surprised to see two '60s types on the stoop but regrouped quickly. "You're early," he quipped. "Halloween isn't for another two months."

"You should see me in my fedora," Andy laughed. I recognized it as a phony laugh but it appeared to fool Wisk. "May we come in? I thought you'd want to hear how things worked out with Braddock."

"Well, I'm kind of busy right now …" As he mulled it over, his curiosity won out. "Okay, sure. Why not?"

"Great." Andy smiled broadly and we stepped inside. My smile wasn't so broad. I didn't find it wise to be out of public view with a man who may have recently helped plan my murder. For that matter, with a man who may have helped plan *any* murder *ever*.

Andy was playing the role of Wisk's best friend and Wisk was buying it. "Should you be opening your door at night to strangers without your gun in your hand? Where is it, anyway?"

"It's in the desk drawer." Wisk acted nonchalant.

"Bring it out." Andy reacted with matching nonchalance. "I'll show you a trick for answering the door."

"No, that's okay." Wisk was not cooperating. I guessed he was recalling what happened the last time Andy had gotten hold of his gun.

Andy was undaunted. "Anton, I'm not going to deprive you of your handgun—I just want to show you this one technique. We'll worry less about you after we leave town."

Andy turned and nodded at me, and I smiled fondly at Wisk. "Andy's right, we would worry." I didn't clarify what we would actually be worrying about.

Wisk did not seem happy, but he gave up arguing. He disappeared into his bedroom and emerged holding his gun. He grew interested as Andy showed him how to handle it so a visitor couldn't see it. When the lesson was over, instead of giving the gun back to Wisk, Andy set it on the table where he could see it and reach it first if he had to.

"Thanks for helping me improve my gun handling skills, but what did you want to tell me about Braddock?"

"Well, first of all, sorry we left you hanging the other night back at the hotel," I said. "Anyhow, we are leaving town soon and thought we should tell you about Braddock in person."

"So, you really are leaving?"

Was I wrong, or was that the best news Anton Wisk had gotten in some time? I assured him that Andy and I were returning home. The news seemed to relax him.

Andy was still playing Wisk's buddy. "Come on, we want to buy you a drink. Let's run down to Gardner's Basin for a drink and maybe a quick bite. Have you eaten?"

"I had soup." Wisk patted his stomach and sighed as if he'd just finished Thanksgiving dinner.

"That's not enough. Come on." Andy poured on the charm. "The Back Bay Ale House has great margaritas and the best raw bar around. You like oysters? I love oysters. And clams, fried clams. Whatever you want. We can tell you the whole story. You must be curious!"

"Well …" Wisk hedged.

"My treat. We won't have another chance to tell you the whole story. We've seen what good work you do—maybe we can talk about a donation to the center."

Wisk couldn't resist a free meal and a possible donation.

"Let me run to the bathroom and then I'll be ready." As Wisk disappeared into the bathroom, Andy picked up the gun and deftly unloaded the bullets into his pocket.

Chapter 43

On the short ride to Gardner's Basin, I sat in the back of our rental car while Andy bonded with Wisk in the front. I felt I had Andy's back. I didn't actually have a plan for protecting him, but I had confidence that if Wisk tried to cause any trouble I could take him.

Andy found a good parking space near the Back Bay Ale House, and the hostess found us an even better table. It was downstairs, but we still had a nice view across the inlet.

"It certainly is a beautiful night," Wisk said. "I live a pretty quiet life and don't get out very often. However, I think I'll live it up a bit this evening." He ordered a beer and, at Andy's insistence, an appetizer sampler.

Andy began gaining Wisk's confidence by sharing some of the details of my close call on the boat with Ward Braddock. I'd grown bored with repeating them so I didn't mind listening. I threw in a comment or correction as needed. By the time his beer was half gone and his food was in front of him, Wisk seemed very relaxed. Then, Andy offered what appeared to be a good-natured jibe.

"Anton, I have a bone to pick with you."

"Oh, really?" Wisk seemed amused at first, but when he looked up from his food at Andy's face, his amusement gave way to confusion. Evidently,

Andy had an actual bone to pick. It could have been something as simple as leaving the seat up when he used the toilet in our hotel room, which by the way he did. The bone, however, turned out to be considerably larger than that.

"Anton," he said with a nod in my direction, "this woman means the world to me. For the last six years she has been my anchor in life. I don't know how I could live without her."

My eyes misted over even though I suspected his loving words were just part of his plan to trick Wisk.

"I don't take kindly to people who put Meg's life in jeopardy, and that, Anton, is what you did."

Wisk protested. He sputtered a lot of syllables that never came together to form any words.

Andy continued. "We will check phone records for our room and for your cell phone, and when we do, I'm fairly certain we will find a call on one of them just after Meg called you from Café Monet. The calls may trace to Ward Braddock's personal phone, but I think it's more likely the call went to a disposable device, possibly the one found among Braddock's possessions."

It was a bluff, but a good one.

"What would that prove?" Wisk tried to hide his concern.

"It would prove that you tipped Ward Braddock off about where to find Meg, convinced him that she knew too much, and not just about what happened in 1964, and that she presented a threat to him that needed to be eliminated."

"That's ridiculous. I didn't know I'd be in your room that night."

Wisk could see the visit heading downhill and tried to shovel as much into his mouth as he could so he didn't have to say more.

Andy was undeterred. "True. That was a bonus. But, you did know Meg would be at the Artistical and you shared the information with Braddock."

"You could never prove that even if it were true, and I'm not saying that it is."

"Oh, we could prove it, but that's not my job, although the police would be interested in why you were so eager to help. I'll be satisfied with an apology to my girlfriend."

Girlfriend sounded so silly in that context, I thought. Silly, but accurate.

Wisk stopped eating. He spent a minute wiping his lips and then another wringing his hands. I saw a switch toggle in his head and knew he'd just come up with a plan. I was a little worried about it since his last plan almost sent me to the bottom of the ocean.

He started to talk. "Look, I have found you both to be reasonable people. You have seen the good work I do here. You understand the need for my services and accomplishments."

Wisk looked from Andy to me and back searching for agreement. I nodded. I could give Wisk that. When he wasn't killing people, he did very good work.

Andy was not so easily placated. "What does that have to do with what we're talking about?"

"It has everything to do with it. I am too valuable to be lost to the community because of some legal wrangling. I understand that there will be some questions about what happened in 1964, and I will be happy to answer them. Certainly, no one will want to deprive this city of my services because of errors in judgment I made half a century ago."

"I'm not talking about 1964," Andy said.

Wisk took a moment to answer. "The minute I heard that Paulsen Braddock was running for governor, I knew I could take advantage of the situation—not for my own benefit, but for Absecon Hope and all the people it helps." He put his hand on his chest in a gesture seen frequently in paintings of the Christ figure. "I am interested in money only for what it can do for my organization, and for what it allows my organization to do for people who need help."

This level of honesty could not be good. I feared that Wisk was on his way to a confession. If so, his openess had to be part of his plan. Had Andy noticed?

Andy spoke in a serious voice. "I'm not talking about extortion."

"I need to explain. I never meant for Meg to get hurt. I always had the best intentions. When I spoke to Braddock on business matters, it's possible—I can't be sure—that I mentioned Meg."

There was no doubt in my mind that his claim of uncertainty constituted a bald-faced lie.

Wisk leaned in close. If I had to cover the topics he did, I wouldn't want the entire restaurant to hear what I said either. "Don't you see? I am guilty of nothing more than naiveté. I should have watched every word I said to Braddock."

"Especially after what happened in '65 when you said too much to him about Charles Speakes." Andy tried to hide his sarcasm. He was not completely successful. "Anton, you told us that you suspected all along that Braddock was responsible for Charles's death. You even suggested he'd tried to kill you. If I were you, I would have been damn careful not to speak out of turn."

Wisk stammered and while he never quite formed a word, he was still trying to claim that he never meant me any harm.

Andy wasn't buying whatever Wisk was trying to sell. "Anton, you put Meg in danger," he said with a penetrating glare.

"What was I supposed to do?" Wisk's reserve burst like a dam. "Everything would have been fine if it weren't for Buddy Boyle. Lucy Abbott told me she was sure Boyle took money from Braddock to keep quiet after his wife disappeared. It seems that, five decades later, Mr. Boyle suddenly developed scruples. Just my luck, Boyle had a brush with death not long before young Braddock announced his intention to run for governor that inspired him to speak up." Wisk shook his head disapprovingly. "Paulsen Braddock's political aspirations offered Boyle a way to hurt Braddock and assuage his guilt over taking his hush money."

This time when Wisk shook his head, I think he was expressing amazement that someone would feel guilty about taking Braddock's money.

"Did Lucy Abbott tell you that?" I asked.

"No, she hadn't kept in touch with Boyle over the years."

"Then who?" Andy asked.

"I got the story from Ward. When I called him with my latest business 'proposition,' he complained that I was no better than Boyle, except that the aggrieved widower wasn't taking any more money because now he wanted revenge. Boyle had decided to destroy young Braddock's dream of becoming New Jersey's next governor, not to mention any chance at higher office." Wisk shook his head. "Ward was convinced Paulsen was on his way to the White House."

"He told you all that?" I found it amazing, although Braddock had told me as much. Of course, at the time he thought I'd be dead within a few hours. Maybe he'd had a similar plan for Wisk.

"For the most part," Wisk said. "What he didn't tell me I pieced together."

"So to prevent Buddy Boyle from rocking the boat, you started sending laced drinks to his home?" Andy asked directly.

The blood drained out of Wisk's face, but he couldn't seem to stop talking. "I really thought Braddock would wear Boyle down and the guy would take more money, but that worried me too. Braddock was rich but he couldn't support the entire population of Atlantic City. Boyle had already gotten his share. He was only interested in personal gain. My money went for good. If anyone deserved more money, it was me. I had to do something."

I hoped Andy felt as wary as I did about the easy flow of information coming from Wisk. The man had a plan.

"It took me a day or so to work out the logistics. If Buddy started to slowly get sick, he would think the cancer was back. If he died, it might look like natural causes, or if anyone looked more closely, they might think suicide. I simply restarted the shipments that he had received when he had cancer. For three weeks, I added a little something to the drinks. Pesticides for cramping, ethylene glycol for nausea, headaches, disorientation." He turned to me and explained. "Antifreeze."

I guess he assumed that, being female, I didn't know that antifreeze contained ethylene glycol, tasted sweet, and was easy to conceal in someone's drink. He assumed wrong.

"Once it was established that his health was deteriorating, I would deliver a lethal dose."

I wanted to ask if he'd considered the possibility of someone else drinking the concoction, but I tried a different tack. "What if his doctor figured it out?"

"I'd met Buddy Boyle through Absecon Hope, and on more than one occasion he'd sworn never to go through cancer treatment again—the cure was worse than the disease, he said. I did wonder if his son could change his mind about seeing a doctor, but doubted he could convince him in less than three weeks."

"If he'd gone to the emergency room, an astute nurse or physician might have recognized the symptoms," Andy said.

"Just in case, I went to his garage to plant some antifreeze, but his garage door was open when I got there and I could see a couple of jugs of the stuff right from the curb. It was almost too easy.

"I mean, ethylene glycol really does a job on you. He would eventually have become so confused that he wouldn't even be able to say if he drank it or not." He seemed to find the thought amusing. "It would look like Boyle, facing a relapse of his cancer and unwilling to endure the pain and suffering of the disease or to undergo further treatment, consumed the lethal dose himself."

He looked at me for confirmation. All I could think was how sick Wisk was. What made him think I could possibly understand *anything* he'd done?

"If you think I enjoyed doing it, you're wrong. I really had no choice. I couldn't let Absecon Hope suffer because of Buddy Boyle's perverse need to ruin Ward Braddock."

Perverse? I thought not, but didn't argue.

"If Braddock didn't need to hide his past, he might not have continued funding us. Of course, with his passing, the center will be well taken care of through his will—my good work will continue."

"But Lucy Abbott?" I asked.

"She committed suicide," he snapped.

"Why now? She was going to be a grandmother."

"I don't know, but I can't regret that she's dead. If Paulsen Braddock's run for high office got Boyle riled up, it might have done the same for Lucy. She'd seen dollar signs before. Why wouldn't she see them again? Especially if she craved some big bucks for the little brat. College money—like the offspring of that little cretin could go to college. God, Lucy couldn't even get the filing right. I ask you, is it so hard to remember that P comes before Q? Not at Absecon Hope, it doesn't."

"Maybe she wasn't that dumb. What if she got suspicious about Buddy Boyle's death? You wouldn't want her asking questions," Andy countered. "I can see why you thought you had to kill Lucy Abbott."

"Why I might *want* to kill Lucy Abbott. We all know she killed herself."

"No, we all know that she *didn't*," I said.

He eyed me with impatience.

"And the police too," Andy added.

Wisk's impatience turned to fear.

"You should have been a little more understanding of Lucy Abbott's situation." I came off a bit on the sanctimonious side.

"I am *exceedingly* understanding of *everyone's* situation. That is what makes me so good at my job."

I think Wisk believed his own hype.

"Then you should have given some thought to how she would feel about having a new grandchild." I still heard that sanctimonious sound.

"Why would I?" Wisk asked.

I glanced at Andy. His face seemed to ask, Yeah, why would he?

"Think about it. Lucy understood how dangerous the world could be and not only because of what she witnessed fifty years ago. In her work at the center, she saw the victims of some horrible deeds. She witnessed the worst of mankind."

"Your point?" Wisk asked.

Your point? Andy's face asked.

"You should have known that she would be extremely concerned about her new grandchild's safety, especially since her daughter would continue to work."

"Why would I care?" Wisk scowled.

Andy's expression asked the same question.

"Because, given her concern, she would buy something that would offer a little safety for her daughter." I paused for effect. "A nanny cam."

"A nanny cam," Andy confirmed.

"Not only would she buy a nanny cam for her daughter, she would check to make sure it worked."

"Right." Andy backed up my story. "She would test it."

"And what better way to check a surveillance camera than to set it up in your own house to see how well it worked."

"No better way," Andy agreed.

"A nanny cam." Wisk sounded disheartened. He'd been undone by a nanny cam.

"A nanny cam." Andy and I spoke in unison.

If I were Wisk, I would have worked harder to see if we were bluffing. He didn't. He accepted that we had seen the murder played out on the video from the nanny cam.

The fear settled in on Wisk's face. "Look," he leaned in, and Andy and I mimicked his move. "I didn't want to kill Lucy but I couldn't let her hurt the center. We were struggling enough as it was. We have a lot of competition."

"You mean gangs?"

He looked at me as if I were crazy. "No, other community service organizations."

I'd always viewed nonprofits as partners working together for the common good. Apparently not.

"I was worried about what Lucy might do, but I *knew* what Boyle was up to. I planned to deal with Lucy once Boyle was out of the way. Then you showed up. I had to accelerate my plan."

With a detachment that I found frightening, Wisk calmly related his story of visiting Lucy at her home. "I said I dropped by to discuss some sensitive Absecon Hope business. I brought breakfast including cranberry juice laced with cyanide. Lucy loved cranberry juice. Of course, she thought the juice tasted a little odd—I'd loaded it with sugar to cover the cyanide taste—but she drank it anyway." He almost smiled at his luck, making the hair on my neck stand up. "It's a shame, but think of how the center would have suffered if Braddock's story came out."

He didn't seem to be confessing so much as explaining why his every move had been the *right* thing to do for the center. He hadn't been disillusioned by his experiences in the world of politics. He'd been hardened and emboldened. He'd learned the Ward Braddock way of getting what you want.

Nonetheless, he had to realize that his statements constituted a confession. The easy flow of information had to be part of a strategy that I didn't understand. How could letting us continue to live be part of it?

Wisk reached into a jacket pocket. Across from me Andy shoved a hand inside his own coat. Wisk's hand emerged holding a handkerchief, though not to wipe tears away because he had shed none. He blew his nose noisily and I saw Andy relax. Wisk returned the hankie to his pocket, and when his hand reemerged, we saw the gun. He immediately slipped it below the table.

"Don't move, Mr. Beck. I have this pointed at your girlfriend." Again, the term sounded ridiculous, but what would I have preferred? Partner? Significant Other? Actually, I thought he could call me pretty much anything he wanted as long as he didn't shoot me.

"Over the course of my career at the center, I've had the opportunity to relieve more than a few 'guests' of their illegal handguns. It wasn't something they'd want to see in a police report." Wisk made a good point.

"You can't shoot us here." Andy sounded confident. But then why shouldn't he? The gun was pointed at *me.*

"I don't plan to," Wisk huffed. "We're going back to the center now. Please just cooperate."

The man was delusional. Andy would disarm him in the time it would take us to reach the car, let alone return to the center.

"It won't make any difference if you kill us, Anton," Andy pointed out. "The police will have all the evidence they need to convict you.

"If you kidnap or kill us it will only increase the police pressure," he continued. "Just go ahead and make your getaway while you can. I'm not risking my life or especially Meg's to stop you. There is nothing I can do." He pointed to himself, not just for emphasis but, I realized, to hit the phone in his breast pocket.

After thinking over Andy's proposition for what felt like a very long time but was probably no more than five seconds, Wisk stood and said, "If either of you move or make any effort to follow me, you'll be sorry. Now, if you'll excuse me ..." He bowed quickly, turned, and began his flight with an impressive burst of energy. We saw that energy expire as he reached the restaurant's parking lot. He was headed toward the inlet at a remarkably slow pace for a supposedly fit septuagenarian.

"Where do you think he's headed?" I asked.

"Just taking it on the lam, I guess." Andy did not seem at all concerned about the fleeing culprit. Pulling a small digital recorder out of his pocket, he grinned at me and said, "I took the liberty of recording our conversation, which as you know is perfectly legal in the great state of New Jersey."

"Did I say anything dumb?" I asked.

"You were *magnificent*," he beamed.

"I put my buddy on alert, to watch for a text from me." Andy checked his outbox. "If the cops aren't here in a few minutes, I'll go after him, before he gets out of sight. On that route, his only option is circling around the building, and I can easily cut him off at the pass." He shook his head. "I expected him to be in better shape."

"Me, too. He told me he swims every day."

"Uh oh, he's headed for the water—I'd better get moving." Andy dropped a hundred dollar bill on the table. "Take care of our check."

As Andy started after Wisk, I watched as the older man climbed onto then stumbled along a raised cement wall bordering the dock area near Scales Restaurant. His effort was clumsy but successful, it appeared, as he jumped off the wall and disappeared from view. Andy reached the wall a few seconds later, just as diners at their waterfront tables leapt to their feet and ran to peer over the wall.

Chapter 43

"Someone call 911!" Andy yelled over his shoulder.

"I've got it covered, Andy," a female voice shouted in reply.

I turned to see a contingent of police led by a statuesque woman in a navy-blue pantsuit rushing to the water's edge.

The waitress was nowhere to be seen and I didn't wait for a check. Sprinting toward the gathering crowd at the waterfront, I reached Andy in record time. As I climbed the wall to stand beside him, I saw several police officers leaning over Anton Wisk, who was screaming in pain as he writhed on a deck about six feet below.

"Ouch," was my only comment.

Chapter 44

As Andy and I gave our statements to the police, EMTs rolled a ranting Anton Wisk to the ambulance. When he spotted the two of us, he pointed and bellowed, "This is all *their* fault! They made me do this! They're crazy! *Crazy*, I tell you!"

As I watched Wisk's display, I commented to Andy, "I am very, very hungry."

"Catching killers can do that to a girl." He turned to the officers. "Are we good to go?"

The cops released us, but we didn't go far. We got a waterfront table at Scales, the restaurant disrupted by Wisk's escape attempt. Andy suggested a Manhattan so we could get back to 1964, but we settled on margaritas, a 21st-century specialty of the dockside restaurant, along with an order of shrimp. When our drinks arrived, Andy raised his glass. "Before we return to that earlier time, let me toast you."

"Cheers to that." I clicked my glass against his.

Andy paused. I sensed he was reluctant to go on. "I know you've noticed that I haven't been myself lately. I haven't been quite straight with you over the past couple of weeks."

Uh oh. I fought to keep my expression impassive.

"It is true that I don't like office work and that this security audit has worn me down. But there's more." Andy wouldn't let his eyes meet mine.

Johnny had warned me, but I didn't listen. I wouldn't listen.

"Our life in the Bahamas is great."

I waited for the big *but.*

"We live in a beautiful place. We are both well paid, and, since our jobs feed and house us, we get to stash most of the money away."

I knew all this. I wished Andy could bring himself to get to the part I *didn't* know. I was a big girl; I could take it. I might pass out but I could take it. When would he get to the *but*?

"I'm the one who took you away from your old life and dragged you into mine. I take full responsibility for that. When I lured you away from your plans for a career change, I thought I was doing something good."

"But … ?" I almost shrieked it. I couldn't wait any longer.

He appeared startled. "But," he paused, "Maggie, I hate working security."

Every muscle in my body relaxed. This was the big reveal?

"I was worn out from my years of being self-employed, never knowing what was next. There was plenty of excitement but a lot of anxiety, too. Taking a steady job seemed like a good idea at the time, especially since it was in paradise. You thought it was a good move, right?"

I nodded.

"I became a PI because I like living outside the lines, and now I find my life is devoted to making sure people don't take one ridiculous misstep over those lines. I don't want to do it anymore. I'm going to resign." He let out a deep breath. "There, I said it." As he looked at me at last, there was apprehension in his eyes.

"That's it?"

"That's your reaction?" He seemed amazed, maybe even disappointed.

"I understand," I said, and I did. "Something's been making you miserable, Andy. You say it's your job and that you want to quit it. That makes perfect sense. Have you thought about what you want to do next?"

"If I stayed in my job, we could probably keep our place in the Bahamas." Unless of course Andy planned on leaving me alone there. I still felt a twinge of doubt.

"If you keep working for the Artistical, we could stay in the cottage," he echoed my thoughts, "but I was wondering ... would you mind moving on?"

Okay. I was still part of his plan. "We've built a nice little nest egg, Andy, and that's what nest eggs are for. A rainy day, or in the case of the Bahamas, a relentlessly sunny day. Where is it you want to go?"

"If you're willing, I thought we could sail around for a few months while we figure it out."

"That sounds great!" I said enthusiastically. We could discuss the "where" later, though I suspected he was thinking his boat in the Caribbean. I was thinking a rented boat in Greece.

His smile was as broad as I'd seen it in weeks. He reached for my hand and we sat looking out over the water to the lights of the marina hotels.

"I wonder what happened to the shrimp we ordered." I sighed.

"You know, Maggie, I like to think that Buddy and Betty might have sat in a spot like this and admired the moon just as we're doing now."

"And ate shrimp?" I glanced back to the restaurant looking for the waitress.

"And looked into each other's eyes like this," he said.

I turned and felt as mesmerized by the cool green eyes as I had the very first time. It had been a while, given that I did not have the ability to see through Andy's eyelids. Something else was going on; he was flirting with me and I was responding. Especially when he said there was a gift involved.

"I planned on giving this to you at the Knife & Fork when we were still in 1964."

"A present from 1964?"

"Exactly. Since I thought we would be spending tonight back then, it occurred to me that people in those days might look askance at our living arrangement. So ..." He reached into his pocket and pulled out a box, a very small box, wrapped in silver and dwarfed by the big, if somewhat squished, white bow on top. "I thought I should give you this tonight."

I smiled as I took it from his hands. "You really went all out on our trip to the past." I ripped off the paper and flipped open the box all the while gushing in what I thought might be 1964-appropriate fashion. "Andy, this is gorgeous! Where'd you borrow it?"

"I didn't borrow it, Maggie, I bought it."

"That's amazing—it looks so real."

"It *is* real."

"It can't be. This looks like two carats worth of diamonds."

"With the baguettes it's 2.05."

I was shocked into silence.

"You once told me you thought emerald-cut diamonds look best with a bathing suit. So, I thought given our new lifestyle that it would be the best cut."

"You bought me a diamond ring? When you're about to quit your job? You didn't need to spend all your money on me!"

"I've had a special fund for this for some time. I ordered it a month ago, and this morning I drove to Philly to pick it up."

"It's beautiful," I said, cradling the box in my hand. "But if this isn't the right time for an expensive gift then I think—"

He interrupted. "You're a little slow on the uptake, Maggie. I'm asking you to marry me. Maybe I got carried away by the domestic fervor of pre-sexual-revolution America, but I've felt for some time that I'd like to spend my life with you. Officially, I mean." He gave me a sheepish grin. "Now, you know I'm not comfortable with emotional displays, so if you could just say 'yes' and put it on your finger, I'd appreciate it."

"You want to marry me?"

"I didn't think that would come as such a shock to you, but yes. And before you ask why, which I am pretty sure you will, let me tell you. Not only are you the only girl I know who ever got kidnapped, tied up with nautical knots, and taken out to sea, you are the only girl I know who *would* get kidnapped, tied up with nautical knots, and taken out to sea."

"Thanks …" I thought the compliment over. "But that kind of thing only happens because I hang out with you."

"No, it happens because you want to help people and you're open to whatever happens."

"I really wasn't that open to being thrown overboard," I corrected him.

He shook his head. "Nah. You take things in stride. And you'll take the next situation in your stride. I like that. I need that."

"Will I have to continue having near-death experiences just to keep our romance alive? That strikes me as more than a little kinky."

He leaned closer. "I want people to know you're my wife." He said the word without flinching. I was impressed. "For some time, I've been worried you might run off with one of those millionaire celebrities you take care of in the Bahamas."

"You can see me, right?" I asked.

He nodded.

"And you've seen the girls those men bring with them? In general, they have a lot more man-made material inside than they're wearing on the outside."

"Look," he said a bit gruffly, "if you don't want to marry me, I can take the ring back." He reached for the box and I slapped his hand away.

"I love this ring!" I slid it across the table to Andy. "Here, you put it on me." I extended my left hand with its bright red 1964 nail polish.

He slid the platinum band down my finger and squeezed my hand.

"You *really* want to marry me?" I asked.

"Yes, I do. Do you want to marry *me*?"

"I do."

A big smile spread across his face. "So, you see, Maggie, good things could and *did* happen in 1964." Looking directly into my eyes, he kissed my hand and said, "Let's just hope we can be as happy for a very long time in our century as Buddy and Betty were for a very short time in theirs."

Andy doesn't go for romantic that often, but when he does, he really hits the nail on the head.